Death is the Cure

Death is the Cure

Nicola Slade

ROBERT HALE · LONDON

ISBN 978-0-7090-8955-1

Robert Hale Limited
Clerkenwell House
Clerkenwell Green
London EC1R 0HT

www.halebooks.com

2 4 6 8 10 9 7 5 3 1

Typeset in 11/14pt
by Derek Doyle & Associates, Shaw Heath
Printed in Great Britain by the MPG Books Group,
Bodmin and King's Lynn

For the Slade, Forster and Barnes families, with love

ACKNOWLEDGEMENT

Thanks to Jeff Behary, of *The Turn of the Century Electrotherapy Museum* in Florida, who patiently answered all my questions about early medical electrical treatment: any errors are mine.

Thanks also to Linda and Liv who read the manuscript and laughed in the right places and to Keri Thomas who designed my website and runs it so brilliantly.

DRAMATIS PERSONAE

CHARLOTTE RICHMOND
> A thankful widow who needs to look over her shoulder while watching her step

ELAINE KNIGHTLEY
> An invalid who does not enjoy poor health

COUNT DE KERSAC
> An elderly Breton gentleman who believes in ghosts

ARMEL DE KERSAC
> A younger Breton gentleman who believes in fairies

MARIANNE DE KERSAC
> An echo from a distant past

LADY BUCKWELL
> An echo from a different and more recent past

MR JONAS TIBBINS
> If curiosity killed the cat, what did it do to Mr Tibbins?

CAPTAIN HORATIO PENBURY
> A jolly tar suffering from trouble amidships

SIMEON CHETTLE
> A neighbour with an unhealthy interest in dead things

LETITIA MONTGOMERY
> A landlady with a lot of legacies

DORA BENSON
> A fount of knowledge: a governess who is always right

MELICENT DUNWOODY
> A fountain: a governess who is always wronged

REVD DECIMUS ATTWELL
> A clergyman who is, no doubt, the father of his flock

MEHITABEL ATTWELL
> An overprotective mother who takes her duties seriously

JONATHAN RADNOR
> A medical man whose treatments are electrifying

Other people in Bath and at home in Hampshire: assorted maids, butlers, footmen, nurses, police inspectors, brothers-in-law, sisters-in-law, grandmothers-in-law, husbands and a fat spaniel.

CHAPTER 1

'Oh my goodness, what on earth. . . .' For a moment Charlotte Richmond assumed the man on the ground must be drunk but reason told her otherwise. At three o'clock in the afternoon? In a genteel city such as Bath? And in a respectable mews?

Besides, the man was wearing good, sober clothes, smart clothes, in fact. He looked to be a gentleman and he looked to be extremely dead.

A moment's horrified intake of breath was followed by a second moment of blind panic. Charlotte's life-long response to trouble was to run away unobserved, disappearing silently and swiftly in the opposite direction, but she stifled the impulse. Was he hurt? Was he indeed dead? Her unruly sense of the ridiculous ambushed her even at such a moment, fuelling a rising hysteria. Dead? Surely the horrid red stain spreading across his chest was evidence enough?

She bit her lip, ignored her instinct to escape and made a rapid search for his pulse which revealed no sign of life and, as she hesitated, wondering what she should do, she realized she was not alone in the mews that led off the adjoining street.

Summer 1858
'For heaven's sake, Lily.' Charlotte Richmond reached out a hand and took the hairbrush from her brother-in-law's wife. 'Don't dare to touch Agnes's hair, it took me an age to pin it up.'

She sighed as she surveyed the bride. Agnes Richmond, spinster of the parish of Finchbourne near Winchester, was never going to be a beautiful bride. Blushing, certainly; indeed Charlotte feared that her discreet application of rice powder would have no effect in disguising the unbecoming purplish crimson of Agnes's hot, eager face.

'I think you should brush it out and start again,' declared Lily Richmond, pouting. 'That wreath of white roses doesn't suit her in the least; she looks so very like a startled horse.'

Charlotte's fingers itched to slap the complacent pink face so close at hand. Thank God Agnes had been fluttering at the attendant maid and had not heard her brother's wife utter what Charlotte had to admit was a harsh but true description of the bride. Poor Agnes; nature had been prodigal with some gifts – her height and rampant good health, the heavy frame, the abundant dark hair and the expressive, slightly prominent dark eyes. Why had not Providence followed this with a less angular, less undeniably equine face, or a manner more suited to a well-bred young woman than Agnes's galumphing bounce? And would it have been such a chore to have thrown in just a trace of feminine charm and grace, queried Charlotte, thinking poorly of Providence.

'Charlotte?' Agnes lifted a plaintive face to her friend and sister-in-law. 'What was Lily saying about my wreath of roses? Do you think they will do?'

'Of course they will, you goose. Ignore Lily, she's just fretful because it's so hot and sticky.' Charlotte forestalled a protest from Lily by addressing her with guile. 'Lily, dear, why don't you go and sit downstairs in the drawing room where it's cool? In your condition we dare not take any risks and it's so hot upstairs. I'm persuaded Barnard would wish it, dear.'

Mollified by the attention paid her and the suggestion that at five months pregnant with the heir to the ancient manor of Finchbourne she was far more important than the bride, Lily consented to take herself off downstairs where she proceeded to torment her large, bovine husband, Barnard, by hinting at her delicacy. Splendidly resistant to imagination or nervous strain, Lily had taken in her stride the catalogue of obstetrical disasters sketched out by Old Nurse, the resident prophet of doom. Her husband, however, was of a more squeamish nature and had developed a tendency to recall urgent estate matters at such recitals.

'Thank God, that's got rid of her,' Charlotte let out a soundless, unladylike whistle. 'No, Agnes, I won't apologize for being unkind, Lily can be a complete pest sometimes. Now . . .' She beckoned the bride. 'Stand up and let me take a good look at you, my dear.'

Agnes Richmond, the only daughter of the manor, lumbered to her feet and stood in an awkward pose in front of the long cheval glass, her face purpling with embarrassment as she looked at her reflection.

'I look so *large*,' she lamented, then she brightened as she surveyed her sister-in-law. 'Now you, dear, you look delightful in that bronze silk shot with emerald; it brings out the green in your eyes and that little wisp of a bonnet is charming with your hair smoothly plaited up like that.'

'You could be right,' agreed Charlotte, staring with frank curiosity at herself in the looking-glass. 'I really don't look quite so brown-complexioned as usual, do I? For once I look quite passable.'

Agnes cried out at this and received a fond pat on the shoulder. 'Enough of singing *my* praises, I want to take a look at the bride. You look lovely,' pronounced Charlotte, gilding the lily out of kindness. 'That very dark amber silk is perfect, just the right colour for you and ideal for the half-mourning we eventually decided on.'

'Oh, Charlotte. . . .' Agnes was reminded of the reason for the half-mourning. 'I sometimes forget how you must be suffering, dearest. I'm so selfish in my own happiness that it is sometimes hard to remember poor Frampton's death. How dreadful of me – for so young a widow, you're such an example of courage to us all.'

Charlotte gently disengaged the now moistly clinging Agnes and pushed her down on to her chair again.

'Now, Agnes, you know we have agreed to put all that behind us. Frampton would not have wanted to spoil your day and I – I have my own memories of your brother that I will endeavour to set aside.'

And so I shall, she thought grimly. I will bury my memories

of my late husband as surely as he lies buried in the churchyard and when I pass his grave on the way into church later today I am quite certain that my only emotion will be one of intense relief that he can never clamber out of it again.

Two hours later Charlotte stood in a pew beside the grandmother of the bride, affectionately watching Agnes marry the object of her heart's desire, The Reverend Percy Benson, newly appointed vicar of the parish. Charlotte considered the groom objectively; he was scarcely the hero of most young women's daydreams. His puny frame, his thinning hair, the bobbing Adam's apple, all contributed to a less than ideal picture, but Percy had a kind heart and most important of all, he adored his lumpen bride.

'Looks a poor fing, don't 'e?' The cockney whisper sounded loud in her ear as Lady Frampton, widow of a wealthy merchant knight and paternal grandmother also of both Charlotte's late husband as well as Barnard, the squire, leaned her ponderous bulk sideways. 'A rasher of wind, my dear, late 'usband would have called him and no mistake. Still,' – she gave a gusty sigh – 'he'll do for Agnes, poor soul, she's no oil painting and she'll never catch a better one. I suppose 'e does 'is best.'

In accordance with the Richmond family tradition, Lady Frampton's only son had taken his wife's surname on marriage to the heiress of Finchbourne. His wife, Charlotte's mother-in-law, now travelling on the Continent, had graciously allowed her husband to bestow his family name on his firstborn son, Frampton Richmond.

The cool peace of the twelfth-century church always brought Charlotte comfort and ease and now she took a cautious look around. As befitted a quiet wedding where the family was in mourning, there were few guests and the pews were less than a quarter full. As the visiting clergyman, the bishop's own chaplain – dispatched to perform the ceremony as a personal favour to the influential and wealthy Richmond family – reedily intoned a prayer, Charlotte ticked off the guests according to her remembered list.

The family, of course: Barnard and Lily, now firmly ensconced as lord and lady of the manor. Lily was resplendent in a virulent purple silk crinoline of alarming proportions which just about disguised her increasing girth while Barnard looking, as ever, benign and bull-like, was the perfect squire, so unlike his late and unlamented elder brother. Lady Frampton, a proud grandmother and dear friend to Charlotte, armour-plated in her black brocade upholstery, topped with a heavy flared cloak in silk plush and lined with a surah silk, wheezed her way cheerfully through the singularly inappropriate hymn, *Victim divine*, which Percy had rather defiantly pronounced to be his favourite.

Charlotte pursed her lips at the lines in the second verse:

Thou standest in the holiest place, As now for guilty sinners slain;
Thy blood of sprinkling speaks, and prays,
All-prevalent for helpless man...

I can identify Percy as the 'helpless man', Charlotte mused with an inner smile, but I can hardly imagine that he sees himself as a victim.

Very well, who else was present? A strident soprano voice clanged at her from across the aisle and she heaved a despondent sigh. Oh yes, Percy's elder sister, the estimable Miss Dora Benson, arrived only a day earlier and already looking alarmingly settled in the draughty barn of Finchbourne Vicarage. A covert glance at Agnes's brand new sister-in-law made Charlotte's heart sink. Oh Lord, poor Agnes. Dora showed every indication of wanting to remove permanently to Finchbourne and where better to take up residence than in the ten-bedroomed home of her younger brother? Agnes could hardly plead shortage of space, so was the bride, just lately released from bondage by her overbearing mother's departure to take the cure at a spa on the Continent, to fall under the thumb of yet another strong-minded older woman? Dora had looked askance at Lily Richmond's clashing splendour while she smoothed down her own dove-coloured silk poplin with an air of complacency, her skirt a modest bell rather than the monstrous metal cage which supported Lily's purple flounces. Like Agnes and Charlotte herself Dora was a tall woman, fair haired and built on sturdy lines and looking altogether larger and more imposing than her unimpressive clerical brother.

If I have to listen to many more of Dora's improving lectures on every topic under the sun, Charlotte vowed, I might have to develop a migraine now and then. She continued her surreptitious review of the congregation and again her brow furrowed as she remarked on the wispy figure drooping two rows behind her. Like Dora Benson, this woman was a governess, but there the resemblance halted. Melicent Dunwoody had none of Dora's splendidly impervious self-possession. Indeed she wilted if anyone so much as glanced at her. Where Dora spoke up loudly and confidently, *knowing* her every pronouncement to be correct, and not merely correct but positively welcome, Miss Dunwoody whispered on a half sob, qualifying every statement with a watery: 'Well, perhaps I could be mistaken. . . .'

And she cried, oh lord how she cried; Charlotte felt damp at the memory.

'Why does Miss Dunwoody weep so?' She had questioned Agnes, in a discreet whisper, on the previous afternoon, following her introduction to the lady.

'Because she is so sensitive.' Agnes had also succumbed to her handkerchief after fondly embracing her former governess. 'She feels it greatly that I wished her to be at my wedding. I'm afraid, by her own account, that many of her late pupils have slighted her, so our attention is particularly gratifying.'

'Really?' Charlotte had shot a sceptical look at the frail figure draped in rusty black. 'If she cries like that all the time I shall be inclined to slight her myself. Will she cheer up, do you imagine, or shall we be inundated for the next couple of days?'

'Oh.' Agnes stared at her sister-in-law. 'Did I not I tell you, dearest Charlotte? No, of course, there's been no time. Dear Barnard has told Miss Dunwoody that she must make a good

16

long stay at Finchbourne and not even to think of seeking a new situation until she is quite rested. You must have heard her say that her most recent employer treated her scandalously by refusing to believe that her husband was making eyes at poor, dear Melicent. Such nonsense, as if she would make up such a thing. Why, the poor soul has an artificial leg!'

In the church, watching with benevolent affection as Agnes, with a blush of royal purple, became Mrs Percy Benson, Charlotte's lips twisted in a smile as she recalled the conversation.

'Why on earth should that make any difference?' she had demanded. 'He could still have made sheep's eyes at her, though I can't see why anyone would wish to do so, she is hardly a beauty. But are you sure, Agnes? An artificial leg? Has she always had it, even when she was living here?'

'Oh no, dear, such a tragedy.' Agnes was only too happy to drip tears at Charlotte once she had checked that the subject of her conversation was safely out of earshot and being fussed over by the hospitable Barnard. 'It was about a year after she left here, about twelve years ago; she was injured very terribly in a carriage accident and the doctors were unable to save her leg. Poor Melicent almost died and although her then employers paid all the medical bills and gave her a small endowment, she felt they treated her very shabbily. I believe they blamed her in some part for the accident as they said she had encouraged their son – a rather dashing Oxford man – to drive too fast. Melicent said it was no such thing, of course, rather that the son had become too fond of her and was reciting poetry at the time and so did not realize how quickly he was driving.' Agnes had issued a gusty sigh. 'Poor Melicent. I fear she has all too frequently been the focus of attention from gentlemen acquainted with her employers, sometimes indeed, from gentlemen within their households. Dear Melicent is always at a loss as to how it is. She is such a dear soul, you know, and so helpful, she positively burns to be of assistance, but somehow her employers never seem to appreciate her and her delicate feelings are always lacerated.'

17

Regarding under her lashes the drooping Miss Dunwoody, Charlotte took leave to doubt that so many gentlemen had made unsolicited advances to her. Apparently Melicent's first charge as governess had been to the five-year old Agnes, with the additional chore during the school holidays of supervising the thirteen-year-old Frampton and his brother, who was a few years younger. And a thankless task that must have been, shuddered Charlotte. I imagine Barnard as a noisy, lumbering, grubby little boy trailing in the wake of his brother who, even then, was probably a monster. I wonder less, though, that Agnes is such a watering pot now that I have encountered her governess; the woman is a positive fountain.

Suppose Melicent to be eighteen at least when she took up her post at Finchbourne twenty-five years ago, Charlotte gave her fingers a surreptitious shake as she counted; she must now be at least forty-three. Another sidelong glance confirmed her earliest impression: Melicent was even plainer than Agnes but with none of the latter's awkward, affectionate ways. Short, skinny, rabbit-toothed and pasty-faced, Providence had bestowed no favours at all on Melicent Dunwoody; small wonder she had invented some feminine charms for herself. Oh well, Charlotte thought, with a tolerant sigh, she can practise her wiles on the neighbourhood; she won't trouble me. Gran and I will be moving to our own house in the village soon.

Lady Frampton nudged Charlotte at this point.

'Get a move on, gal,' she hissed loudly, her best teeth whistling and rattling loudly. 'They're off to the vestry and you'll be wanted to sign the register. Stop day-dreaming there and shift yerself.' She gave Charlotte a further push, urging, ' 'urry up, will you? I'm sharp set and wanting my vittles.'

In the vestry Charlotte suffered the tearful embrace of the new Mrs Percy Benson and allowed Agnes to drip tears on to her neck. 'Come, Agnes,' she remonstrated at last. 'Dry these tears and let me shake Percy by the hand. No,' she warned, as a fresh outburst seemed impending. 'I warn you, one more bout of weeping and I'll throw a bucket of water over you, I promise you.'

'That's what I so admire about you, Charlotte,' a low, amused voice came from behind her. 'You're always so tactful.'

Charlotte whirled round to see a warm smile and a hand outstretched in greeting, as a tall, brown-haired man in his mid-thirties nodded to her.

'Kit! Mr Knightley? When did you arrive home from London? I thought you were quite certain to be detained beyond the wedding.'

'Yes,' he nodded, still holding her hand in his firm clasp. 'I had telegraphed Elaine to that effect but my business matters suddenly drew to a conclusion this morning and a new idea came to the fore, so I jumped on to the first train heading south.' He checked and shot her a grave look. 'Did you see Elaine last night? Was she well? I came straight to the church and haven't been home yet, though I won't stay long after the wedding.'

'I can do better than that,' Charlotte reassured him in an undertone. 'I was up very early this morning and took Lady Frampton's dog for a walk over to Knightley Hall to enquire after Elaine's health. I can inform you, sir, that your lady wife is in excellent spirits and assures me that she is in fine fettle.'

He gave a wry smile, releasing her hand as he turned to nod a greeting to his old schoolfriend, Barnard Richmond, then took a step back towards her. 'And how much of that am I to believe, Charlotte? We both know that my wife can be astoundingly untruthful about her state of health, if she doesn't want me to be worried.'

'I know.' Charlotte laid her hand briefly on his arm. 'I believe she was as well as she has been lately. I know that's small comfort, but truly, Kit, I don't think she is actually any worse just now.'

He smiled and moved away to congratulate the bride and groom, his welcome assured as patron of the living and a prime mover in their engagement. Charlotte cast a brief glance at his retreating back and sighed. Elaine Knightley, her dearest friend, was dying, of that there was no doubt. The only question was how long it would take her.

*

19

Several days after the wedding Charlotte took her usual roundabout route over the commons and hills a few miles south of Winchester, to visit the Knightleys. A fresh breeze made the countryside inviting, and the atmosphere at Finchbourne Manor was becoming oppressive, to say the least.

'For heaven's sake, Gran,' Charlotte had exclaimed after breakfast. 'How can Lily, the least patient and long-suffering of women, bear that dreadful creature weeping and wailing all over her? I shall take to violence, I promise you, if Melicent Dunwoody sobs over me one more time. The woman is a bottomless well of tears and she turns them on at a moment's notice.'

'I 'ave to admit that she's a tedious wench,' agreed Lady Frampton, leaning back in the comfortable armchair positioned in the bay window of her bedroom where she could keep an eye on the comings and goings of visitors and family as they journeyed up the short front drive. 'But she don't bother me, I'm bound to say as much in 'er favour.'

'Of course she doesn't bother you,' Charlotte burst out. 'Because you are a very clever old lady, darling Gran, and you hide yourself away up here where even that encroaching watering pot dare not intrude. But I have no such refuge and it seems to be every five minutes that I'm waylaid about some slight that has been her lot. Yesterday it was the butler, poor Hoxton, who had offended by forgetting to offer her a second glass of wine at dinner. This morning it was Lily's maid who "talked back" to Miss Dunwoody, when all she wanted was a little assistance in rejuvenating her best – her *only* silk gown – she being too poor, sadly, to afford another. I gather Lily's maid was brutally frank in pointing out that she owed service to her own particular mistress only.'

Charlotte flung herself around the stuffy, comfortable bedchamber, dark with its Elizabethan oak panelling. She wondered for a moment whether to wrestle open the small, leaded casement window, partly obscured by heavy brocade curtains, but knew that such an action would bring the old lady's wrath down on her head. 'I swear to you, Gran, that I feel a truly murderous desire at least five times a day, to throttle that woman!'

Lady Frampton clapped her hands in amusement but offered no sympathy. 'Get on with you, you silly wench, I think you must be feeling liverish. Go for a walk or something and get rid of these megrims in your silly 'ead. As far as I can make out Barnard allowed Melicent Dunwoody to weep and wail over him until he agreed in self defence that she could stay and not even Lily can shift him from that stance. You know, we all know, 'ow bull-'eaded 'e can be when he's forced into a corner, so you might as well admit defeat.' She shifted herself into a more comfortable pose and closed her eyes, her large capable hands folded over her imposing belly. After a moment she opened them again. 'What, you still 'ere, madam? Be off with you, I'll warrant Mrs Knightley would enjoy your tale of the wedding goings-on.'

'So there you are, Elaine.' Charlotte sprawled inelegantly but comfortably on the cushions of a long wooden chair in the rose garden of Knightley Hall where her friend lay shaded from the afternoon sun. 'Lady Frampton shooed me off without ceremony to talk to you, rather than interfere with her afternoon nap.'

'I'm delighted that she did so.' Elaine Knightley's grey eyes gleamed with affection as she looked at the younger girl; so much more relaxed now compared to the taut anxiety that had been noticeable on her arrival in England only three months ago at the end of April. 'How did Agnes bear it all? Did she weep? How foolish of me, of course she wept! How did she look? Kit, dreadful man, had no idea at all what the wedding dress was like, or how Agnes carried herself. All he could tell me was that the food served at the wedding breakfast was a vast improvement on previous repasts he had suffered at the manor.'

'I'll take that as a compliment.' Charlotte nodded with a complacent smile. 'Lily drove the kitchen staff mad, in this her first entertainment since assuming the mantle of Lady of the Manor, and she harried and chivvied the kitchen and the gardeners and all the maids into laying on a feast fit for a royal wedding. At least, that was what Cook declared it to be and when I remember the peculiar, universal brown tinge to all the food that was served up at the manor on my arrival in this country, I feel a glow of pride at my patience in teaching Cook how to dish up food that is neither brown, burnt or boring.'

'Indeed, my dear girl, you have worked miracles,' Elaine agreed, shifting her position slightly, with a barely perceptible frown. As Charlotte started up, Mrs Knightley shook her head, with a forbidding glance. 'No, it's all right, I'm quite comfortable now. Sit back in your chair and relax. Tell me about your plans; when are you and old Lady Frampton to move into the house in the village?'

'That's another irritation.' Charlotte sighed in frustration. 'First of all the house Barnard has offered us, Rowan Lodge, was to be fumigated after the previous tenant's cats had colonized the place. After that came the decoration and now, at this late stage, Barnard informs me that there's a new problem with the kitchen drains which may take weeks to resolve. And worse even than all the rest, as the house is next door to the vicarage, the drainage problem is common to both houses, so Dora Benson is to take up residence at the manor this very afternoon. Not to mention poor Agnes and Percy Benson when they return from their honeymoon on the Isle of Wight in three or four weeks' time.'

She leaned over the side of her chair to pick a handful of daisies and started to loop them into a chain. 'I tell you, Elaine, I'm already having to watch my tongue with Miss Dunwoody, but when Dora Benson becomes resident in the house, I think I shall certainly need a scold's bridle – for myself if not for her. The woman is a walking history book, which is perfectly admirable; I like history myself, but not morning, noon and night. If that were all I could bear her, but she is bent on *improving* us along with it. When she came to tea yesterday she even tried to contradict dear Gran on some point about Queen Caroline in spite of Gran informing her haughtily that she had seen with her own eyes the poor lady barred from her husband's coronation. Even though Dora was routed, I could see that she still felt a glow of superiority. She will be quite impossible in the house, all day, every day.'

Elaine's smile had an absent air as she looked suddenly thoughtful, but she made no comment and Charlotte continued, 'Do you know, Dora has actually had the impertinence to scold the servants for calling me Miss Char? She informed me, in her calmest, most superior voice, that such a form was quite incorrect and that I should be addressed as Mrs Frampton Richmond. I bit my tongue and replied politely that the servants and I were perfectly conversant with the correct forms of address, but that we were all happy and comfortable with the more friendly style, so she countered this by remarking that in that case, they should pronounce my name with a soft *Ch* as in *Char*lotte, instead of a hard one – Char short for Charlie – as they do.'

Charlotte grinned at her friend across the low garden table between them. 'I'm thinking of hiring myself out as a lady's companion for a few months just to get away from the manor. I tell you that but for the fact that Barnard would be so mortified and hurt, I promise you that is exactly what I'd do.'

'Really?' Elaine sat up with a surprisingly vigorous movement. 'Are you in earnest, Char? Oh, not about hiring yourself out, I realize that was a joke, but about wishing you could have a change of scenery for a while?'

'I . . . suppose so.' Charlotte also sat up and stared at the sudden colour in her friend's normally pale cheeks and at the sparkle in her wide grey eyes. 'Why, what is it, Elaine? Do you know someone who would like me to help them? For you know I would be more than happy to do what I could. . . .'

'Yes, my dear goose.' Elaine smiled. 'Before your very eyes you see a woman who stands in dire need of a congenial companion for a week or so, possibly even as much as a month, but certainly no more than that. Will you come with me to Bath, Char? To keep me company so that Kit need not dance attendance on me? I know that he would trust you to take the greatest care of me, as he would trust no other, and although he

23

threatens to leave the harvest and the men to their own devices to be at my side, I know it will break his heart if he has to do so at such a busy time. Will you come with me?'

'With the greatest pleasure. You know that. I've always dreamed of going to Bath for when I was a child in Australia my godmother used to tell me stories about the city's delights and her adventures there as a young girl.' Charlotte was intrigued. 'But why Bath? And why now? Do you have a sudden whim to visit the city? Or is it a long-standing desire?'

'Oh no, it's just Kit.' Elaine sighed and moved her hands in a fluttering gesture of despair. 'He has come home from London full of some wonderful new medical advances and treatments now available in Bath that he insists I must try. I've tried to remonstrate with him, but he's convinced himself that this medical galvanism, or Faradism, or whatever it is called, will succeed where all else has failed and I just can't dissuade him.' She shifted restlessly again and met Charlotte's concerned gaze with a level and noncommittal stare. 'He's filled with such enthusiasm and hope that I cannot bear to disillusion him even though I know, and so does he in his heart I'm quite sure, that there is no treatment that will bring me a miracle cure. I can think of nobody else whose company I should so relish, so will you come with me, dearest Charlotte, in order to put Kit's mind at rest about me?'

It was as well that Charlotte had the excitement and interest of planning her first trip away from home since her arrival in England in the spring, for the two invading governesses failed signally to hit it off and little more than a week later Lady Frampton prophesied that it would soon be open warfare between the two women.

'Before those two are done it'll be parasols and pin-cushions at dawn, you mark my words, it's as good as going to the play,' she chortled in high glee, when Charlotte escaped to the old lady's room one afternoon. 'Did you 'ear 'em at each other's throats this morning, Char? First Miss Melicent tells a tale, with sighings and gaspings, of some deathly ailment she's suffering,

24

then what must 'appen but Miss Dora wades in, all brisk and bullying, and tells 'er she ort to be out in the fresh h'air to cure 'er ills.'

She snorted with amusement. 'Well, Miss Melicent won that bout when she laid a trembling 'and to 'er bosom and declared 'ow greatly she envied Miss Dora's robust health.'

'Don't remind me, Gran.' Charlotte sighed and smiled at the memory. 'They're at each other's throats again in the drawing-room even now, which is why I ran away. The Lord only knows how Lily puts up with them, but she seems to thrive on the squabbles. I could almost suspect her of setting them at each other deliberately just for the fun of it. If only Dora could contain herself and forbear from lecturing *me*, I could tolerate her quite well. She's perfectly correct about Melicent's silly fads and fusses – even though she does have a false leg she could quite easily walk about the garden and the park. Just a gentle ramble daily would blow some welcome fresh air through her empty head.'

She leaned back in her chair, stretching lazily. 'Thank heaven for the Knightleys and Elaine's invitation to Bath,' she purred. 'I swear it's only that prospect that stops me boxing Melicent's ears and being so plainly rude to Dora that even that monument of self-satisfaction could not fail to recognize the insult.' She shot the old lady an amused glance. 'You'll be safe enough, Gran, so I shan't commiserate with you for a single minute. You can always plead your age and infirmity, but my heart bleeds for poor Agnes, she'll never be able to escape. Poor dear, she'll come home expecting to move straight into the vicarage and settle down to married bliss with Percy, and instead she'll walk straight into a hornet's nest!'

'Quite right, you needn't commence to worry about me, young Char.' Lady Frampton wheezed and chuckled, her eyes half-closed and slitted in amusement, her cheeks – already rosy – assuming an alarming brick-red hue. 'My shoulders are broad enough, the Lord knows, and I'll keep an eye out for our Agnes. If she starts to suffer, mark my words I'll make my views strongly known to Barnard. He's a kind-hearted lad and turning into a proper squire now he's let alone to get on with it. He won't let them distress 'is only sister.'

She heaved herself round in the low, comfortable chair, upholstered in a delicate pale blue, incongruous when set against the vast, big-boned bulk that was quite undiminished by her eighty years.

'Tell me what arrangements 'ave been made so far,' she commanded. 'What 'as Mr Knightley decided about travelling? Do you plan to take the train from Winchester to London and then to Bath?'

'I'm not sure,' Charlotte confessed. 'That's the most direct route but I think Kit is reluctant to expose Elaine to the rigours of travelling across London to Paddington. He says the capital is a stinking pit at the best of times and at its foetid worst in August.'

'Strong words,' commented Lady Frampton with a haughty sniff and a glare of disapproval. 'I'll 'ave you know, young woman, that I lived all my life in London till a few years ago and you can see it didn't do me no 'arm. Still, I suppose Mrs Knightley is in delicate 'ealth, poor soul, and it wouldn't do to take chances, so I can't blame 'er 'usband. What alternative does 'e propose?'

'Several,' Charlotte explained. 'We could drive to the junction and take the train to Salisbury, changing there to link with the main line to Bath, or we could, as I understand it, take a veritable cross-country trip, zig-zagging merrily on our way to our destination. I shan't care at all, the only train I've ever travelled on was from Southampton to the junction here, on my way from the boat when I first arrived in England. It will be an adventure to go to Bath by train, whichever route Kit and Elaine decide on.'

She grinned down at the old lady. 'I have three particularly pressing reasons for visiting Bath, Gran.' She ticked them off on her fingers. 'First of all I am only too happy to act as companion to dear Mrs Knightley. She has been the best possible friend to me since I arrived in this country and it gives me great pleasure to think I can be of some assistance to her.

'Secondly, it will afford me both pleasure and relief to escape the clutches of the warring governesses here at the manor. And thirdly' – she sighed a little, but shook herself – 'I can't help but wish my godmother could be with me, and Ma, of course. They brought me up on Miss Austen's novels and would be delighted to know about this trip, so I shall do it for them.'

Standing on the platform at the station in Salisbury, in the neighbouring county of Wiltshire a couple of weeks later, Charlotte recalled her words to Lady Frampton and gnawed at her bottom lip in anxiety as she positioned herself behind Kit Knightley, hoping that his broad-shouldered frame might conceal her from view. Why does that man stare so? she fretted, and shrank in retreat under the brim of her new straw bonnet so that the inquisitive stranger a few yards down the platform would be unable to see her face.

She had not noticed him in the bustle of their arrival at the station, she had been too occupied in helping Elaine's maid and former nurse to settle her charge on a seat in the shade while Kit Knightley and the steady, middle-aged footman who was to travel with the ladies – returning home once they were settled – oversaw the removal of the various trunks, valises and hatboxes from the carriage to the train.

Elaine had waved her away. 'Charlotte, I promise you that I'm well taken care of.' She laughed at her younger friend. 'Go and explore the station, or take a look at the train, I know you're in a fever of excitement. No, really, I mean it. How can I possibly be tired already? I had a good night's sleep at the White Hart after that decorous carriage drive from Finchbourne to Salisbury yesterday and this morning I've not been allowed to do so much as lift a finger.'

Reassured on this point Charlotte had ventured closer to the engine to marvel at the hardiness of the driver and fireman, working in all weathers. Today was so hot, she thought, fanning herself gently, that the railwaymen would relish the breeze in the open cab. The driver, seeing her friendly interest, called down to her and boldly invited her to climb up and join him.

'Better not,' she told him with a rueful look at her fresh

chestnut brown poplin with its modest crinoline. 'What a wonderful view you must have from up there.'

As so often before, Charlotte's approachable manner gained her a friend, together with a great deal more information than she really required regarding pistons and steam, and the driving wheel which, she gathered, was the monstrously high wheel at present dwarfing her.

Rescue, in the form of Kit Knightley hove in view, but, as Kit strolled down the length of the platform to join her, she was suddenly struck by the expression on the face of a bystander. A man of middle age, middle height, middling looks, his clothing respectable but undistinguished, he raised his head and stared at Kit with a bright-eyed interest as he passed, then cast a thoughtful look at Charlotte herself.

'Well, Char?' Kit Knightley smiled as Charlotte broke off her conversation with the engine driver and turned to greet him. 'Still excited at the prospect now you come face to face with the steaming titan?'

'More than ever,' she declared with a little wriggle of anticipation and raised a laughing face to the engine driver who called down a friendly farewell. 'To think we'll be in Bath in just a few hours and how much more comfortable it will be for Elaine than to be jounced around in a carriage. Not that your carriage isn't a very elegant one,' she added, by way of a hasty disclaimer.

He laughed at her. 'However well-sprung my carriage, it can't compare in comfort to the train, especially with the footrests they usefully provide for invalids.' He sobered suddenly and took her hand, saying in an earnest voice, 'Char, you will look after her – and yourself – won't you? I feel I am really obliged to get home and see poor Randall; the place can't run at harvest time without a bailiff so I shall have to act for him, and he's one of my oldest friends besides. I shan't rest until I see for myself that his injuries aren't life-threatening.'

'Of course we'll manage,' Charlotte assured him. 'And, of course, you must go – poor Mr Randall must be in a ferment of worry as well as in great pain. Who could have foreseen such an unfortunate accident stemming from a mere rut on the track?'

'The rutted track was the beginning, certainly,' he agreed, turning to walk back with her towards the seat where Elaine was waiting. 'But no more rutted than usual. For the life of me I can't understand why a cart that has travelled that road a dozen or more times should suddenly decide to lurch so disastrously to the side. Pinned between a stone wall and the cartwheel, with the weight of a heavy wagon laden with sheaves behind it, it's a wonder poor Randall wasn't killed. In fact, it's a miracle he survived with no more than a broken leg and bruising.'

When Kit bent to address his wife, Charlotte noticed the stranger again. He was still staring at them, his eyes narrowed now with a keen interest as he seemed to single her out. A shudder, barely concealed, ran through her; and throughout the business of getting Elaine comfortably settled in the first class carriage and making sure that the luggage was securely stowed Charlotte strained her memory. No, she concluded, as Kit took his affectionate farewell of his wife and cordially shook her own hand, the man was a complete stranger. Charlotte had an excellent memory for faces, developed in part as a precaution during her adventurous youth in Australia in the train of her charming but erratic stepfather. The man across the way was certainly unknown to her, but was she equally unknown to him?

She stood at the carriage window to watch the last minute hustle and bustle and saw that the stranger was now surrounded by a crowd of late comers all jostling each other as they attempted to board the train.

Suddenly there was an outcry, screaming and a loud shout of alarm and Charlotte gasped as she saw that the man she had been observing so unobtrusively was now hanging half over the platform, held only by the strong arm of a porter while he and other passengers reached out to a young lady who had apparently fallen on to the railway line.

'What is it, Char?' Elaine was anxious.

'I can't quite see . . . I wonder if I should go and help? Oh no, I think it will be all right.' Charlotte craned her neck out of the window, all semblance of ladylike behaviour banished by curiosity and a feeling of unease. 'A young woman fell on to the track but they've managed to rescue her and . . . yes, she's being carried to the ladies' room.'

She withdrew into the carriage to reassure Mrs Knightley. 'I give you my word, Elaine, although her dress looks to be bloodstained there is a busy bustle about her, so I think she must be injured, but not fatally. There are no glum faces – rather they are all agog with excitement at the drama.'

She looked at the eager faces a little way up the platform. No, there was no grief there, so the girl's injury must be unfortunate rather than life-threatening. But what of the inquisitive stranger? Yes, he was there still, rubbing ruefully at his strained shoulder, with a grim frown dawning on his face as he conferred earnestly with the porter who had hauled him to safety. As she stared at him anxiously, the stranger raised his head, his expression still puzzled and angry. He caught her eye and his face cleared as he gave a little nod, and turned away from the porter, pausing only to slip something into the willing hand. The crowd of onlookers engulfed him again and she lost sight of him, but she thought the man had hastened to board the train which was now about to leave.

Watching the crowd as the train drew out of Salisbury Station Charlotte chewed at her bottom lip. What an unfortunate incident and what a mercy the young woman seemed to have escaped serious injury, though Char shuddered at the thought of all that blood. But what of the man who had been watching Charlotte herself? Was he on her trail, about to destroy her happiness by revealing the past she hoped to have buried?

CHAPTER 2

Bath! I'm actually here, in Bath; if only Ma could see me now. Charlotte kept her raptures to herself as she leaned back against the elegant cushions of primrose silk in their well-appointed private sitting-room. Her companion looked across the room, with a smile of warm affection.

'Well, Charlotte? Does it live up to your expectations?'

'Beyond them,' Charlotte confessed as Elaine Knightley nodded in amused sympathy. 'Far, far beyond them! I stood like a gawk, staring at the bustle of people as we were waiting outside the station, feeling as if I were in a dream.' She shook her head with a slight, rueful smile. 'It's no use, I really must stop expecting to walk into the pages of a novel, for even if we were to come across him, Mr Darcy might well be taking the waters and the hot bath for his rheumatism! And after all, here I am with Mrs Knightley. What a pity your name is not Emma.'

Elaine's smile faltered for a moment. 'That was always the plan, you know, that we would name. . . .' She bit her lip and turned her head away and after a moment Charlotte continued, striving for her previous light-hearted tone.

'That puts me in mind of something I forgot to mention before. Are you sure it's such a good idea for you to come to Bath? I fear that a baking hot September might not be the best time for you to try the treatments.'

'My dear.' Elaine shrugged and pouted at Charlotte with a mixture of amusement and resignation. 'How could I argue with my husband when he was so pleased with himself for making the arrangements? Even when he knows. . . . I'm sorry to leave

31

you to brave the company alone, Char,' Elaine broke off her sentence then smiled at the younger girl, changing the subject. 'But I promised Kit faithfully that I would, under no circumstances, overdo things on our first night.'

'Wouldn't you be more comfortable in bed, Elaine?' Charlotte had noted the violet shadows under her friend's eyes, but she made the suggestion warily. Elaine rarely made any reference to her infirmity herself, nor did she tolerate any discussion of her health by others.

'Probably,' admitted the other woman, turning to smile and nod at her maid who was waiting for instructions. 'Do you hear that, Jackson? I promise to go to bed shortly and with no fuss. In the meantime, Mrs Richmond will cluck over me just as much as you would yourself, while you get my bed ready for me.'

'As you wish, ma'am,' came the quiet response, followed by a quick frown in Charlotte's direction. 'I rely on you, Miss Char, if you'd be so kind, to keep her from excitement, it does wear her out so. I'll be back directly.' At Charlotte's nod of reassurance the older woman left the room with a heavy tread and an anxious backward glance at her mistress.

'Dear Jackson,' Elaine was amused. 'She can never forget that she was my nurse and has looked after me since I was a month old. I can tell she approves of you though, Char, because she insisted there was no need for you to bring a maid and that she could manage for us both. This is a mark of signal favour, I'll have you know. *And* she calls you Miss Char, even though she is usually a stickler for the correct forms.'

She settled herself more comfortably on the *chaise-longue* by the window. 'How fortunate that we have our own sitting room, I can lie here and watch the world go by whenever I wish. Now, do tell me about Agnes. I'm so glad she and Mr Benson returned in the nick of time for you to see her before our own departure. How did she seem? And was she disappointed not to be going straight to the vicarage?'

'If she was, she made no mention of it.' Charlotte grinned. 'You know Agnes – she sees the hand of Providence in everything, though I suspect a few days in the company of her sister-in-law and the weeping willow may challenge even her pious resignation. No, what was preoccupying her more than anything was the fact that she had spent much of the honeymoon month recovering from her seasickness on the ferry crossing to Cowes, short as it was, and that even now, she still suffers from a recurrence of that same *mal-de-mer* every morning even though she is on dry land!'

She waited for her companion to digest this information and smiled in sympathy at the outburst of giggles.

'Oh no, already? Poor Agnes, has she really no idea? Who would have thought Mr Benson had it in him! Did you say anything to her, Char? Surely someone should mention to her what she is really suffering from?'

'I'd have said something, of course, had I not been coming away the very next day but as it was, I've left it to Lily who at least can sympathize with her, and to Lady Frampton who will apply robust common sense to any vapours that Melicent, the weeping willow, succumbs to upon hearing the news.' As Jackson reappeared, wearing a look of determination, Charlotte rose and kissed her friend. 'I'll leave you in peace, dear Elaine, and go to satisfy my curiosity about our fellow inmates.'

'Char!' exclaimed Elaine in laughing protest. 'You simply must not call them inmates, Waterloo House is not an asylum, you know. Remember one of Kit's cousins stayed here in the spring of last year, which is how we knew of it. He recommended it to us as a most comfortable house with congenial fellow guests, an accomplished cook and an attentive hostess. Mrs Montgomery is a widow, I gather, and when she inherited this great barrack of a house, a year or so ago, alas with very little income, she hit upon this splendid idea of catering solely for invalids. Kit's cousin jokes that she even retains her own medical practitioner, but that was just his fun, though he insisted that there seemed to be doctors at the door almost every day.'

'I know.' Charlotte paused at the door, with a mischievous grin. 'You told me so, my dear, and I'm sure it's all perfectly respectable, but I confess I'm intrigued at the prospect of a houseful of invalids, all here to endure some form of treatment. What in the world do you suppose they all talk about at dinner? Not too detailed a catalogue of ailments, I do trust.'

It was a new experience, Charlotte reflected, to enter a room crowded with strangers and not to feel a constraint, a nervous awareness of her situation, or at least, she thought with a wry smile, a little less constraint than usual. It was simply the height of unlikelihood that she would encounter anyone who had known her in Australia. It was another world, another life, so surely there could be no one in Bath who could point a finger and denounce her?

In spite of her bravado she experienced a moment of unaccustomed shyness and, biting her lip, she made her way across the dark gold-coloured carpet to where her hostess stood in anxious consultation with a stout gentleman in his late fifties.

'Ah, Mrs Richmond, how do you do?' Mrs Letitia Montgomery, a small, faded blonde woman of uncertain age and protruding blue eyes, was all gracious hospitality. 'I was glad to hear that Mrs Knightley had decided to rest. I always encourage my guests to take things steadily in their first few days and an early night is by far the best course for her after a long journey, don't you agree?'

'Quite, quite,' interposed the gentleman by her side. 'Rest, that's the key, soon have the lady feeling more the thing, hey?'

As Charlotte nodded politely in reply, Mrs Montgomery hastened to perform the introduction.

'Do forgive me. Mrs Richmond, this is Captain Horatio Penbury, one of my most welcome regular guests.'

'Yes, indeed.' Captain Penbury bent his large red face over Charlotte's hand, with a flourishing bow. 'That's Horatio St Vincent Penbury, at your service, ma'am, named of course after the battle of Cape St Vincent and its glorious victor, word having reached my father of the victory even as my mama was lying in.' He nodded jovially across Charlotte to his hostess. 'I'm afraid you must put up with me, as here I am again, to try the waters and the new treatments. I have a musket ball lodged inside me, don't y'know,' he confided to Charlotte in a loud whisper. 'Fit as a fiddle most of the time, then, by Gad, sick as a cat. That was the war with the Americans, y'know. I was a midshipman; just a young stripling but I got my wound by an unlucky shot from the USS *Chesapeake*. That was in 1813, a long time ago. It happened during the engagement when we captured her from the Americans,' he added proudly.

'Quite so, Captain. Oh, Captain, please don't sit on that gilt chair, it was left me by my great-aunt.' Mrs Montgomery hurried Charlotte away from the abashed captain towards a man in early middle age, accompanied by an elderly man and a small girl. 'Mrs Richmond, allow me to present Monsieur le Comte de Kersac, together with his son, M. Armel de Kersac and Mlle Marianne.' A frown creased her brow and she fluttered at the younger man. 'Oh, M. Armel, if you would be so good as to take your arm from the mantel? The Chinese vase by your elbow there was left me by my grandmama. . . .'

Charlotte dropped a decorous curtsy and made polite small talk with the two men while she scrutinized them under her lashes. The elder Frenchman was a short, spare man with an air of melancholy about him, while his son, who moved away hastily from the ornately carved brown and orange-streaked marble mantelpiece, was built on a much larger scale, and was a cheerful-looking man in his early forties. Both men spoke excellent English as did the little girl, who whispered that she was ten; she was built like her father, quite a tall child but fair-haired where his hair was brown, and her blue eyes lacked his twinkling humour.

'Well, *madame*?' enquired the elder gentleman. 'Now that you see us, do you think that you will like us?'

'I beg your pardon, *monsieur*,' she blushed. 'I didn't mean to stare.'

'No.' He smiled at her kindly. 'You were summing us up, were you not? I think you are used to making up your mind quickly whether you are in the presence of friend or foe – so tell me, I am curious. How have you classified *us*?'

His acute assessment startled her and she felt a sudden tremor of alarm. Surely I can't be so transparent, she fretted but he touched her hand in a brief, gentle reassurance. 'Pray do not be anxious, my child,' he said quietly as he drew her slightly to one side. 'It is merely that I recognize certain attributes. When one has been very much afraid,' he added, in a low voice that was indistinguishable to anyone standing near them, 'It leaves a mark that is unmistakable to a fellow sufferer.' He nodded and moved away as their hostess continued her round of introductions, leaving Charlotte feeling shaken and intrigued, but also slightly alarmed, by his remark.

'Here we have a neighbour of yours, I believe, Mrs Richmond.' Mrs Montgomery presented Charlotte to a man with a thatch of very dark hair, who looked to be somewhere in his forties. A heavy, unbroken eyebrow fought a jutting chin for dominance of his face but the forbidding and rather ape-like appearance this might have suggested was belied by an expression of undaunted and cheerful optimism. 'Mr Simeon Chettle, who has broken his journey home to Finchbourne to recruit his strength by taking the waters and trying the new medical treatments.'

'You look surprised, Mrs Richmond.' With a polite smile of enquiry Charlotte took the eagerly outstretched hand. 'Indeed you may, for although I do habitually reside in Finchbourne, I have been touring the Continent for the last six months and the fatigues of the journey sent me here, to dear Waterloo House, before I take up the reins again.'

'I believe I know your house. It is just at the end of the village, is it not?' Charlotte remarked, having worked out who he must be. 'Out on the road to Winchester, the imposing red-brick residence with the charming clump of silver birch trees to the side? I'm happy to meet you, Mr Chettle, and sorry to hear that you are so tired by your journeying.'

'Thank you, thank you.' Mr Chettle looked gratified at her description of his house – in truth a bleak-looking barn – and he nodded gratefully over the hand he retained in his own sadly clammy grasp. 'I had embarked on my tour with high expectations, you know. It was to be a tour of discovery, concentrating on funerary monuments and mourning customs on the Continent, as this is my great interest.'

Charlotte blinked but maintained an air of interest while gently withdrawing her hand. It took her all her resolution not to wipe it surreptitiously on her skirt.

'Alas, although the first two months of the trip were an outstanding success, my dear mama, who always insisted on accompanying me upon my travels, was taken ill near Innsbruck and succumbed to a paralytic seizure that sadly took her from me.'

'How truly dreadful for you,' Charlotte commiserated with him. 'I do hope you felt able to continue on your pilgrimage? I'm sure that your mother would not have wished you to curtail your investigation, even in such sad circumstances.'

'My dear Mrs Richmond,' he cried in admiration. 'Why, you have chosen the very word. It was, it became indeed, a "pilgrimage" as I took care to follow every arrangement of our itinerary. As you rightly suggest, dear Mama would have wished nothing less. Indeed, during my initial unbridled grief I did consider taking Mama in her coffin along with me on my travels, so little did I wish to be parted from her, but luckily I fell in with an English clergyman who had been most inconveniently delayed in Innsbruck by the unfortunate and premature demise of his own wife. He represented to me the difficulties of such a proceeding and offered to conduct my dear mother's funeral service.

'By then I had consoled myself that Mama would be happy for me, in the interests of my lifelong research, to experience a Tyrolean interment.' He gave a gusty sigh and looked disappointed. 'Sadly, the service was very plain as he turned out to be an evangelical and very low church, so there was none of the ceremony and colour of our own dear High Anglican church at Finchbourne or, indeed, that of the more usual Roman Catholic obsequies prevalent in that part of Austria.'

'Oh dear.' Charlotte felt that some response, however inadequate, was necessary. 'How very unfortunate. I do hope you were able to pursue your interests later on?'

'Oh yes,' he responded happily, beaming at her from under

that heavy black brow. 'Rome was of particular interest, of course, especially the catacombs, and I have many little mementoes of my visit. I found it was quite easy to purchase small grave ornaments and mourning devices. I shall have a delightful time cataloguing my souvenirs when I return home. I am happy, too, to be able to inform you that I attended, in person, no fewer than sixteen funeral services when I was on my travels.'

He rubbed his hands with glee and Charlotte wondered, with detached interest, if the gentleman was conscious of his own unpleasantly clammy grasp. He nodded round at the rest of the guests, or at least those who had not found it prudent to move away. 'I made no distinction between denominations either and was able to compare the various services, to the advantage of our own system of belief, of course.' He edged closer towards her with an air of concern mingled with a sudden eager gleam of interest. 'But I believe I have not offered my condolences, my dear young lady. I understand you are but recently widowed? I was only slightly acquainted with Major Richmond, but, of course, he was abroad so much with his regiment.'

Charlotte, taking a backward step as unobtrusively as possible, murmured polite gratitude but it was of no use. He surged forward to loom uncomfortably close as he continued, taking her hand again and pressing it with damp fervour between both of his own: 'I feel it very much that I was not able to attend the funeral,' he assured her. 'You must tell me all about it.' He nodded again, eagerly thrusting his large face even closer to Charlotte's own. 'I make it my business to attend the obsequies of all my acquaintances,' he told her earnestly. 'I feel it is a kind attention and I know that it offers comfort to the bereaved. I tell you sometimes the grieving relatives are so overwhelmed with grief that they cannot attend sufficiently to the wants of the visiting mourners. When that is the case I make certain that I introduce myself to everyone present, whether known to me or not, and I can assure you that sometimes gentlemen have been struck silent at this attention. It is very gratifying.'

'Indeed, sir, I can readily believe it must be.' Charlotte was grateful to her hostess when Mrs Montgomery whisked her away with an apology to Mr Chettle followed by a small scream of protest.

'Oh, Mr Chettle,' she shrilled, scuttling towards a small ormolu table. 'Pray do not disturb my little arrangement of *objets d'art*. Those little porcelain animals and boxes are Meissen and were left to me by a dear, dear friend, now sadly departed.

'Let me present you to Mrs Attwell and her son,' she urged, having satisfied herself that Mr Chettle had proved obedient and was looking abashed as he slunk towards the imposing bay window which was draped in opulent gold velvet curtains that matched the gold in the flocked and figured wallpaper. She led Charlotte to a pair of chairs at the fireside where a lady, surely on the shady side of seventy, sat with a choleric-looking younger man, as wide as he was tall, in clerical dress at her side. Their relationship was evident in the similarity of features and in their large-boned figures although the lady lacked her son's height and could frankly be described as squat. The reverend gentleman, although probably no more than one or two and forty, displayed a domed skull as innocent of hair as the fine ostrich egg Charlotte had owned as a child and the wisps of hair that dared to escape the lady's sternly utilitarian cap showed a faded auburn that matched her son's bristling eyebrows. There was no mistaking their kinship and their expressions too, evinced an identical curiosity at greeting a stranger.

The lady inclined her neck very slightly and extended two stubby fingers as she shook hands but the trace of a frown creased her brow as she cast a further, appraising look at Charlotte, then she took over the introductions from her hostess who bustled away. 'My son,' she said, her rather harsh voice softening as the clergyman rose. 'The Reverend Decimus Attwell. We are in Bath for a short visit while Decimus consults various doctors.'

Decimus Attwell's small brown eyes lit up as he surveyed Charlotte and he moved closer to her, ignoring a disapproving maternal sniff and stretching out an inordinately large hand which, as a surreptitious downward glance confirmed, matched his inordinately large feet. 'My mother coddles me to a degree,' he confided, with a louring glance at his parent. 'I had a bad bout of pneumonia in January and am finding it difficult to shake off the weakness it engendered. The warmer weather is helping, but that wasn't quick enough for my mother, so here we are. My parish is in Leicestershire, quite a distance, so we are making a stay here, three weeks at least.'

Mrs Attwell frowned more deeply. 'I wish you would not treat your illness so flippantly, Decimus,' she reproved him, then turned to Charlotte with a slight baring of her teeth. 'I understand you are not seeking medical attention yourself, Mrs Richmond. Mrs Montgomery says you are here with a friend.'

During dinner Charlotte found herself seated beside Mr Chettle who, while leaning a little too closely towards her, enlightened her about the funerary customs of the ancient Etruscans, along with some passing, and detailed, references to the disembowelling and embalming to be found in many cultures, customs which he assured her he greatly admired. On her other side sat Captain Penbury who gave her a very full account of the engagement between the Royal Navy and the United States Navy on the occasion of the capture of the USS *Chesapeake* in November 1813, as well as some interesting and distressing information on the unpleasant consequences entailed upon carrying around a musket ball inside one's anatomy. Discretion overcame his eagerness to describe his symptoms quite in every particular however and he bent once more upon his depressing invalid diet of grey gruel.

Released to the comparative safety of the drawing-room once more, she was just deciding to make her escape on the ground of fatigue and of wishing to attend to Elaine, when Captain Penbury hailed her.

'My dear Mrs Richmond,' he bellowed, in his bluff quarter deck style. 'Allow me to present my new acquaintance and one of our fellow guests at Waterloo House, Mr . . . ah . . . Mr Jonas Tibbins, it that not correct, sir? Been dining out elsewhere tonight. A visitor to our shores from the United States, no less, but latterly from our fair capital city, so he tells me.' Captain Penbury then ruined the encomium he had bestowed upon London by adding, 'Dreadful place, mind you, not surprised you've headed west to get away from it. Inhabited largely by foreigners and criminals, it's my belief.'

'Delighted. . . .' Charlotte began, then faltered into silence as she gazed into the eyes of the man who had been watching her with such keen interest on Salisbury Station earlier that day.

'But my dear young lady,' Mr Tibbins broke off his suave greeting, to exclaim, 'you are looking very pale; may I be of assistance?'

'No, no, pray do not be concerned, sir,' she hastened to assure him. 'It is merely that I am rather tired after a long day's travelling. A night's rest will certainly restore me.'

He gave a sympathetic nod and looked at her again, more closely. 'But surely we have met before, ma'am?' He frowned as she shook her head wordlessly, her mouth too dry with a moment's sudden panic to speak. 'Ah, I believe I recall the occasion. We were fellow travellers on the train from Salisbury. That is it, I remember now.' His eyes narrowed and he looked at her with such renewed interest that she had to summon all her powers of self-control not to shuffle guiltily under his scrutiny.

'Are you recovered, sir,' she managed to speak without croaking, 'from that unfortunate accident? I saw you bravely rescuing that young lady; how fortunate that she did not fall under the moving train.'

'Indeed.' His voice, with the faintest of drawls, sounded slightly absent as he continued to gaze at her. 'The lady suffered a flesh wound only, I believe. Did you . . . did you happen to observe what actually happened, ma'am? How she came to fall like that, I mean?'

'I fear not.' She shook her head and he pursed his lips. 'I assumed it was the press of the crowd, people boarding the train and others bidding them farewell.'

'That must be so,' he agreed, though his slightly balding forehead was still creased by a frown, then he made a visible effort and smiled at her. 'I was on my way back to Waterloo

House after a day or so away and when I first observed you, ma'am, you were standing on the platform with a gentleman, your husband, no doubt?'

Paying no attention to her denial Mr Tibbins looked round the room. 'Indeed, that is he, is it not? The tall gentleman in conversation with our hostess? Pray allow me the honour of an introduction to him.'

'Oh no.' Charlotte hastened to put him right. 'I am a widow, sir, and the gentleman you saw this morning is married to my friend, Mrs Knightley who has dined in her room tonight, being an invalid. That gentleman with Mrs Montgomery is a French count, I understand. I believe he is here with his small daughter and his elderly father.'

'A French count?' Mr Tibbins, already scrutinizing the other guest, now straightened up, his eyes alight and eager. 'I must make his acquaintance, if indeed, we are not already known to each other. I have many business interests in France and am often to be found in Paris.'

Later, in her room, Charlotte thoughtfully plaited her hair for the night and bit her lip. I really must not allow myself to panic so, she decided. How likely is it that someone from my childhood in Australia will turn up in Bath to unmask me? Or from my travels in India last year. The devastation wrought by the Mutiny can cover a multitude of sins, even mine, if anyone should question me. Besides, I have certainly never visited America and nor did my stepfather, but the mere recollection of her alarm was causing her heart to pound more rapidly even now.

What a relief that he lost interest in me so rapidly. Charlotte blew out her candle and climbed into bed. But he was certainly more than usually interested in the younger M. de Kersac, I wonder why? And he was right; I suppose there is a superficial resemblance between my fellow guest and Kit Knightley, from a distance at least. Thank heaven I was able to make my excuses to Mrs Montgomery and escape shortly afterward. I was mistaken this time about his interest, but am I never going to be able to relax? It seems as though the past is always just around the corner, waiting to trip me up.

*

Next morning Charlotte looked in on Elaine before going down to breakfast.

'Before you ask, Char,' smiled her friend, 'I slept most of the night and am feeling rested. There's no need for you to telegraph to Kit, or for him to come galloping to my rescue. And you need not sneak a sidelong look at Jackson either: she'll confirm that I am perfectly well.'

The maid gave her a grim smile and nodded to Charlotte. 'I wouldn't go so far as to say that, exactly, but she's none the worse for the journey, Miss Char. You go and get something to eat.'

All the other guests at Waterloo House were gathering at the breakfast table, obviously eager to avail themselves early of the medical delights on offer in Bath. Captain Penbury greeted Charlotte with one of his flourishing bows, cut off rather abruptly by a groan as he bent a little too vigorously. Mr Chettle leaped to the door when he spotted her as did the younger French count. Both gentlemen, however, were forestalled by Mrs Montgomery who glided forward and greeted Charlotte with her anxious but hospitable smile.

'Do come and sit here, Mrs Richmond,' she beamed. 'No, no, not just there, I do beg of you, that seat is always kept empty in honour of my dear late husband. Here you are. I'm sure you will be comfortable between Mr Tibbins and M. de Kersac. I wonder, do you speak French at all, though, of course M. de Kersac speaks English most delightfully?'

Charlotte contented herself with a deprecating smile as she took her seat, ushered thence with great ceremony by the imposing footman. One of her stepfather's maxims slipped into her head: *Always keep something back, Char. No need to enlighten all and sundry as to your intelligence or abilities. Sometimes indeed, it can be advisable to appear a dull bluestocking but on other occasions it might be better to be thought of as a sweet young thing without a thought beyond fripperies. Either way you should never give a hint that you might have more brains in your little finger than most men have in their whole bodies.*

In fact Charlotte spoke French almost fluently having learned the language from her godmother whose despairing mother had been wont to declare that *at least Meg could boast of one of the accomplishments expected of a lady*. Charlotte gave a reminiscent smile; the countess, Meg's mother had not, fortunately for her own peace of mind, survived to hear of Lady Meg's rather less ladylike habits which had culminated in her hasty departure from England. Sometimes, too, there had been lessons from various elderly French people, all claiming to be aristocrats who had fled abroad from the Reign of Terror. Lady Meg had been privately scathing about some of these claims and had once descended in wrath upon a lesson, declaring the teacher's accent to be quite unacceptably plebeian for her god-daughter. Charlotte recalled with a fond smile that her mother, Molly, had run into the street after the old lady, to thrust half a loaf and a few pence into her hand, to soften Meg's accusation.

Charlotte found herself giving the elderly French gentleman a slight curtsy as he resumed his seat beside her. Even Meg could have had no doubts about his aristocratic antecedents, Charlotte decided, but the gentleman from America and London, on her other side, received only a polite inclination of her head.

Do I like him? She pondered the question as she applied herself to her meal. Because I just don't know and that's not like me; I usually weigh people up before I pronounce judgement. Mr Tibbins however, makes me feel uneasy and has done so from the moment I clapped eyes on him and I simply don't know why. She recalled an old woman in Freemantle, said to have been born in the Highlands of Scotland, who once complained that one of her neighbours gave her a *'cauld grue'*. That's it, she decided; the American gentleman, although he seems perfectly pleasant, gives me a *cauld grue* and whether unfairly or not I do not trust the man.

To do him justice there was nothing unpleasing either in the man's appearance or his manners. He was of medium build, medium height and of undistinguished appearance with a pleasant voice that held, Charlotte thought, the merest trace of what she supposed must be an American accent. He was solicitous in looking after her needs and engaged her in light conversation, enquiring after her plans for the day.

'I don't know yet,' she told him. 'I'm here with my friend who is to try various medical treatments so until she is happily situated I can make no plans for my own entertainment. Besides,' she added, 'as today is Sunday I expect we shall spend the day very quietly, recovering from the exertions of the journey, though I certainly hope to attend a service in Bath Abbey if it proves possible.'

The old Frenchman on her right ate silently and sparingly, apparently absorbed in his breakfast, but Charlotte was aware of a keen intelligence and a wariness about him. She recalled his remark of the previous evening: '*When one has been very much afraid, it leaves a mark that is unmistakable to a fellow sufferer.*' Well, he was right about me, she thought. During this last twelve months I have lost the mother and stepfather I adored; I've been alone and penniless, one of the enemy in the middle of a country torn by war; forced by circumstances into marriage with a dreadful and frightening man; and finally, when I allowed myself to believe that I was safe at last, I found myself embroiled in a mystery and threatened by a murderer. I wonder what great fear it can be that M. de Kersac remembers? I imagine it is probably the French Revolution; he must surely be old enough to have lived through the Terror and that, without question, would have 'left its mark' on him.

Her other neighbour eventually laid down his knife and fork, wiped his mouth on his napkin and smiled round the table at his fellow guests.

'How pleasant it is for me to return as a guest to Waterloo House after my brief sojourn elsewhere and how fortunate I feel to have discovered such an agreeable residence in the first place,' he announced in a confiding manner and with a genial nod towards his hostess. 'I have been travelling widely in England since I landed and a chance meeting with a charming lady when I was lately in Brighton told me of this house. I believe she was

45

an acquaintance of yours, dear Mrs Montgomery. We must have a cosy talk about her soon.'

Charlotte, buttering her toast, surprised an expression of utter dismay on the face of her landlady; a face that seemed suddenly wary, much older, pale and drawn. However, the lady had herself well in hand and merely murmured a commonplace rejoinder. What perplexed Charlotte more though, was the distinct air of quiet satisfaction that Mr Tibbins radiated as a result of this interchange.

On the opposite side of the large mahogany table Captain Penbury and Mr Chettle were discussing their various travels abroad, with the sailor advocating the benefits of a sea voyage, while the younger man spoke up in vigorous defence of the health-giving heat of Egypt where he had spent a period of several months, some ten years previously.

Mr Tibbins, whose hearing was evidently acute, cocked an eager ear to this conversation and Charlotte had the oddest feeling, almost as though he was happily checking their remarks against some list in his head. Presently he broke into the talk himself, with some anecdotes about life in America before he returned to their topic. 'So, gentlemen, you have both enjoyed the delights of the eastern Mediterranean climate?' he enquired. 'Did you enjoy Alexandria at all, Mr Chettle? I believe there is a flourishing trade, both legal and otherwise, in the many relics to be found pertaining to Cleopatra, that beautiful lady of legend whom age cannot wither.'

Mr Chettle's face darkened; his jaw jutted forbiddingly and his overhanging eyebrow loomed in a frown as he gave a curt nod in reply and addressed himself to his breakfast. Mr Tibbins gave a slight nod of satisfaction and turned to the other guest. 'And what of your own travels, Captain?' His smile deepened as he observed the sudden fidgeting that overtook the naval man. 'Were you by any chance engaged in the Battle of Acre?'

The man from London shook his head and sighed at the other man's abrupt denial. 'No? Perhaps a relative of yours took part? What a stirring battle that must have been. Only eighteen years ago and so fortunate – fewer than twenty of your gallant British sailor boys killed, against more than a thousand of the enemy. How one would have cheered to see such courage and derring-do among the British officers.'

Again, Charlotte was puzzled as he assumed that same enigmatic smile while the bluff Captain Penbury's already weatherbeaten red face was suffused with an even deeper terracotta glow.

At this point Mrs Montgomery resumed control of her breakfast table and not a moment too soon, decided Charlotte. Their hostess herself still wore a look of wary concern while Mr Chettle was frowning at his half-eaten mutton chop, his appetite apparently vanished, and Captain Penbury, who had subsided from his turkey-cock bluster, was downing his weak tea with an air of imperfectly assumed indifference. The cause of all this unrest, Mr Tibbins, sat peeling an orange with perfect unconcern.

'We are expecting a most distinguished new guest,' Mrs Montgomery told them, determinedly not letting her glance fall on the disruptive gentleman. She cast a gracious smile round the table and said smugly, 'A Lady Buckwell has written to engage a sitting room and a bedchamber for a month and she is bringing her own maid. Apparently she is an elderly lady who wishes to reacquaint herself with the delights and diversions of Bath which she knew in her youth.'

Charlotte readily understood her hostess's air of complacent satisfaction. An elderly lady with her own maid, staying for a month and obviously well-to-do, was a catch indeed, particularly at this time of year when most visitors headed for the country rather than a hot, stuffy city and Bath was thin of company. Bath had sunk into genteel shabbiness since its heyday in the Regency, so Mr Chettle had informed her the previous evening, and even Waterloo House, occupied as it was with invalids all year round, had at least one or two bedrooms still vacant, so Lady Buckwell could have her sitting room without difficulty.

'What plans do you have for today, Mrs Richmond?' Mrs

Montgomery addressed Charlotte with a kindly condescension, interrupting herself to let out a tiny scream of dismay. 'Oh, pray, Mr Tibbins; I beg of you do not move that vase. It is Sèvres and was bequeathed to me by my first husband's mother's cousin. It is one of my most precious possessions.'

Charlotte was secretly amused to note that even Mr Tibbins's customary bounce was a little subdued at this admonition and that he snatched his hand away looking like a guilty schoolboy.

'I've just been telling Mr Tibbins,' she explained to Mrs Montgomery, 'that I hope to be able to attend church, but that I can't settle on any excursion until I've discovered what my friend, Mrs Knightley, is doing. She must see her medical adviser before any plans can be made.'

'Very wise, very wise,' boomed Captain Penbury, who clearly could not bear any discussion of symptoms and treatments that did not allow him to take part. 'And who might Mrs Knightley's medical adviser be? I should call myself honoured if the lady would let me be her guide, if she has not yet decided on her course of treatment.'

Charlotte was spared the necessity of answering as the captain, diverted, broke off their conversation as he stared past her out of the window.

'By George,' he exclaimed, his face alight with interest. 'Talk of the devil—' He broke off in some confusion as Mrs Montgomery's slightly protuberant blue eyes rested on him in glacial disdain. 'Harrumph, beg your pardon, ma'am ... but there, just outside this house is the latest and most sought after medical man in Bath. And, by heaven, he's just walked up the steps of this house. Now there, Mrs Richmond,' – he turned eagerly back to Charlotte – 'that's the fellow your friend should see. What was his name now? Rumble? Runcorn? Aye, he has them all queuing to consult him on the latest treatments so I fear Mrs Knightley might not stand a chance of seeing him.'

The maid entered and bobbed a curtsy to her mistress. 'Beg your pardon, ma'am, but Mrs Knightley would be glad if Mrs Richmond would look in on her. I've just shown Mr Jonathan Radnor to Mrs Knightley's sitting-room.'

*

The electrical medical practitioner in whose revolutionary methods Kit Knightley was placing such trust bowed over Charlotte's hand and turned back to his patient.

'As you will have heard, dear Mrs Knightley,' the young man smiled, 'I trained under Mr Frederick York who practised here in Bath until three years ago. Like Mr York, I was initially apprenticed to a chemist but then completed further studies under Mr York's auspices before proceeding to Paris for further practical experience. Mr York, however, specialized in galvanism which certainly had some successes but which, in my opinion, causes too great a degree of discomfort for the patient.'

'Discomfort?' Charlotte interrupted with a sharp query and was aware of Jackson shuffling her feet slightly where she stood protectively behind her mistress. Charlotte was also aware of an approving nod in her own direction from Jackson, as she spoke up further. 'Mr Knightley didn't mention any discomfort when he arranged for this treatment.'

'No, no, Miss, er, Mrs Richmond.' Mr Radnor hastened to explain, his brown eyes meltingly sincere in his handsome face. 'That was in the past. The method I use is known as Faradism.' He frowned for a moment then continued, 'I suppose the simplest way I can describe it is that I use electricity to stimulate a response in the patient's muscles. This response, when used judiciously by a skilled operator, can have a markedly beneficial effect upon the nervous system in chronic patients.'

Elaine's sweet smile betrayed none of the despair Charlotte knew her to feel. Both women were aware that no stimulus of muscular response would benefit Elaine in the long run; that her condition was beyond medical help. Elaine refused to discuss her symptoms, but Charlotte was well aware that her friend was suffering increasing bouts of internal pain, besides the long-standing delicate condition of her heart that was responsible for her bodily weakness. Both women, however, knew that at home in Hampshire, Kit Knightley was clinging desperately to the belief that this radical new treatment would restore his wife completely to health and neither of them could bear to shatter his faith.

'I suggest a restful morning, Mrs Knightley,' the electrical specialist was advocating. 'As I understand you spent most of yesterday travelling, we will take it very steadily.' His gently superior smile grated on Charlotte, but she noted that Elaine seemed a little soothed by the young man's attentions; she was certainly listening with interest to his suggestions. 'In bed, if you please, although this afternoon it will be acceptable, if you feel your strength equal to it, to rest upon this comfortable-looking day bed so conveniently to hand by the window.' He bowed again and Charlotte hid a smile at Elaine's equally ceremonious nod.

'I fear I must forbid any attendance at church, dear lady, and tomorrow morning I would like you to remain in bed until noon. In the afternoon I will send round a bath chair with a respectable and reliable man to push it. It is a little cooler today and I am assured that we can expect a health-giving breeze tomorrow so I'm sure you will feel all the better for some fresh air and new interests.'

He gave her an approving smile. 'On Tuesday at about eleven o'clock, I would like you to come to my treatment rooms just off Milsom Street down towards the Pump Room and we shall commence treatment. If your maid could pack several loose nightgowns I think you would find that the most comfortable garb.'

Charlotte saw the young man down to the entrance hall, asking further details of how long the initial treatment would take and whether Elaine would need extra rest afterwards. As they spoke together under the suspicious eye of Mrs Montgomery's mother's brother's portrait, the ubiquitous Mr Tibbins descended the stairs, admired himself in the mirror, stroked his modest side-whiskers, added a tilt to his hat, gave a preliminary twirl to the cane he carried on every possible occasion, and sauntered out of the front door, with a graceful nod to Charlotte. His gaze fell on her companion with mere mild curiosity at first until a spark lit his eye and he stared with avid interest before going on his way with a jaunty spring in his step.

'Who . . . who was that?' The dapper young medical man was looking distinctly alarmed. 'Mrs Richmond, who was that gentleman who has just gone out?

CHAPTER 3

Elaine Knightley professed herself content with the programme suggested by her new medical adviser.

'Frankly, my dear Char,' she admitted. 'I shall be only too glad to stay in my room today and am happy to postpone making the acquaintance of my fellow guests. No, I'm not ill, don't look so anxious. I am merely tired after the journey and all the excitements before we left home. Why don't you do as you suggested and make your way to the abbey? I remember it as a beautiful building and you will enjoy the literary and historical associations, but do try to concentrate on the sermon too!'

Charlotte grinned and nodded in agreement and Elaine went on, 'What would you like to do this afternoon?' As Charlotte shrugged, Elaine looked thoughtful. 'In that case, if you have no decided preference, perhaps we could spend a peaceful afternoon exploring this box of novels that has just been delivered to me? Kit, bless him, sent them an order. If you would read aloud to me, I confess I should enjoy it very much, perhaps after tea? Kit is no hand at reading aloud which is a pity as I do enjoy lying back and listening, so it would be a great pleasure if you would do the honours.'

The service in Bath Abbey was inspiring but try as she might Charlotte's efforts to concentrate upon uplifting thoughts were interrupted by memories of her mother and Will Glover and digressions into remembered passages from various much-loved novels. The other guests at Waterloo House jostled in Charlotte's thoughts also, in particular the disturbing Mr Tibbins who seemed to upset his fellow residents merely by opening his mouth. But nothing he said was impolite, mused Charlotte as she listened with half an ear to the sermon, her eyes demurely on the prayer book in her lap. She cast her mind back and could only recall fragments of what had seemed to be mere social niceties. She was only too aware, however, that he was keeping her under observation nearly all the time and could only be grateful that his interest appeared to be benign. In fact, during their brief conversational encounters she had begun to find him a sympathetic and amusing fellow guest, happy to relate tales of his life in New York and other cities in America where he seemed to have travelled extensively.

It was a puzzle, but, she sighed, she had a greater puzzle to hand. After the service Charlotte strolled down towards the river and sat down on a convenient bench, delving into her reticule and pulling out a much creased letter. A frown marred her smooth brow as she read the pointed calligraphy for quite the twentieth time.

My dear Madam,

I thank you most humbly for the good wishes you graciously convey to me from my old friend, Dr Perry, now your neighbour in Hampshire. It was a delightful surprise to have news of him and I am only too happy to be of service to a friend of his. Sadly, however, I am unable to satisfy your request for information regarding the birth, in Bath, of a female orphan in late November of the year 1819.

As my old friend told you, I have a particular interest in female delinquency which is a scourge upon the fair name of womanhood and upon receipt of your kind enquiry, I betook myself to make enquiries on your friend's behalf. Alas, the registers of the Female Penitentiary here in Bath proved to be of little assistance in your quest as there is no record of a female orphan, Molly Wesley by name, having been born to any of the unfortunate women confined there. Nor, dear lady, was there any female child born during a month either side of the date you gave me.

It is a grievous admission for me to be obliged to make, dear

Mrs Richmond, but I am unable to serve you further in this matter. Should you wish, on your acquaintance's behalf (and what a fortunate female she must be to have so solicitous a friend) to investigate further, I can only suggest that there existed at that time several small homes for orphans, run by charitable persons.

I remain, with deepest apologies for so inadequate a response to your cry for help,

Your humble servant,
Jas Yolland

She had said that there were three particular reasons for her delight in the proposed visit to Bath but in fact there was a fourth, which she had confided to only one other. The notion, when it struck her shortly after Elaine's welcome invitation, had seemed heaven-sent. Bath was where Charlotte's mother, Molly Glover, née Wesley, had been born – in an orphanage – she had told her daughter. It had seemed such an obvious proceeding to Charlotte to make discreet enquiries about that same orphanage and when she had confided the bare bones of her problem to Dr Perry, the Finchbourne physician, he had been triumphant when he unearthed the address of his old acquaintance.

'Prosy old bore,' he had confided to Charlotte. 'But if there's anything to be found, he'll ferret it out for you.' He had cocked an inquisitive eyebrow at her. 'Someone you knew in Australia or India no doubt?'

Well, she sighed, as she folded the letter and slipped it into her bag, that avenue is closed off to me but I am certainly not abandoning my quest. As Mr Yolland says, there were, and probably still are, some private institutions. My difficulty will be in discovering them and seeking out anyone who has any recollection of nearly forty years ago.

Elaine's proposed programme for their entertainment was carried out to their mutual benefit, Charlotte reading aloud with brio and Elaine applauding at particularly dramatic moments. Once or twice Charlotte faltered in her performance but she pulled herself together and was confident Elaine had noticed nothing untoward in her manner. Charlotte, however, had much to consider and was glad to fall in with the suggestion that she should forego the delights of dinner with her fellow guests and share Elaine's supper in their sitting-room.

It had been such an oddly frightening little incident, she recalled, when she was able later to sit in her own room and reflect on the event.

She had taken an early tea in the drawing-room of Waterloo House, accompanied by her hostess who dispensed the beverage from a massive silver urn, along with Mrs Attwell and the son she kept so firmly tied to her apron strings, Mr Chettle, and the bluff captain whose ponderous gallantries were as trying in their way as the unpleasant descriptions of funeral customs which she reluctantly suspected were her Hampshire neighbour's attempt at charming her.

As soon as it could not be condemned as impolite, Charlotte gathered up her shawl and reticule, bade a pleasant farewell to the assembled company and swiftly left the house, seeking some fresh air. Sadly, fresh air was hard to come by as the city sweltered in a damp heat that made her buff muslin dress cling unpleasantly, but she persevered and managed a fairly brisk walk along the river. It was on her return towards Waterloo House that she crossed the road, turned a corner and came upon a gentleman on one knee, in the act of rising up from the pavement. He looked dazed and reached into his pocket for a handkerchief which he pressed to the side of his head.

It was Mr Jonas Tibbins.

As she halted, surprised and alarmed, Charlotte saw that the American was staring at the red stain that was spreading across the white linen he held, and forgetting her reservations, she rushed to his side.

'Sir? Mr Tibbins? Can I be of any assistance?' She fished out her own handkerchief from her reticule and he allowed her to exchange it for his own bloody one. 'There,' she frowned as she dabbed tentatively at a nasty graze above his left ear. 'I think the flow of blood is ceasing now. I'll fold this handkerchief into a pad and you should hold it there for a few minutes more.'

55

His obedience was alarming, but she saw that although he was still pale and a trifle stunned, his eyes were alert and he was frowning more with concentration than with pain.

'Lean against this wall, sir,' she advised, giving him a gentle push so that he had no course but to comply. She took a further look at the wound and opined that it only needed to be washed now and some basilicum powder applied as a further protective measure. He made no reply and she touched his arm.

'What in the world happened, Mr Tibbins?' she asked, and when he shook his head gingerly, she insisted. 'Don't be foolish,' she admonished him. 'I have no intention of mentioning this incident to anyone, least of all our fellow inmates. . . .' She stumbled, remembering Elaine Knightley's admonition. 'I mean our fellow guests,' she continued, aware of an amused flicker of appreciation from her companion. 'However, I am perfectly aware that there is a half brick lying in the gutter a couple of feet away from where we stand, and that the wound you are nursing could very well have resulted from that half brick being thrown at you.'

He turned his head deliberately, to stare at the brick she indicated, and then to stare at her with dawning admiration.

'You are a remarkable woman, Mrs Richmond,' he said, with an odd half smile of what looked like satisfaction. 'And you are quite correct in your deduction. I believe that the brick there, that you have so cleverly observed, did indeed make contact with my head and that it was aimed deliberately at me.'

He glanced round at the throng of passers-by and raised an eyebrow. 'Five or ten minutes ago,' he said. 'I was alone on this side of the street and there was a mere straggle of pedestrians over on the other pavement. I believe that someone spotted me as I walked up the hill and decided upon opportunistic action. He must have concealed himself in that alleyway yonder, providing himself with a handy weapon, ah . . . the brick, in fact. Then he took his chance that with so few persons around no one would observe his assault upon me.' His mouth twisted in a wry smile. 'As indeed appears to be the case,' he said. 'You were certainly the only person to come to my assistance.'

He had shrugged off her further offers of help and had accepted, with some relief she thought, her assurance of complete discretion. But when he left her to resume his journey, she was struck by a thought. Bending to pick up the offending half brick and examine it, she was shocked though not surprised to find traces of blood and hair on it.

Charlotte set out to explore Bath armed with a guide book that she had dutifully bought the previous week on a last minute trip to Winchester where she had stocked up on a new cap or two, as well as some summer gloves and stockings. 'I'm going to explore Bath today,' she said lightly to Elaine, but said nothing to her friend of Mr Radnor's anxious looks at the sight of Mr Tibbins upon the previous morning. No need to set up doubts in her mind about her new medical practitioner, Elaine was reluctant enough as it was about the whole enterprise. Nor had she mentioned the astonishing attack on the American.

As she wandered down Milsom Street, marvelling at the quality and quantity of the shops, she idly turned over and over in her mind the various conversations she had witnessed with the surprising Mr Tibbins and other people, both on Saturday night and again yesterday morning. She had only fleetingly encountered the other residents since Sunday morning but her recollection was quite clear. Mrs Montgomery had looked suddenly old and defeated somehow when Mr Tibbins spoke to her in that confidential, familiar manner, Charlotte thought, but why? There had been mention of someone in Brighton, but why should that disturb the owner of Waterloo House? And Mr Tibbins had unsettled Captain Penbury and Mr Chettle too. Charlotte recalled the captain's gruff uneasiness when some far off battle or other had been tossed into the conversation. What could that have meant? And her newly encountered neighbour from Finchbourne had looked distinctly uneasy at the reminder of his visit, many years earlier, to Egypt.

To cap it all there was the surprising reaction of young Mr Radnor, otherwise so pleased with himself and his luxuriant whiskers and moustachios which emulated the style of Prince

Albert; so confident too, of his ability to cure his patients, or at least to charm them out of their fees, she thought with a cynical grin. Yes, that complacent smile had been wiped off his handsome face and an anxious frown had quite disfigured those regular features, and all because a middle-aged tourist from America, who might not be all he purported to be, had taken a second look at him.

Oh well, she decided with a philosophical shrug. What do I care as long as Mr Tibbins has no interest in me? But he is a man to watch, she faltered, a man to be wary of, with that intense curiosity about his fellow guests. Such a man might think nothing of ferreting out snippets of information about anyone he met, to store away for future reference. He might even, she pursed her lips, try to find out about the history of an eminently respectable and innocent – oh yes, definitely *innocent* – young widow visiting Bath with an invalid friend.

Certainly I must avoid too much conversation with him, she determined, but reluctant as she was to face it, she was aware that Mr Tibbins had held her under a certain scrutiny on each occasion of their meeting in the halls and corridors of Waterloo House. For some reason though, that close watch did not resemble the keen, and slightly, mocking observance that characterized his dealings with the other guests. No, Mr Tibbins's round, ingenuous face bore an expression of interest and something like approval as he watched her.

He had looked at her with a similarly approving regard when she had pointed out the half brick in the road and informed him of her belief that it had been thrown at him. Why was he pleased with her? What could it possibly matter to him whether she were observant or no? And there was the most intriguing question of all, why in the world had someone troubled to throw a brick at him in the first place? Certainly the American had brushed aside her concern and laughed it off as of no importance, but Charlotte's mind was busy with possibilities and unanswerable queries, the greatest of which was: had the supposed accident at Salisbury Railway Station indeed been an accident at all?

She had racked her brains in an effort to recall what she had seen, but she was no clearer in her mind now than before. She had spotted Mr Tibbins in the throng of passengers about to board the train, along with their friends and relatives all eager to bid them farewell. Had he been standing beside the young woman who so nearly could have been crushed by the train? Had – Charlotte bit her lip in anxiety – had someone pushed that girl by mistake, having meant to send Mr Tibbins on to the track?

It was inconceivable that Mr Tibbins himself should not be concerned upon that point and she felt some relief that his deliberations must surely deflect his interest from her. A slight anxiety niggled at the back of her mind nonetheless and Will's words echoed in her memory: *If anyone starts to show too great an interest, Char, keep your head down and your nose clean.*

Fortunately so far his interest in her still seemed friendly, but Charlotte had observed other occupants of Waterloo House huddled in what appeared to be reluctant and resentful discourse with their fellow guest. The previous evening Charlotte had put in a brief duty visit to the drawing room before slipping out to dine alone with Mrs Knightley and she had seen both of the Counts de Kersac buttonholed, separately, by Mr Tibbins, apparently no worse for wear and with his mouse brown hair combed forward to conceal his wound. Receiving no encouragement from the French gentlemen he had moved on to the burly clergyman, the Reverend Decimus Attwell who had given him a testy glare and lumbered away growling. Mr Attwell's stout and sour-looking mother had, in Charlotte's hearing, snapped, 'Leave us alone,' when Mr Tibbins had bowed goodnight to her.

Walking along Milsom Street with her nose in her guidebook Charlotte almost walked into a tall gentleman who was striding along with a purposeful air.

'I do beg your pardon, *madame.*' It was the younger of the two French inhabitants of Waterloo House. 'Oh, *mais* – but it is Mrs Richmond, is it not? I am sorry to be so clumsy, do forgive me.'

'But there's nothing to forgive.' Charlotte hastily pocketed her book as she laughed up at him and held out her hand. 'I plead guilty to being a world away. I have been assiduously following the instructions of this excellent guidebook and have already trodden on a terrier, stumbled over a small urchin and grievously offended an elderly gentleman who objected when I walked into him. Of the three' – she gave a reminiscent smile – 'I fancy the urchin was the most vociferous. But my absorption in Bath history is no reason for knocking you into the road, sir, and I must take care not to risk life and limb, mine or anyone else's!'

He bowed over her hand and retained it for a moment as he smiled down at her, admiration plainly written in his amiable features. Not a handsome face, she considered, gently removing her hand, but a very kind one. He looks as if one could trust him. The conclusion startled her. Kindness was not a quality she usually sought when covertly examining a new acquaintance; she was more accustomed to weighing up the chances of being unmasked, or at least, the unmasking of her late stepfather, the beloved but decidedly unreliable Will Glover. No, kindness had not often come her way, particularly not in a man. Or trustworthiness.

He was still standing there in front of her on the pavement when an irate elderly woman berated him and he moved guiltily to Charlotte's side. 'I understand that your friend will be taking the air this afternoon.' At her blink of astonishment he laughed ruefully. 'Yes, I know, there are no secret *rendezvous* for the guests at Waterloo House, dear lady. I did not mean to pry however, rather to enquire if you and Mrs Knightley plan to visit the Pump Room later today. I enquire because my father and daughter have asked me to escort them there and, as we are strangers in Bath, it would be pleasant to meet some acquaintances.'

She smiled and returned a noncommittal remark but he pressed her. 'I do apologize, Mrs Richmond, but you see Marianne has taken a fancy to you – I do hope you will not take offence. It is the first time she has expressed an interest in anyone since . . . since her mother and brother died more than a year ago.' His large head drooped and he looked dejected, but brightened as she gave him an enquiring glance. 'Yes, my wife and seven-year-old son, *petit* Armel, both died of a fever. It was very sudden and Marianne almost died too; she has not yet fully recovered her strength which is partly why we decided to visit Bath. My father, too, is to take the waters, to see if they will alleviate his rheumatism.'

'I shall be delighted to meet you in the Pump Room,' Charlotte told him. 'As long as Mrs Knightley has no other plans.'

'So there you have it, Elaine,' Charlotte was eating a light meal in Elaine's sitting room again instead of mingling with her fellow guests. 'If you have no objection I have engaged us to visit the Pump Room so that you can make the acquaintance of a very quiet, elderly French count, his son who is also a count, but not at all high in the instep, and the little girl who looks to be rather delicate.'

She paused, holding a piece of bread and butter in her hand. 'I can't tell you what a relief it is to eat in a room that isn't papered and curtained and carpeted in dark gold. All the rooms downstairs have the same paper, a heavily figured flock in a dull yellow ochre and the curtains are all heavy velvet to match. The effect is opulent but oppressive, particularly when the temperature outside is so high. I much prefer these light pretty chintzes and silks.'

Elaine smiled as she nibbled daintily at a slice of cold lamb. 'An elderly French count sounds an interesting prospect and as devotees of Miss Austen we certainly must greet our new Bath acquaintances in the Pump Room – where else? Can we cast the younger count as Mr Darcy perhaps? I trust he won't turn out to be a Wickham or a Willoughby.'

'Not a Darcy.' Charlotte looked thoughtful. 'As I said, he's perfectly approachable; friendly even. And no' – she recalled that odd moment when she had sensed Armel de Kersac was a man to be trusted – 'definitely not a villain, he's a very nice man.'

Elaine said nothing but she looked amused and Charlotte read her thoughts. 'And no, you need not look so demure, my friend. I have no interest in looking for a new husband as you are well aware. You know that I'm only too thankful to have rid myself of my first one. Never mind why young ladies used to visit Bath in former days, nothing could be further from my mind than snaring myself an admirer.'

'It might not have been your intention, Char,' murmured Elaine, as they sat in the Pump Room later that day, 'but you have secured yourself an admirer, nonetheless. The younger M. de Kersac is very markedly showing an interest in you.'

Before Charlotte could respond the little French girl sidled towards her and shyly took the hand outstretched to greet her. 'Well, Marianne? Did you drink up your water? Do you feel better?'

'I did not like it, *madame*,' whispered the child, still clutching Charlotte's hand. 'It is not . . . it is not nice.'

'Oh dear,' Charlotte stood up. 'Then I had better pluck up courage and taste it too; I cannot come to Bath and refuse to take the waters. Elaine, you stay there and I'll bring you a glass.'

Accepting a tumbler of water from the serving woman, Charlotte tasted it and wrinkled up her nose in surprise. She turned to smile at Marianne's grandfather who was resting close by. 'Goodness, surely it would be better to bathe in this water than to drink it?' she laughed.

'My dear young lady.' He raised his glass in a toast. 'I believe you are expected to do both, but preferably not at the same time. I trust it will restore your friend to good health though for your part, I do not believe you are in need of a cure.'

'No indeed.' It was the younger Frenchman who sounded out of breath having hurried across the wide hall on seeing Charlotte talking to his family. 'Do forgive me, I had to have a word with someone.' He seemed dashed when he realized Charlotte already had a glass of pump water but brightened at a thought. 'Allow me to help your friend over to us. It won't take a moment.'

His father watched him and gave a slight sigh. 'It is good of

Armel to take time away from the farm at this time, but he felt it imperative that Marianne should try the waters. I think, myself, that the cure began when she was taken away from home, from surroundings that held sad memories, and that all the child needs is fresh company and new experiences.'

Charlotte smiled down at the child beside her but addressed the old man. 'Where in France do you live, M. de Kersac? Did you have a long journey?'

'We are Bretons, my dear, from near Pont l'Abbé far to the west; we live at the coast so it was a relatively easy journey, sailing from Brest to Plymouth and thence to Bath.'

'Breton? Does that then explain M. Armel's unusual name?'

'It was a custom in my wife's family to name the eldest son, Armel, and I was content to carry on the tradition. The name is said to mean "a prince of the bear" but my wife always maintained, mistakenly, I suspect, that it was a variant of Arthur, who was, as I am sure you are aware, known to legend as The Once and Future King.'

A muscle quirked the corner of the old count's mouth and Charlotte wondered if he was smiling at some inner thought. When he raised an eyebrow at her questioning glance she was convinced that he was amused for some reason but he said no more.

Armel de Kersac brought Elaine's chair over to them and over second glasses of the famous water, taken with heroic determination to suffer the benefits, they discussed their journeys.

'Mrs Knightley's husband was also unable to leave his harvest,' she told Armel, explaining that his father had told her about their journey. 'Do you have a large farm? I spent many summers helping with harvests in Australia when I was a child, I'm sure Marianne enjoys it too.'

Brushing aside their interest in her background – how stupid of me to say that, she scolded herself, now I'll have to trot out the usual story – she asked again about the farm in Brittany.

'It is just a large farm now,' Armel explained. 'During the Revolution my grandfather, who was an invalid, kept quietly at home and, as he was an estimable landowner and loved by the peasants, the *manoir* was not destroyed. Since his death my father has run it as a farm rather than an estate in the old style.'

'It seemed expedient to do so,' remarked the elder count, in his dry way and Charlotte shot a glance at him from under her lashes. *Expedience*. Yes, that would be her own way of doing things, she concluded. Do what is necessary to survive; do not draw attention to yourself; get through it at all cost; do not allow anyone close. I wonder, dare I ask him?

'*Monsieur*? I wondered . . . might I presume to ask if you were affected in any way by the Revolution, living so far away from Paris, even if the troubles did not destroy your home?'

Armel de Kersac cast an anxious look at the elderly count and made as if to intervene but his father held up an imperious hand. 'No, Armel, Mrs Richmond is not displaying vulgar curiosity and I have no objection to her questions.' His son subsided, a look of astonishment on his pleasant face as the older man turned to Charlotte. 'No, my dear, do not look so abashed. I told you when we first met that we have much in common, you and I.'

Charlotte freed her hand from the child's and stretched it out to the frail old man who took it in his own. Her wordless sympathy seemed to move him and he blinked once or twice before continuing. 'I was in Paris,' he said, speaking with difficulty. 'My mother was imprisoned and I was taken from her when I was a small child. When she . . . was sent to the guillotine I was taken to Brittany, to the Manoir de Kersac, which has been my home now for many quiet years. I have no happy memories of that part of my childhood, indeed much of my recollection is blurred and fragmented, so it is not a period I dwell upon with any pleasure.'

'A stirring tale indeed.' The jovial voice with its trace of a transatlantic accent them made them all jump. Mr Tibbins was surveying them with a beaming smile, his gaze flickering inquisitively from Armel to the elderly count. 'There can be few men still alive, *monsieur*' – he bowed to M. de Kersac – 'who were part of that time of terror. And you are from Brittany, I understand? I was visiting there myself, only a few weeks ago. Ah, how many noble warriors from that beautiful province perished gallantly, continuing to fight in the royalist cause.'

'Not only in Brittany.' Armel de Kersac reminded him. 'My wife's family came from the Vendée, further to the south and there the royalists fought bitterly for many years after the Revolution. It was a sad time for all of France.'

'Indeed it was,' agreed the other man with a pious sigh as his eyes, alight with that unsettling, burning curiosity, darted round the group again, resting once more, for a fleeting moment, on the stooped but elegant figure of the old count. 'I'm sure there are many tales to be told of heroism and disgrace alike, from that dark time.'

There was nothing in his words that anyone could find to object to yet somehow Charlotte felt a shiver of unease. Something lurked in his eyes; a gleam of surprised satisfaction that she thought had not been there when he first joined them. She thought he had started a little when he observed the three de Kersacs together. He stood now, at his ease, absently twirling his ebony cane as he looked down at the little girl with a paternal air.

'What a very beautiful child, M. de Kersac.' He addressed Marianne's father, his tone congratulatory. 'She does not resemble you, I think? Such luxuriant fair hair and with such notable light-blue eyes. No doubt she is the image of her mother.'

'No.' Armel looked puzzled but answered readily. 'Her mother was small and dark.'

'Ah.' Mr Tibbins prepared to take his leave, his air now one of extreme self-satisfaction, as he nodded in friendly fashion to the assembled company. 'I am sure then that the young lady is a throwback to a grandmother perhaps, or even, perhaps, a great-grandmother.'

It seemed an innocent enough remark, Charlotte considered later that night. So why should the elder Comte de Kersac suddenly look so bleak, his blue eyes pale and chill as he stared after the American's retreating back?

*

'Mrs Richmond?' Some twenty minutes later Charlotte was startled to hear herself addressed by the American himself. Elaine Knightley had returned to Waterloo House to lie down, but insisted that Charlotte take advantage of the slight breeze that had arisen and enjoy herself in the fresh air. The shops, however, had proved a greater lure and she was now standing outside a milliner's admiring a delightful but most unsuitable white straw bonnet with a spotted veil and trimmed with a large pink rose.

'I beg your pardon, young lady.' The surprising Mr Tibbins could exercise considerable charm when he wished and for some reason that seemed to be his present desire. 'Pray forgive me for interrupting your reverie, but it has occurred to me that we might have some interests in common, you and I.'

Charlotte felt the blood drain from her face and in her instinctive turning away from him she glimpsed her perfectly white reflection in the milliner's many-paned window. Fear gripped her and she had to take a deep breath before she could face him again.

'I . . . do not understand you, sir.'

'I have been *maladroit*.' He was all contrition. 'Allow me to explain myself. You must understand, Mrs Richmond, that I am engaged in an investigation which is at a very delicate stage of proceeding and that I have a proposition to put to you about which, should you choose to be less than discreet, a great many careful schemes and plans would come to naught.'

Fear dampened even Charlotte's ever ready curiosity and she scarcely took in his words, but she managed to assume a look of polite interest while surreptitiously stepping backward to lean against the nearest wall. He did not, to be sure, seem to be threatening her with physical violence, or at least, not at this moment. He wore an animated air, one of interest and not the blandly ingenuous expression she had observed previously when he dropped his little darts in the ears of her fellow guests.

She opened her mouth to offer some polite excuse or other

when a faint rumbling she had already remarked, suddenly sounded like thunder and she found herself grasped roughly by Mr Tibbins and pushed aside, just as a heavy handcart, laden with iron cooking pots, hurtled past them, its lumbering path halted as it crashed, cauldrons clanging on the road, accompanied by shrieks and lamentations, into a wooden stall piled high with fruit and vegetables.

The noise was indescribable, with the stall holder wailing in fear and anger, the bystanders scandalizing at the tops of their voices, and the sound of heavily booted feet as the owner of the cart clattered down the cobbled street exclaiming in horror. Even when he halted at the scene of devastation the carter did not draw breath but continued to maintain that his cart had been properly secured at the top of the hill.

'I'll take my Bible oath,' he announced to all and sundry. 'Man and boy I been bringing they pots and pans every week to Bath, and my old dad before me, and strike me dead if I ever left the brake off in my life.' He paused as the crowd agreed loudly that this was the case, then he took up his tale once more. 'Up on the 'ill it was. I stopped to give the time o' day to some fellow, and God 'elp me, off down the street went my cart. The pity of it is I'll never find out who took my brake off, there being such a press of people up there, ladies and gents too, but there was some varmints of boys I saw, and I'll warrant they done it.'

Charlotte, meanwhile, was gasping as she tried to catch her breath. Mr Tibbins had glanced up just in time, she realized, and had thrust her aside, but in doing so he had cannoned into her, forcing the breath from her body. Well, she gasped to herself, it was a fair exchange for her life. A hasty glance at the shattered planks that had formed the stall gave her an intimation of the damage such a heavy object travelling at speed could have done to her.

'Sir,' she gasped. 'Mr Tibbins, I must thank you for—'

'Hush.' He brushed her thanks aside. 'I must think. Why should a cart which had been secured suddenly take wing? I suspect that the carter is correct; someone deliberately kicked off the brake, or, more likely, bent down and did it quietly, unnoticed in the crowd, and sent that cart headlong down the hill. But why? An accident – or something else?'

Charlotte was glad to sit down; her legs felt weak and when she tried to raise the brandy to her lips, her hand shook so badly that she had to set the glass down for a moment. Mr Tibbins, she observed, looked to be in a like condition. 'Time for a little restorative,' he had said decisively, looking up and down the street, settling on this small hotel nearby, with a public room suitable for a lady. 'You have had a shock, Mrs Richmond, and so have I. Pray join me in a glass of brandy to calm our nerves.' She managed a sip and then another and was comforted by the fiery warmth; it emboldened her to pose the question that was burning in her brain.

'You spoke of something other than an accident,' she said bluntly. 'Was that cart aimed at you, Mr Tibbins? Was this another assault upon you?'

She was pleased that he made no pretence of not understanding her; that he did not brush aside her concerns, or play the bluff gentleman protecting a fragile woman. He stared at his glass and then returned his gaze to her own face.

'I believe so,' he answered. At her faint sigh, he rallied and smiled a little. 'It was a singularly inept attempt at injury though, was it not? Such a missile as that cart must be notoriously difficult to aim precisely in any direction at all.'

She made no comment, but returned to her own earlier deliberations.

'Was that the third attempt upon your life in the last few days, Mr Tibbins?' she asked, keeping her voice and manner calm and composed.

Again he gratified her by accepting her intelligence without question. 'The second attempt, certainly,' he agreed. 'I have racked my brains about the accident at Salisbury but I can see no reason for anyone there to attack me. I am forced to the conclusion that it was as it appeared. An unfortunate accident resulting from a sudden surge of movement on an already overcrowded platform.'

Charlotte nodded slowly, sipping her brandy. 'I, too, have tried to remember everything I saw,' she told him. 'I noticed you earlier on the platform and then lost sight of you when Mrs Knightley and I were settling ourselves in our carriage. By the time I could look out of the window there were more people boarding the train and I glimpsed you only briefly. I am quite certain, though, that you were not very near that young lady who fell, because I noticed when they lifted her that she was wearing a white straw bonnet with a rather large bright yellow flower in it, and I had definitely not seen that before.'

His interest was caught. 'You consider, do you, ma'am, that if she had been pushed in mistake for myself, she would have been standing close beside me? Indeed she must have done so, or there could have been no mistake.' He looked almost disappointed as he continued, 'Well, then, so be it. We must conclude that it was merely an unfortunate accident. That time at least. . . .'

He called for the waiter and took another glass of brandy, but Charlotte smiled and shook her head. 'So you believe, sir, that the half-brick and the cart were both deliberately aimed at you?'

'As I said just now' – he shook his head in bewilderment – 'both attempts were singularly inefficient as a means to murder.' She gasped and his mood lightened at once as he grinned at her. 'That must be considered as a motive, dear lady, but I'm inclined to think that both efforts were in the nature of a warning shot across my bows, to use the nautical language of the gallant Captain Penbury.'

Her eyes were round with astonishment. 'But why would anyone wish to murder you, sir?' she asked with interest. 'I have certainly been aware that some of our fellow guests are perhaps a little annoyed at your – um, shall we say slightly intrusive curiosity? But that's not. . . .'

He held up his hand to stop her, while nodding in agreement. 'I think the time has come for me to explain certain circumstances to you. I am pretty sure I can rely upon your complete discretion else I should not venture upon such an undertaking. But I know that you have made no mention of that little *contretemps* yesterday and I believe I can trust you.

'In the course of my business undertakings,' Mr Tibbins continued. 'I have found it politic to deal with many ... ah, secondary, agents, in a surprising number of places across the globe, both in America, in Great Britain and across Europe. I have not hitherto encountered anyone whom I should wish to appoint as my agent in the Antipodes but you, my dear young lady, appear to be the ideal candidate. Shall you be returning to Australia in the near future?'

The relief was almost as frightening as the fear she had suffered when he first accosted her not long ago, before the cart came upon them, but years of practice came to her rescue and she was able to look him straight in the eye. *Don't hold on too long, Will said. An honest look is invaluable, but keep on too long and you can unsettle people. A brief manly glance – or a demurely feminine one – and you're instantly trustworthy.*

'You want me to be your spy?' she asked baldly, frowning at him and shook her head slowly. 'It's an intriguing offer, Mr Tibbins, but I have no plans to leave this country. But tell me,' she asked, her curiosity roused, 'what do you obtain from these agents of yours?'

He shrugged his shoulders, still looking at her with that impersonal, appraising stare. 'I set them riddles to solve in connection with my own business and in the course of obtaining answers for me they invariably come into possession of a surprising amount of information about a vast number of individuals. Whenever I spend any time in a new town I like to discover what I can about my companions. Is it not Shakespeare who speaks of "a snapper-up of unconsidered trifles"? You could thus describe me. It is astonishing what secrets people hide and how useful those secrets can be to another person.'

In spite of herself Charlotte was interested. This man's creed appeared to resemble that of both her stepfather and her godmother neither of whom had ever neglected an opportunity to listen to gossip, *in case it came in handy*.

'Is that what you have been doing here in Bath, sir?' she asked, then remembered something. 'But what were you actually doing on Salisbury Station when I first saw you?'

To her surprise, his eyes narrowed in a smile of considerable satisfaction as she spoke, as if she had fulfilled his expectation, and he answered her quite candidly.

'I had been staying at Waterloo House for a week when I received a message that someone most nearly concerned with my primary business was thought to have been seen in Salisbury so I repaired there at once. Sadly my informant was mistaken so I returned to Bath where I am happy to say I begin to make real progress.'

He was silent for a moment and Charlotte took this as her cue that he had finished speaking, so began to rise.

'Stay one moment, Mrs Richmond, if you will be so kind?' She resumed her seat and turned an enquiring gaze upon him, intrigued to see that he was apparently struggling with some decision.

'I believe I can trust to your discretion, my dear young lady,' he said in a quiet tone far removed from the jocular, teasing familiarity of his address to his fellow guests at Waterloo House. 'I am rarely mistaken in a character and I believe you to be a woman of resource and intelligence, possessed of an enquiring mind, sharply observant and able to make rapid judgements concerning situations and persons who might pose a threat to you.'

He paused for a moment and Charlotte stared at him in astonishment. He smiled and continued, 'Have you ever heard of Pinkerton's Detective Agency in the United States of America?' When she shook her head, mystified, he nodded and began to explain. 'It is a private organization, very similar in aim to the forces of law and order, but it is privately managed. I spent more than twenty years in the service of the law of this country, firstly as a young Bow Street Runner and remained with them when they combined with the Metropolitan Police Force, ending up as one of Sir Robert Peel's famous Bobbies.'

'You are a policeman? An English policeman?' Charlotte prayed that he had not heard her sharp inward breath and that her colour had not altered.

'I was a policeman,' he corrected her. 'And yes, I am English by birth. As to the police I can honestly say that I was an excellent policeman, as all my superiors save one told me so.'

'And what of that one, sir?' She had control of herself once more and summoned up a smile that combined slight amusement with scepticism.

'Ah, that one, my dear.' He twinkled at her. 'That was rather unfortunate. The one dissenter to the chorus of praise they lavished upon me was the husband of a rather jolly lady who enjoyed flirting with danger – and with me.' He pursed his lips and looked rueful. 'Sadly the gentleman held an exalted position and he urged me to consider my future in the force. Suffice it to say that my resignation was the safest option, but I did not wish to abandon my life of investigation and when I heard of the new investigation agency started by Pinkerton in America some few years ago, it seemed an excellent idea. I was already in that country as I had earlier made the trip across the Atlantic Ocean to seek my fortune and had succeeded in a modest fashion, but I still hankered after a life as a thief catcher so I visited Allan Pinkerton to observe his methods. Pinkerton offered me a job almost on the spot and I have prospered exceedingly with his organization. Nowadays I am a specialist regarding this part of the world so I am frequently to be found in both England and in Europe. And, as I previously informed you, I have agents reporting to me from all across the globe.'

She drew in a deep breath and stared at him with open interest. 'And you would like me to become one of your detective agents, Mr Tibbins?'

He nodded. 'Detection has a fine long provenance, Mrs Richmond,' he informed her. 'Besides the famous Bow Street Runners, there was an age old tradition of *thief taking*, where a private individual could employ the services of the thief taker to seek recompense for some wrong. That, in essence, is what my employers offer. It can be profitable and satisfying in equal measures.'

She was fascinated and forgot to be afraid of him. 'And you enjoy the hunt, sir?' she asked.

'I bear malice to no man, or indeed woman,' he said. 'What I do possess is an inordinate amount of curiosity towards my fellow creatures and in the course of my police work I observed many cases of injustice and far too many felons escaping from their just deserts so the work I do now is immensely satisfying. Too satisfying, some might say, for I confess I take a mischievous delight in teasing and unsettling suspects; such methods can bring rapid results, you see.'

He grinned suddenly and raised an eyebrow. 'You, my dear lady,' he said lightly, 'would be astonished at the thoroughness of my investigations. When I was commissioned by a client who now deems it safer to reside in America than in his native country, to seek out a certain person, I discovered that the same person was expected to visit Bath at this time and to reside at Waterloo House. Naturally I made a reservation for myself at the same establishment, arriving a little prior to my quarry. Once here I set about portraying myself as a gentleman of leisure, interested in old buildings and in history, and taking note of everything out of the ordinary. In short, I play the part of an enthusiastic and talkative tourist from the New World and as such I am received with warmth and a certain amount of patronage.

'To my delight I received notice that yet another person who was sought by a different client would also, as it happened, be visiting Waterloo House, so I have great hopes of killing two birds with one stone, as the saying goes, at the cost of one set of expenses.' He smiled at her and she realized that she was softening towards him. It was hard not to be disarmed; after all he had, as he had told her, recognized her own good qualities.

'As an example of the way I work,' he told her. 'I sent detailed information as well as descriptions, where I possessed such knowledge, of everyone staying at Waterloo House, or expected in the period of my visit, to my office in London and have already received some most intriguing snippets of information about our fellow guests. Yes, my dear Mrs Richmond' – his tone took on a teasing amusement – 'even you and your invalid companion have come under our scrutiny when I heard that your arrival was anticipated, and you will, I am sure, be glad to hear that there is "nothing known" against either the beautiful young widow or the equally beautiful invalid lady.'

Charlotte was grateful that Mr Tibbins did not appear to expect a response to his jocular remarks as her heart was pounding so loudly she knew she could not speak. He turned to her once more.

'Will you not consider my proposition, Mrs Richmond? I believe you would enjoy life working confidentially as one of my sub-agents, financed to travel the world in style, in pursuit of intelligence for clients and reporting to me. For example, in my present concern here in Bath, money is not a consideration and criminal activity is not, thankfully for my own profit, confined to the so-called criminal classes.'

This most unexpected interview had taken up a scant three-quarters of an hour since the incident with the cart but Charlotte felt as though several hours had passed and she felt overwhelmed by this encounter. She shook her head and he shrugged, but as she was about to bow in farewell, an outrageous idea struck her.

'I am content with the life I have,' she told him, 'but I wonder if you would be willing to undertake a very small commission for me while you are in Bath?'

He looked astonished, but when she explained about her search for the history of her 'friend' he cocked his head and surveyed her with bright intelligent little eyes.

'For you, Mrs Richmond,' he said lightly. 'I'll do it. It's not my usual line of work, but it'll take me right back to my early days as a Runner.'

She furnished him with the few details in her possession and after some discussion he shook her hand, adding, 'I shall live in hope, dear lady, that you will change your mind for I believe that we could do business together. My agents need to be intelligent, observant and discreet and a particular requirement is that they should be fluent in the French language.'

He broke off and laughed at her, but not unkindly. '*Au revoir, madame,*' he nodded, smiling broadly at the dismay on her face as she realized that a few minutes earlier he had slipped into speaking French and that she replied, unnoticing, in the same tongue, as a matter of courtesy.

The guests of Waterloo House gathered as was their custom for a glass of sherry served in Mrs Montgomery's dainty little crystal glasses. Charlotte was a trifle surprised when she first saw them; surely, she thought, they must have been a bequest from some relative and therefore too precious to use.

'How kind of you to admire them, Mrs Richmond.' Mrs Montgomery looked gratified. 'I could never, of course, allow anyone to use the twist stemmed thistle glasses left to me by Mrs Hamish McDonald, my second cousin once removed. Those were the very glasses used by her grandfather shortly before he was hanged, drawn and quartered after the Jacobite rebellion, in an unfortunate mix-up as he should, of course, have been beheaded, being a gentleman. He used to toast 'The King Across the Water' with those very glasses. Do take a look at them – through the glass, of course, they are not to be touched – there in my Sheraton cabinet that came to me from dear Lady Cumbernauld.'

'Ah, the prince, the Young Chevalier himself – Bonny Prince Charlie as he was known to his admirers.' Mr Chettle elbowed his way into the conversation, planting himself firmly between Charlotte and Mrs Montgomery who, however, thwarted his intention by removing herself to the other side of the drawing room and urging more of her guests to take a glass of sherry. 'Yes, indeed. Why, I visited the memorial to the late Stuart princes only this spring when I was in Rome.' He pinned Charlotte firmly to the spot by his eager gaze, the better to commence his lecture. 'The memorial is, as you may not know, dear Mrs Richmond, situated in the Basilica of St Peter, and takes the form of a truncated obelisk, made in marble by the celebrated sculptor, Canova. It is a sad spot; a place of reflection, to make even the most loyal subjects of Her Majesty ponder on the melancholy history of those unfortunate exiled royal gentlemen—'

'Exiled royalty? Spongers one and all,' broke in a sharply decided voice, startling Charlotte and causing even Mr Chettle to abandon his lecture as they turned to stare at the newcomer.

'I have encountered many exiles,' pronounced the elderly lady who stood in the doorway to the drawing room. 'Exiled kings, queens, princes, duchesses, counts, barons and the like and I tell you frankly, not one of them had two ha'pennies to rub together and every one of them was glad to trade his illustrious presence at a party in return for a square meal, a glass or two of champagne, and a bit of bowing and scraping.'

Charlotte had to bite her lip as she observed the effect of the lady on the assembled guests. Small of stature and, in spite of her immaculate paint and powder, probably not far short of her allotted three score years and ten, the new guest presented a figure of astonishing elegance. Her crinoline of dull gold silk was wide and swaying, though she cast a startled and disdainful glance at the only too similar gold of Mrs Montgomery's furnishings, and the shawl draped over her arms bore a lustrous gleam that spoke eloquently of money. She wore emeralds in her ears, at her throat and on her fingers and in the beautifully dressed hair, the improbable golden colour of which matched her dress as closely as the emeralds matched her eyes.

Mrs Montgomery rushed forward to greet her latest guest, Lady Buckwell, and marshalled everyone into a line so that she could present them all. Charlotte was further amused to see that both Captain Penbury and Mr Chettle bowed low over the lady's hand in due deference to her force of character. When it came to the de Kersacs' turn to be presented the elder count bowed and smiled as he raised the lady's hand to his lips.

'I must endorse your remarks, *madame*.' He nodded with a slight smile as he met Charlotte's amused grin. 'That is a stern but sadly only too accurate description of many exiles I have encountered. But you need have no fear of us, my lady, my son and I are merely visitors to these shores, for the purpose of taking the waters in Bath and will be returning home long before we can have need of trespassing on your goodwill.'

'And yet . . .' The interruption came in the voice of the

surprising Mr Tibbins and tonight the note that always struck Charlotte as knowing and arch and with its constant hint of secrets known and relished was particularly pronounced as he surveyed the company with a lurking hint of amusement in his small, shrewd eyes. 'And yet, in many ways it could be said that we are all exiles here, are we not, Count? Even those fortunate enough to have been born upon the shores of this blessed isle, could be termed in exile from past lives, past loves, past hopes and dreams, is that not true? Remember the words of Psalm 137: *By the rivers of Babylon . . . we wept when we remembered Zion.* What do we think of, I wonder, when we ourselves remember Zion?'

The old Breton gentleman stiffened and turned away without comment while Charlotte jerked her head up to stare at the detective. Exiles? That's certainly true of me, she told herself. Not only am I an exile from my homeland, but I am exiled from my past, from Ma and Will and everything that made me what and who I am. Is that what the psalm is about? Loneliness – and remembering?

When it came to Charlotte's turn to make her curtsy she had composed herself and looked with frank interest at the older woman, and with a puzzled impression that they had met before. No recollection sprang immediately to mind and she was about to relinquish her place when Lady Buckwell, who had returned Charlotte's stare with a puzzled frown of her own, clutched at her arm in sudden distress, a weakness which she hastily masked.

'What is it, ma'am?' Charlotte asked in a low voice. 'May I help you to a chair?'

'No, no, it's nothing,' came the reply in an irritated tone, then she stared again at the tall, dark-haired young woman in front of her. 'No.' She shook her head decisively then continued in an undertone, 'You – there was a momentary expression – I was reminded of someone, that's all. Someone from another time, another world.'

'Lady Buckwell kept us all entertained at dinner,' Charlotte told Elaine next morning before going down to breakfast. 'I'm sure some of the guests believed her to be romancing when she told tales of scandalous goings-on at foreign courts, but there was a reminiscent gleam in her eye that suggested it could all be true. She's a splendidly unembarrassed lady and I was amused to watch her reeling in all the gentlemen.'

'What? Surely not your admirer too, Char?' Elaine lifted a laughing face as Jackson plaited and pinned up her flaxen hair.

'I'm afraid so. Even Count Armel is a little in her thrall.' Charlotte heaved a mock sigh. 'The other two ladies present were rather less inclined to take her at face value, though of course Mrs Montgomery is obliged to pin a pleasant smile on her face at all times, however outrageous her guests' behaviour. I could see she was biting her tongue and as for Mrs Attwell, the parson's mother, she positively simmered with rage which she suppressed, fortunately. I gather from the few remarks she has addressed in my direction that she and her son are very Low Church and of a puritanical persuasion and they both seem constantly on the brink of an explosion of rage, so bad temper must run in the family. I thought she should explode in horror when her ladyship casually dropped into the conversation a mention of the Prince Regent, an unmentionable undergarment, and an adventure with some gypsies. I was so glad you were not present else I should have disgraced myself and as it was I was obliged to conceal an outbreak of giggles.'

'You are rather taken with this naughty old lady, are you not, Charlotte?' Elaine was now arranged in a comfortable chair to await her breakfast. 'I think you like her.'

'Yes, I do,' Charlotte confessed. 'Though within limits. She has a very merry twinkle and a spicy tongue, but I suspect she would be the very last person one would wish to trust, or to turn to for help.'

There was no sign of Lady Buckwell in the breakfast-room. No, thought Charlotte; I imagine it takes a long time for her to be arrayed in costume, painted and powdered and bewigged and fit to tackle the world. Breakfast was not yet being served, but she took her seat and watched idly as Mr Tibbins engaged Mr Chettle in close conversation. There could be no mistake, she realized: her neighbour from Finchbourne was growing heated and angry although the detective's urbane expression did not alter. With a farewell she could not hear he turned away, only to waylay Captain Penbury with precisely the same effect. Both gentlemen looked furious yet apprehensive and if looks could kill, she considered, their tormentor would be doubly dead.

Since their shared adventure and the subsequent surprising and revealing conversation of the day before, Mr Tibbins had, thankfully, let her alone, merely smiling and whispering at tea-time that he had already made considerable progress regarding what he archly called his 'latest case' on her behalf. She was grateful for his forbearance as she was still shaken, not simply by the physical danger she had endured but by the way he had ensnared her into speaking French. My own fault too, she fretted, but thank the Lord he still seems kindly disposed to me. I wonder what it is that he has discovered about Ma? If indeed he has really found anything at all.

As the guests assembled at the table Charlotte observed that there were tiny folded notes on the plates in front of Mrs Attwell and of the old Count de Kersac. She was also aware that Mrs Montgomery took her place at the head of the table as if she were later due to climb into a tumbril, whisked something small and white from her plate, and that her eyes swivelled round to cast a frightened glance at the apparently unconscious Mr Tibbins.

The footman helped Charlotte to a fillet of sole and when she looked up from her plate she saw that Mrs Attwell looked grey with a pinched look about her tightly folded lips. The note had vanished. A glance at old M. de Kersac showed Charlotte that he had opened his own note and that he seemed almost paralysed as he read it. Anxiously she turned to offer assistance but he shook his head and crumpled the note in his hand, then put it into his coat pocket.

Sensitive to his distress, Charlotte bent her head to her breakfast and accepted a second slice of bread and butter that she did not really want, so that he need not engage her in conversation, but all the time she was thinking furiously.

For a brief moment the single word on the old man's letter

had been clearly visible to her. It had read: *Monseigneur*, a title which, as Charlotte was aware through her godmother's dictates regarding social matters, could be applied in equal measure to a prince or a prelate.

She slid a sidelong glance at the elderly man beside her, now drinking a cup of chocolate with apparent unconcern. Prince? There were certainly princes again in France, she supposed, but why travel incognito? The days of the Terror were long gone and the aristocracy fêted nowadays. Besides – a quiet farmer from the far west coast of Brittany? Surely not, but that left the alternative, assuming the note – from Mr Tibbins she was convinced, it smacked of his mischievous style – had addressed him correctly. I had him down at something around eighty, she mused thoughtfully. Could he be older? An ordained priest even before the Revolution? But *Monseigneur* indicated a high-ranking churchman so had his evidently aristocratic blood perhaps ensured a rapid rise into the Church hierarchy? After Napoleon had taken control, France had settled into a semblance of normality – Charlotte recalled her occasional history lessons delivered when Lady Meg was in tutorial mood. The count could have been ordained and risen in the Church quite easily then. But *Monseigneur*? Could he have risen to the top? Might he be a renegade Catholic *cardinal*? A renegade cardinal who was now accompanied by an entirely unsuitable son and granddaughter?

How ridiculous. She stared unseeing at her plate, a frown of exasperation creasing her brow. It is far more likely that it is some silly joke of Mr Tibbins's if indeed it was he who left those notes in the first place. Princes and prelates indeed.

Her speculation was interrupted by the appearance of some letters on a silver tray which was placed in front of Mrs Montgomery.

'Good gracious, Mrs Richmond.' She fluttered in Charlotte's direction. 'Here is a request for rooms for two of your friends, or could they possibly be family members, I wonder? At any rate, Mr Barnard Richmond requests rooms for Miss Benson and Miss Dunwoody who will arrive today. He states that a letter from him is on its way to you, Mrs Richmond.'

Before she could assimilate the disaster about to befall her, Charlotte's attention was attracted by the detective from Pinkerton's Agency who stood up, laying his napkin on his plate and bowing to the ladies, and directed a significant glance in her own direction as he spoke.

'I must beg your pardon, Mrs Montgomery and ladies and gentlemen,' he announced. 'But time and tide wait for no man, as the saying goes, and I must be about my business. Pray excuse me, I must bid you good morning.'

Obedient to his casually lifted eyebrow Charlotte made her own excuses and followed him unobtrusively from the room. He met her in the entrance hall where he was yet again admiring his reflection in the looking-glass.

'Good girl,' he said, with an approving nod. 'By George, Mrs Richmond, I'll recruit you yet as one of my agents. I've seldom met with a more intelligent pupil.' He laughed out loud at her confusion and continued in a quieter tone, 'I have been busy about your business, my dear young lady. I put out feelers immediately after our conversation of yesterday and by late last evening I had the answer you seek.'

'Already?' Charlotte was startled and a little apprehensive. 'Good heavens!'

'Indeed,' he said with some satisfaction. 'I work quickly. My enquiries led me to an interview with an invalid lady who resides in the city. Apparently she was employed at the period in question, as an under-nurse in a small charitable institution run privately by a Quaker gentleman and is adamant that she remembers the child you named as Molly Wesley.'

At her shocked gasp he raised an eyebrow and shot her a shrewd glance, but made no comment, simply continuing his report. 'Here is the lady's name and address,' he said, handing her a piece of paper. 'If you wish to observe her unaware, I can tell you that every weekday she is wheeled round the city in a bath chair. She takes the same route every day between three and four o'clock in the afternoon and has done so for a year or two. You may be interested to learn that her journey takes her past Waterloo House at precisely a quarter past three o'clock every day.'

He shook his head as she tried to offer him a fee, laughing frankly at her. 'Indeed no, Mrs Richmond. Accept this small office as a *pourboire*, an incentive to changing your mind. And do not hesitate to visit this woman for she is expecting you.'

As she nodded her thanks she was reminded of something and the question sprang to her lips. 'Did you leave those little notes at the breakfast table?' she asked abruptly.

'Again you prove your mettle, dear lady.' He smiled his approval. 'That is an old trick, a lesson for you in how to unsettle the opposition. No need for elaborate subterfuges, a mere word, a hint in the right ear or under the right nose can prove most effective in eliciting the outcome that is desired.' His smile was wry as he went on, 'I must confess that I have only two cases on hand at Waterloo House, though I believe a third is in the offing. However, I have found it impossible to resist a little teasing; you will recall that I mentioned my habit of checking up on anyone I meet? Sometimes, as in the present instance, my researches bring me hints of indiscretions that are not my concern.'

He raised an eyebrow as she frowned and looked disapproving at this admission, then he hesitated, still amused. 'No, I cannot resist the impulse to instruct you, my dear. Another means of eliciting a response,' he added in a confidential tone, 'is to observe your quarry out of his customary habitat, at a party, for instance. That's a grand chance to see a man give himself away.' He made her a mock bow. 'Or *herself*, of course. No one is above suspicion so we must not forget the ladies.'

As he had turned to leave the breakfast-table Charlotte had been aware that several of her fellow guests had followed him with their eyes. Mrs Attwell's face had lost its look of pinched apprehension and burned with what looked like an inner fire. Mrs Montgomery leant back against her chair watching him with an air of exhausted apprehension, while Mr Chettle and Captain Penbury were united in lowering frowns and angry glares.

Now, as she watched Mr Tibbins saunter out of the front door about his business, Charlotte became aware that the Count de Kersac was in the hall, his frail frame vibrating with silent emotion and a swift sidelong glance revealed an expression of chill despair directed at the departing fellow guest.

CHAPTER 4

'Are you sure you really want to attempt this, Elaine?' Charlotte frowned as she observed the preparations for Elaine's first session of electrical treatment. 'Kit would understand if you were to decide against it, I'm sure.'

Mr Radnor practised close by the Pump Room and the Baths and Charlotte had been biting her tongue about her misgivings ever since they arrived and were ushered into the consulting room where the ominous-looking electrical equipment was being prepared. Charlotte had hissed her question to her friend moments before young Mr Radnor handed Elaine over to a sensible middle-aged woman who took her to a small room so that she could change into the loose cotton shift she had brought with her. As Elaine shook her head in answer to Charlotte, the maid, Jackson, closed the door firmly on the nurse and assisted her mistress herself. Meanwhile, the medical man seized upon Charlotte and proceeded to lecture her on his methods.

'Here, Mrs Richmond,' he enthused, eyes glowing with zeal. 'Medical Faradism is indeed a miraculous invention, I have obtained many excellent results from it. Observe these buzzing coils with sponge-covered electrodes attached to them. These are dipped into salt water and introduced to the skin and the electrical currents thus produced make the muscles contract, which is of indescribable benefit to the patient in the way of stimulation.'

Charlotte obediently observed the equipment and concealed an inward shudder, wondering whether Kit Knightley would be so anxious to submit his wife to this ordeal if he had ever attended a session of this new-fangled treatment.

'Today,' continued Mr Radnor, his enthusiasm unabashed in the face of Charlotte's barely concealed distaste, 'I shall place Mrs Knightley in that wooden chair, which is quite an ordinary chair, dear ma'am, you need have no anxiety; it is perfectly comfortable too. Both legs will then be inserted into buckets of water with electrodes and wires. That, I think, will suffice for today, but tomorrow I should like to expand the treatment by placing Mrs Knightley's arms into glass pans with wire and electrodes too.'

'Don't fuss, Char.' Elaine was stoical as Charlotte whispered to her again. 'Mr Radnor says it will only make my muscles twitch and that it won't hurt. And who knows? The electrical currents might have a galvanic effect on my nervous system.'

'Oh no, Mrs Knightley,' Mr Radnor hastened to explain. 'This isn't galvanism; that really *was* an uncomfortable business. You need have no fear of discomfort.'

Charlotte hid a smile as Elaine sighed. She knew how irritated her friend often found herself when confronted by someone who failed to comprehend her jokes. 'Cheer up, Elaine,' she whispered. 'You look dressed for the tumbril in that long white shift. It won't be long and we can go to admire the flowers in Victoria Park afterwards if you feel up to it.' As she laughed, as much to keep up her own spirits as those of her friend, she pursed her lips at that mention of a tumbril. The French Revolution seems to be cropping up entirely too frequently in my thoughts of late, she frowned.

The treatment session proved less uncomfortable than it looked and Elaine stood up to it very well, even assuring Charlotte that she was sure she felt a slight improvement already. Jackson cast a forbidding frown at Jonathan Radnor and assisted Elaine to the small changing room which contained a day bed so that patients might take an hour's rest after their exertions.

Charlotte decided to use the period of Elaine's rest to investigate the former nurse identified by Mr Tibbins and with some trepidation she stood outside a tall, narrow house just around the corner from the doctor's consulting rooms. She paused with her hand on the knocker only to have the door open inward to reveal a thin, respectable-looking woman who asked if she could be of assistance.

'Oh.' Charlotte bit her lip then launched into her explanation. 'I have been told that a Mrs . . .' – she consulted the note Mr Tibbins had handed her – 'Mrs Liddiard, that's it. I should be most grateful if I might have a short talk with her?'

'You'll be the lady the gentleman spoke to Mother about,' said the other woman. 'Pray walk right in. Mother's in the little parlour here. I would be obliged if you would let yourself out, ma'am, when you are ready to leave, as I have to go into town and Mother has not the use of her legs. I've just made her a pot of tea so I'll put out an extra cup for you.'

The back parlour was small and dark but the door opened out into a small area at the back and let in a welcome draught of slightly cooler air as Charlotte and the former nurse sat in companionable ease, Charlotte upright at the table and Mrs Liddiard across from her in a shabby but comfortable armchair.

'Oh no, dear,' she responded to Charlotte's friendly query. 'I was only too happy to help with your enquiry when that gentleman sought me out. A very clever and efficient gentleman he was too. He said he had begun asking about the Female Penitentiary which was where many babies were born; that had led him to search out news of any private orphanages and lo and behold, someone recollected my own name.' She looked delighted at this attention and shook her head several times. 'If you see that gentleman, my dear, I wish you would ask him to furnish you with the name of whoever told him of me. I dearly love to talk of the old days, and welcome company, sitting in here day after day as I do.'

'Have you always been a nurse in Bath?' Charlotte was making polite conversation while she wondered how to steer the reminiscences to the questions that burned in her brain.

'Oh yes, dear. I learnt a lot from my mother who was a children's nurse herself, to a lady near Chippenham, and then I had a few years working at the orphanage here, oh a long time ago; thirty years and more it must be. That was sad sometimes, mind you, but I was fond of the children.'

'The orphanage?' Here it came. Charlotte sat up straight and stared across the table at the other woman, recalling her mother's scanty scraps of information about her history. 'An acquaintance in Hampshire,' she improvised, 'she told me that she believes her mother was born in an orphanage in Bath more than thirty years ago. I asked Mr Tibbins if he could discover anything of her circumstances. Her name was Molly, that was the name, Molly Wesley, I believe. And I understand that she would have been born round about 1819 or thereabouts.'

'Just as the gentleman told me!' Mrs Liddiard's face shone crimson and heartily. 'If ever I heard such a thing. Why, I remember that little girl as plain as day, but your friend doesn't have it quite right, you know.'

She sat back and nodded comfortably across at her visitor while Charlotte struggled to maintain her air of polite interest. Could it be true? She trusted Mr Tibbins's efficiency and if he believed this pleasant stranger had actually known Charlotte's mother, then that was indeed the case.

She felt a surge of gratitude to the Pinkerton's detective, that he should enter so wholeheartedly into her own small investigation when at any moment, she supposed, his mysterious assailant might mount another attack on his person. I could help him, she decided; I could offer to keep my eyes and ears open while I am in Bath, if he would trust me with some of his researches. The prospect excited her but now was not the time so she bent towards Mrs Liddiard once more.

'Ah, there's nothing like a nice cup of tea, I always say, come rain or shine.' Mrs Liddiard sipped with relish then put down her cup and nodded brightly to the girl sitting opposite her. 'As I said, I'm sure I remember that child very well, but she wasn't born in the orphanage, you know. Far from it. I got quite a shock when I started work there and realized who she was. It was a crying shame, that it was.'

'What ... what happened?' Charlotte asked in a faltering

voice, her hands clasped tightly in her lap under the overhang of the table, out of Mrs Liddiard's sight.

'It's quite a tale,' came the answer, and the older woman settled herself more comfortably and began her story, happy to have such an interested auditor. 'I was just a young girl and my first post was as an under-nurse at a lady's house, here in Bath. Not a private household, as such, but something you found a lot in those days; and nowadays too, if I am any judge. I worked for a woman who took in young ladies of good family when they were in trouble, if you understand me.' Charlotte nodded, holding her breath. 'The guests would arrive about a couple of months before their confinement and my mistress would find good foster parents for the babies. Sometimes the young ladies were lucky and their families would make arrangements, but other times my mistress would do so.'

Mrs Liddiard picked up the teapot, cocked her head at Charlotte and poured them both a further cup of tea before she continued, 'Well, I remember that little baby quite clearly because her mother wasn't the usual run of young lady. Dearie me, no. Very fashionable, she was, and open-handed and very impatient to be done with the whole business, not tearful and frightened as they mostly were. And she was married too, or said she was; certainly the other thing we realized was that she had already had at least one child and that again was unusual.' She nodded sagely. 'I remember my mistress saying to me that it was a clear case of a husband away, in the army perhaps. Let me see . . . You said I think that the name was Molly Wesley? It must be the same – I certainly don't recall any other girl at the orphanage with anything like the name. The lady I'm telling you about told us her name was Mrs Wellesley, "Like His Grace, the Duke of Wellington", she told us. And she laughed when she said it. Well, we knew, of course, that the guests never gave us their real names but I remember my mistress saying she wondered if there could *really* be a family connection with his lordship, with her so fashionable and bold.

'We liked her, you know, my mistress and the servants alike, for all her airs and graces and even though we were sure she was no better than she should be. A hoity-toity piece she was, with sandy hair; not pretty, but taking, quite a little woman and one you wouldn't forget. Not the first society lady to find herself in a fix, we thought; husband away, perhaps, as I said just now, and a baby she couldn't fit the dates to. The baby was born somewhere before Christmas, that I remember, because Mrs Wellesley had to get back to London for some great Twelfth Night Ball, and the baby would have been around the six weeks when her mother left for Town.'

'But how did the baby end up in the orphanage?' Charlotte tried to keep her voice calm and to display no unseemly anxiety.

'Mary, that was her name. Little Mary Wellesley, that's right. Well, my dear, it was a sad business. Her mother, as I said, had to be in London at Christmas time so she gave my mistress a good sum of money and asked her to find respectable foster parents for the baby. She would come back to Bath by Easter and would make permanent arrangements then. So off she went and I never saw her again.'

She stared with surprise at Charlotte's shocked gasp. 'I don't mean that the way it sounds, my dear,' she explained, shaking her head. 'She may well have come looking for her baby, but I've no knowledge of it myself. What happened was that the very day after Mrs Wellesley upped and went off to Town, my mother had a fall and I was sent for to help look after my father and little brothers. When I eventually came back to Bath – and that was a year or two later as my mother became an invalid – I found disaster had struck my mistress as she had suffered a palsy stroke and died and the house given up.'

'But what became of the baby, Mary?'

'Nobody knew. No more did I till I obtained my position at the orphanage and found the little mite there. The tale the orphanage had been told was that she'd been fostered but there was no money to pay for her and so the foster parents had given her up. Well, I knew that was a lie; there'd been plenty of money, for my mistress had told me, so all I can conclude is that the foster parents stole the money and got rid of the child. If they hadn't given her right name I'd never have found out that much.'

She cast a shrewd look at Charlotte's pale face and patted her hand. 'There, there, my dear, no use getting upset over an old story. You mustn't think that the orphanage was a cruel place, not like you read about in books; it was a small, private affair. The master was a clerical gentleman, firm man, but fair, and the children were well-treated, taught to read and write and kept clean and healthy. I used to keep a special eye on young Mary and because I knew she was Quality, I made sure she spoke as well as I could manage and kept her at her books too. But there, she must have been about eight years old when I left the place to marry John Liddiard and I never saw her from that time. We went to live over near Chippenham, you see, and I didn't come back to Bath to live with my daughter till after John died, three years ago that was, come next Easter. My health had failed by then and I could no longer live alone.'

To Charlotte's relief she saw that her hour was almost up. The friendly former nurse had poured out so much information that she needed some time alone to digest it all. As she rose and thanked her hostess for the tea and for her time, Mrs Liddiard gave her a shrewd glance and a comforting pat on her arm. 'You can come and talk to me whenever you wish, my dear,' she offered. 'I'm always here except when I go for my drive out between three and four o'clock. Don't you forget now. . . .'

Charlotte wandered aimlessly across Pultney Bridge but today even the fascinating shops failed to engross her. All she could think about was the child who had ended up in the orphanage.

Was that really you, Ma? It was too circumstantial, she thought, to be a coincidence. The name was so similar and the child: 'a pretty little thing, with fair curls, very taking'. In her mind's eye Charlotte could see her pretty little mother with her hair bundled into a snood and with fair curls escaping from the net to frame her face, so unlike her tall, dark and angular daughter.

Fond as she was of Elaine Knightley, it was undoubtedly a relief to be on her own with these thoughts teeming in her brain. Mr Radnor had vetoed Charlotte's suggestion of a trip to see the Victoria Gardens.

'Another time, I think, Mrs Richmond.' He had given her a patronizing nod and, at the same time, patted his patient's hand. 'Mrs Knightley has weathered this morning's treatment exceptionally well and is now looking refreshed, so I wish to build on this success by sending her to the King's Bath to try bathing in the warm water this afternoon.'

'Dear Char.' Elaine smiled up at her anxious companion. 'I really am quite well enough to do this, so please don't fuss. We'll explore the gardens another time and meanwhile, you have the whole afternoon to yourself. You deserve it, my dear, after dancing attendance on me so kindly.'

Charlotte's protestations were brushed aside and so she had set out for a walk beside the river but her mind was too agitated to appreciate the delights of the city and the heat was exhausting, even to a healthy young woman. I shall go back to Waterloo House, she determined, to see if there's a letter from Finchbourne that will explain why I am to be punished by the arrival of Agnes's battling governesses.

It wasn't difficult, she conceded, not difficult at all, to understand why her brother-in-law Barnard might have been driven to so drastic a step. Melicent Dunwoody's constant weeping and hypochondria alone would cause a saint to have a temper tantrum. Combine this with Dora Benson's brisk common sense and total lack of sensibility, as evinced by her brutally frank remarks about Melicent's imaginary ailments, and Charlotte could manage to summon up considerable pity for Barnard and the entire household at Finchbourne.

I'm not sorry for you now though, she sighed, compressing her lips as she frowned. What a thing to do to *me*, Barnard! You could have despatched the pair of them anywhere in the country, abroad even, perhaps to Carlsbad to stay with Mrs Richmond. With a wry smile Charlotte pictured her redoubtable mother-in-law's reaction to such an invasion at the Bohemian spa where she was currently taking the cure, but no, Barnard, she fumed, you had to bundle them off to me in Bath. Her ready sense of humour came to her rescue as she strolled back up Milsom Street, fanning herself with her book as the heat threatened to become oppressive. Perhaps Mr Tibbins will take them off my hands? Perhaps he will engage the warring governesses in a light flirtation to while away the time.

She recollected that Mrs Montgomery had been considerably exercised because she now had only one room remaining that she could allocate to the two governesses. Hmm, that won't please them at all, Charlotte grinned, feeling more cheerful; as long as nobody expects me to share with either of them she hastily qualified her thought. . . .

As she turned along George Street Charlotte heard her name called out in the unmistakable bluff tones of Captain Penbury who was to be seen just coming down one of the hilly side streets. She cast a furtive glance behind her and saw that the gallant captain had been detained briefly by a couple who were asking directions. Perfect. Slipping swiftly into another of the side roads that would take her up to Waterloo House, not far above Edgar Buildings, she congratulated herself on her stratagem. Captain Penbury, who was, she conceded, a perfectly acceptable sort of man, had begun to pay her a little too much attention, a few too many broad compliments on her charm of person. If I can avoid him, she told herself, and keep doing so, perhaps he'll take the hint and leave me alone.

A second loud hail dashed that hope but pretending valiantly that she had not heard him, Charlotte hastened up the hill and realized that she could probably make her way through the mews and so gain entry to Waterloo House through the back door. Darting into the Waterloo House mews she paused to take a breath, head turned to look over her shoulder, and tripped over something lying on the cobbles. Something large and warm. Something wet on the hand she reached down to steady herself with.

'Oh my goodness, what on earth. . . .' For a moment she assumed the man on the ground must be drunk but reason told her otherwise. At three o'clock in the afternoon? In a respectable mews? Besides, the man was wearing good sober clothes, smart clothes, in fact. He looked to be a gentleman and he looked to be extremely dead.

A moment's horrified intake of breath was followed by a second moment of blind panic. Her life-long response to trouble was to get away unobserved, silently and swiftly in the opposite direction. Was he hurt? Was he indeed dead? Her unruly sense of the ridiculous ambushed her even at such a moment, fuelling a rising hysteria. Dead? Surely the horrid red stain spreading across his chest was evidence enough? She bit her lip, stifled her impulse to escape, and made a rapid search for his pulse which revealed no sign of life and, as she hesitated, wondering what she should do, she realized she was not alone in the mews that led off the adjoining street.

Half crouching with his knee upon the ground, and leaning against the wall in the concealing shadow that obscured at least half of the cobbled courtyard, was the elder Count de Kersac. His breath was coming in shallow gasps and he gave every indication of imminent collapse, his face a sickly greenish-white, a frail hand clutched to his chest. Charlotte leaped to her feet from beside the body and hastened over to the old man.

'Why, good heavens! Monsieur de Kersac, what in God's name has happened here? Are you injured also, sir? Pray let me help you. Here, come and sit on this upturned cart.' She looked round but there was no sign of the stable hands who should have been lounging in the vicinity of the coach house. Nor was there any movement beyond the stables, in the small dingy garden of Waterloo House, so she gave the count her arm and steered him to the cart which, old and ramshackle as it was, still provided a place for them both to lean against.

'Well,' she said, blowing out her cheeks in a satisfying, if unladylike, gusty sigh.

'Well indeed,' he said, and she was relieved to see that his cheeks were regaining a little colour and that his breathing was calmer and less ragged. Together they stared wide-eyed at the man on the ground and the old count tilted his head to one side, took a breath and addressed her again. '*Vraiment, madame,* I must make you my compliments!'

'Compliments, *monsieur*?' It was such a bizarre remark in the circumstances that Charlotte turned to look at him in astonishment.

'Indeed, *madame*.' He gave a faint smile of acknowledgement at the slight suggestion of a curtsy that had been dinned into her by her mother and godmother. '*Always, always, Char, make sure you are polite and respectful to everyone but particularly to the elderly. They have more influence than you might think and if there is trouble, it can do you no harm to be thought of as a meek and charming young woman of breeding.*' Her stepfather, Will Glover, had added his own rider to this advice: '*Don't forget, Char, a curtsy is a useful distraction. It disarms the other person and gives you time to consider your position.*'

'Indeed,' he said again, his voice now calm and quiet, only the slightest increase in his elegant accent betraying his perturbation. 'My compliments, *madame*, upon your *sang-froid*. I myself have an unfortunate weakness when it comes to the sight of blood and I confess it overtook me here, but one might almost assume that finding a bloody corpse lying at one's feet was a daily occurrence for you.'

'Not a *daily* occurrence, *monsieur*, I do assure you.' She answered him in the same, almost mocking tone and saw him nod, with a spark of warmth in his pale-blue eyes, as if he admired her composure and recognized her yet again, not simply as he had remarked at their first meeting – as a fellow sufferer – but now, as a realist, practical and useful to have beside one in a crisis, in spite of his unfortunate reaction to the sight of blood.

A crisis! She forced herself to look again at the bloodied figure lying on the dusty cobbles in front of her. She knew him, of course; she had known him immediately and she felt a spasm of sorrow allied with anger, but this was not the time for such emotions.

'Did – did you know this gentleman at all, *m'sieur*?'

There was a very slight hesitation, a small movement of his mouth in a gesture of distaste as he gazed down at the silent, sprawled body of the detective, Mr Tibbins. He shook his head. 'He did not seem to be the kind of man I should wish to claim as a close acquaintance, either dead or alive.'

The sound of brisk footsteps caused her to turn her head towards the road.

'That might well be Captain Penbury,' she said, catching her breath and noting, with relief, that the old gentleman's colour was less livid. 'He was following me and I thought I had escaped him, but that sounds like his tread. We must send for help at once.'

He nodded and she lowered her eyes then turned towards the opening of the alley to await the newcomer. That was when she noticed the ebony stick that Mr Tibbins had twirled so jauntily. It now lay beside him, revealed to be a sword-stick – unsheathed – and a narrow blade, stained with blood, lay several feet away as though flung aside in haste.

CHAPTER 5

'Monsieur de Kersac!' Her voice was urgent. He saw that her anxious gaze was directed at the sword-stick and shook his head, looking suddenly very old and utterly exhausted.

'*Mon dieu*! I fell; I remember tripping over something and I saw it was the body of a man, but that . . . I did not see it. My weakness overtook me then but I thought, I hoped perhaps, that this was some unfortunate accident.'

'No.' She stared sadly at the body of Mr Tibbins. 'Scarcely an accident, he has been stabbed with his own sword-stick.' She caught a glimpse of her own right hand. It was covered in blood, in just the same way as the old count's sleeve. 'You must have done just what I did,' she told him swiftly, holding out her own wrist and retracting it with an apology as his face paled again at the sight. 'As you say, I stumbled upon the body shortly after you did and we both tried to find a pulse.'

'Well, well, Mrs Richmond, here you are. By George you're a fast walker, my dear; good healthy stock, by George, I like that in a woman, so I do. Did you not hear me calling out to you? Hey? I thought I would give myself the pleasure of your company . . . why? What the devil?'

Charlotte and the old Frenchman watched as Captain Penbury repeated the rigmarole of checking for a pulse in a body whose blood was only too obviously no longer circulating.

'What the. . . ? Mrs Richmond? Are you in any way indisposed, my dear young lady? Good God! What a shocking thing for you to discover. And you, *Mounseer*? Here, let me just shout for the constables and find someone to guard this poor fellow ... Why, bless my soul! If it isn't that talkative American fellow who's been staying at Mrs Montgomery's. This will upset the apple cart, my word if it don't, she certainly won't like this at all.'

He rushed hither and yon and in a very short time procured a stolid-looking gardener's boy from a neighbouring building and called loudly in at the door to the kitchen regions of Waterloo House as he ordered the kitchen maid to go running for the constables.

Within a very short time the yard was filled with people, servants from the neighbouring buildings, from Waterloo House itself; some of her fellow guests, attracted by the shouts for the constables, and an assortment of complete strangers thronging around out of curiosity. Charlotte ran a rapid glance round the yard, taking in the solitary pony cart in the coach house and sticking her head briefly into the stable to soothe the old grey pony who gave no sign of being grateful for such attention.

Impressed by the captain's efficiency - who would have thought it? Charlotte was all admiration, she had supposed he was all talk - she took the old count's arm and helped him into the house via the back door, brushing aside the cook's offer of a chair for him.

'You're very kind.' Charlotte gave a smile and a nod. 'But I think M. de Kersac will be more comfortable above stairs in the drawing room. I imagine the constables will want to question him, and me too, and we must make haste to let Mrs Montgomery know this dreadful news if she hasn't heard all the noise and wondered at it. But a cup of tea, perhaps or,' – she exchanged an urgent glance with the cook – 'Maybe a glass of brandy?'

The footman arrived in the drawing room almost as swiftly as did Charlotte and the old French gentleman. Setting the small silver salver on a side table he helped settle M. de Kersac in a high backed chair by the window and handed him a glass of brandy. Charlotte was glad to see that the cook had poured it with a generous hand and, after observing that her own glass was equally full, she determined to take merely a restorative sip.

I must take care, she thought. I have no idea who stabbed Mr Tibbins, but he must have been barely dead when first M. de Kersac and then I stumbled on him; a few minutes before and we should have seen the murder committed. Thank God we did not! She took another sip then set it determinedly on a side table. Getting tipsy on brandy won't do any good. Irresistibly a memory of one of Will Glover's tales bubbled up as she recalled him describing a funeral he had been called upon to conduct. *'The mourners were all roaring drunk,'* he had explained. *'The body was supposed to have been pickled in spirits of rum, in the manner of the late Lord Nelson, of blessed memory.'* Will had been sitting on a fallen log, the sun glinting on his chestnut curls and an arm wrapped casually around his wife. Charlotte, aged about fourteen, was paddling in the shallows of a wide river, somewhere on the east coast of Australia; she couldn't, after all this time, remember exactly where. *'They'd sent for a parson and I was the first they caught up with, but by the time I arrived they had drunk his health in his own pickling fluid. Luckily it had all gone but they plied me with their own poteen, so I was soon as drunk as the rest.'*

Ten years on, Charlotte bit back the tears as she heard his laughing voice: *'The singing of the hymns was particularly fine, as I recall,'* he had reported.

No, a riotously drunken funeral service might well have passed uncensured in the outback, she reflected, but an inebriated young widow in a respectable house might draw some awkward questions down upon her, when considered in conjunction with the blood on her sleeve. And questions, as Charlotte was only too well aware, were something she had been taught to avoid.

Yes, well ... Several other guests at Waterloo House had seemed anxious to avoid questions over the last day or so, particularly those of the late American. She glanced over towards her companion. His colour was much better and he had regained his composure.

'M'sieur?' She waited until Mrs Montgomery had ceased her fussing and fluttering over her most elderly guest and was attending to the other people already congregating in the

drawing-room, drawn irresistibly by disaster, then spoke in a low tone as she attracted his attention. 'Do you not think we should go and change our attire?' She lowered her gaze significantly to his own bloodstained coat and he gave an involuntary shudder. 'There is no point, after all, in exciting alarm and misplaced questioning. I certainly have no desire to be quizzed on matters that have no bearing in this instance.'

There was considerable intelligence as well as that sympathy that always seemed to lie between them in the pale blue eyes lifted to her own hazel ones and he rose at once with a brief nod of comprehension, only the sudden reaching for her arm betraying the agitation which still remained.

'I have said it before,' he murmured, as they moved unobtrusively out of the room, still filling with yet more assorted guests and hovering servants, 'you are a remarkably intelligent and resourceful young woman, and a woman of decision to boot. If you will assist me to the stairs I can manage for myself, thank you.'

In her own room Charlotte was glad to find that Jackson was out and about in Bath somewhere and she breathed a sigh of relief that Elaine was safely occupied in the King's Bath and not here where she could not fail to be disturbed by the turn of events. Closer examination of her dress revealed that only the detachable cuff was stained, but rather than simply stitch in a new, clean cuff, Charlotte gave a slight shudder and donned one of her simple poplin gowns, in the tawny bronze colour that she had decided should serve as half mourning. It was the work of a moment to immerse the cuff in cold water and observe, with satisfaction, the way the blood instantly began to seep out of the fabric.

Back in the drawing-room she discovered Mrs Montgomery dispensing tea to the Comte de Kersac, who now appeared quite composed, and a large, sandy-haired policeman.

Inspector Nicholson's round, blue eyes sparked with interest at the entrance of a young and personable woman and once the introductions had been performed he appeared to think Charlotte needed particular comfort and manly reassurance, taking her hand in his and patting it in an avuncular fashion.

'There now, my dear young lady,' he purred, 'there can be no cause for you to be alarmed; we officers of the law are here to help you. Now pray take a seat, won't you, madam? That's right – that will do well, opposite the old gentleman.' The last was in a loud whispered aside and Charlotte was perfectly aware that the count had heard and was amused by the inspector's heavy tact. The policeman nodded to the Frenchman once more.

'Now then, *mounseer*, if you wouldn't mind just running through that again to get it clear in my mind. You decided to enter the house through the back premises, you say?'

'I am an old man,' was the simple reply, accompanied by the suggestion of a Gallic shrug. 'The road becomes even more steep as you reach the brow of the hill and I wished to avoid unnecessary exertion, particularly on so warm a day.' He paused to acknowledge the inspector's sympathetic rumble.

'I was already fatigued and possibly mopping my brow which must explain why I stumbled so clumsily upon the American gentleman's body without seeing it. I fell to my knees, and then as soon as I had collected my thoughts I looked for a pulse. Alas none was evident so I dragged myself to my feet and managed to reach the shelter of a wall where, I regret to say, my shock and weariness overcame me once more.' He pursed his lips and frowned. 'At that point I beheld Mrs Richmond as she entered the mews.'

'Quite so, quite so, thank you, *mounseer*, that is very clearly put. Well, Mrs Richmond, I've heard what Mounseer de Kersac has to say on the subject and now I should like to hear your tale.'

Clasping her hands in her lap and looking a picture of innocence, Charlotte told her story. Oh lord, Ma, she thought. What *would* you and Will think of all this? Policemen patting me on the hand, elderly French aristocrats treating me as an equal, mysterious American detective agents lying dead at my feet. '*Never forget, Char,*' Will had often reminded her during their all too frequent headlong flights from the law, '*if you have no excuse to hand and nothing convincing offers immediately, you can always have recourse to tears. But mind you use them sparingly and only cry to give yourself time to think. Plenty of time for real tears when the danger is past.'*

Her ever ready, frequently inappropriate, sense of humour almost over-mastered her as she recalled Will's laughing confession that he had himself once been driven to employ an emergency bout of tears. So astonished was his captor and interrogator that he had called for refreshments and during the interval, Will had made good his escape. It had been a close run thing, he told her, but luckily Charlotte had no need of tears or excuses on the present occasion – she was reserving her sorrow for the surprising Mr Tibbins for when she could be private – so she gave her evidence in a sedate and sober voice, keeping her eyes demurely lowered when not required to speak.

'Now tell me, Mrs Richmond,' the inspector enquired. 'Did you see any suspicious individual running from the scene of this dastardly crime? The *mounseer* here says he saw nobody, but your eyes, begging his pardon, are younger and sharper.'

'I saw nobody,' she replied, in a steady voice. 'And heard nothing at all out of the ordinary. There is no other way out of the mews apart from the entrance on to the road. Though there is, of course, that narrow strip of grass to the side of Waterloo House, but that only leads round to the front door. I am not aware whether anyone was seen from the front of the house emerging from that passageway.'

The inspector heaved a sigh and obediently diverted in the direction she had indicated. 'Plenty of witnesses on hand out there to say there was no one who did that.' He harrumphed and gave himself the pleasure of offering Charlotte comfort and support in the shape of a languishing glance and a further pat on the hand. 'There'll be an inquest, of course, but I have great hopes that a deposition from each of you will be sufficient, *mounseer* and madam. But to my mind there's no real doubt. Some common thief, or one of the gypsies from down by the river, saw a chance and took the American gentleman by surprise. My first impression is that he was attacked for there is bruising to his chin and evidence of a wound on the side of his head . . . I beg your pardon, Mrs Richmond. Did you speak? No?

Well, as I say, there is that wound and it looks to me as if he had been punched to the ground, perhaps hitting the kerbstone which would render him unconscious for a moment or so; there is certainly a further wound at the back of the head. At that point my guess is that the dastardly fellow noticed Mr Tibbins's cane and the blade now visible after the fall, and stabbed him with his own sword-stick.'

He shook his head in condemnation of such behaviour. 'It's my belief the villain heard you coming, *mounseer*, for I'm bound to say he had no time to steal anything, as far as we can ascertain. Certainly Mr Tibbins's valuables were still about his person.'

As the inspector rose, beckoning his sergeant and bowing with evident reluctance over Charlotte's hand, a commotion arose at the door to the drawing room. The butler entered with an apologetic cough towards his mistress as he announced: 'Miss Benson and Miss Dunwoody, ma'am.'

Oh good Lord. Her hand flew to her mouth and Charlotte winced as recollection flooded in. The warring governesses! She had completely forgotten the millstone her brother-in-law Barnard had despatched to hang around her neck. And into this house, at this time. She heaved a despondent sigh and crossed the room to support Mrs Montgomery in her ordeal; though, to be sure, the lady of the house had not, as yet, the slightest notion of her impending trials.

'Yes indeed, Mrs Richmond, we had a most pleasant and efficient journey.' That was Dora Benson, sister to the Vicar of Finchbourne. Dora was nodding graciously to her hostess and extended that condescension to Charlotte, her clear, bell-like tones clanging round the room leaving none of the guests able to ignore her. 'Mr Barnard Richmond most kindly insisted upon first class tickets for us and we received every comfort and attention.'

'Oh yes, indeed.' That failing voice, with an irritating, built-in half sob, was Melicent Dunwoody, that dripping fountain masquerading as a woman. Charlotte groaned inwardly. Melicent did not look happy and when Melicent was unhappy, which was most of the time, she took care to ensure that the whole world knew it.

'Every comfort was indeed offered, but I do feel that it would have been a Christian kindness in Miss Dora if she had only allowed me to travel all the way facing forwards. I am so sadly prone to moments of faintness and unease when my back is to the engine. And Miss Dora is in possession of so many facts and figures about the railways, especially about the most dreadful accidents, and she insisted on imparting them all to me and our fellow travellers, that I declare my head is spinning.'

'What utter nonsense—' began Dora Benson in brisk tones, but Charlotte interrupted her.

'I'm sure you will wish to be conducted to your bedchamber, in that case, Miss Dunwoody,' she suggested. 'And you too, Miss Benson.'

'Yes, yes, of course.' Mrs Montgomery broke off her discreet appraisal of her two most newly arrived guests and beckoned the hovering butler from the hall. Evidently emboldened by Charlotte's determined expression, Mrs Montgomery swept the two ladies out of the room and up the stairs. Inspector Nicholson had regarded the scene with a lively curiosity but had evidently decided on a discreet withdrawal.

Charlotte closed her eyes for a brief moment then slipped away to her own room.

'I simply couldn't bring myself to be present when the two of them learned firstly that they were expected to share a bed and, even more distressing, that a corpse had been lately discovered on our own doorstep, so to speak,' she later confessed to Elaine, as they lingered over a glass of sherry in Elaine's sitting room in the hour before dinner was announced. 'I could see that the journey had been a nightmare, what with Dora in full flow of information and Melicent at her most dreary and irksome. Just listen to what Barnard writes:

They are driving me to despair, Char, with their never-ending vapours and scenes. It was bad enough when Miss Dora began to

*instruct Agnes in the behaviour expected of a clergyman's wife,
but when Miss Melicent started in on the house and complained
that the new curtains were deliberately chosen to give her a
fainting turn every time she entered the morning-room, you can
picture Lily's reaction. I am sorry to pass them over to you, Char,
but I could think of no other way of saving my sanity.*

'Poor Barnard.' Charlotte's eyes sparkled as she looked up
from this missive, with its agitated penmanship and liberal
scattering of blots. 'Desperation has given him inspiration. I've
never known him write, or indeed even speak, with such
fluency.'

'Their arrival is certainly inopportune,' Elaine responded with
a smile. 'Now tell me, dearest Char, are you quite certain that
you are suffering no ill-effects? I've listened to your account and
still find it almost impossible to credit such a thing. What a very
disagreeable experience it must have been, to discover that poor,
unfortunate gentleman. So distressing for you, my dear girl.'

Charlotte brushed this aside and turned the conversation,
determined that Elaine should not discover her sadness at this
brutal death. 'But what of you, Elaine? Do you feel you have
received any benefit from today's treatments? I had expected to
find you prostrate upon your bed and that I should be required
to wave the smelling salts under your nose at regular intervals
throughout the entire evening. But you look splendidly well;
there is even a faint colour in your cheeks.'

'I feel very much better than I have for some time,' Elaine
admitted but there was a shadow in the wide grey eyes. 'Don't
run away to telegraph the news to Kit though, I beg of you. I
cannot bear his hopes to be raised untimely and I shall write to
him myself.'

'But. . . .' Charlotte reached out to clasp the delicate hand held
out to her.

'No, Char,' Elaine repeated, her eyes and voice very resolute.
'I am most grateful for this respite and to know, particularly for
Kit's sake, that the electrical Faradism seems to be helping, but
we will wait and see. I know that there is no real . . .' She broke

off her sentence and squeezed Charlotte's hand, continuing with a smile, 'The hot bath was an unusual and interesting experience. You would have found it most entertaining when a very large lady who was in front of me on the steps down from the Pump Room, tripped over the voluminous gown she was wearing and fell down into the water, head first and legs sadly aloft, revealed in all their distressingly naked glory.'

Without further comment Charlotte accepted the abrupt change of subject and Elaine went on with her story. 'One or two people were quite incensed that this adventure had awoken them from their peaceful dozing, but on the whole it seems to have added spice to the bathing. For my part, I confess I was relieved that neither you nor Kit happened to be there for I know you both far too well to hope that either of you could have contained your laughter. Or indeed that you would have even tried to do so!'

Charlotte managed a faint smile though her heart was heavy, then looked up at her friend's next words.'I shall come to dinner tonight, Char,' Elaine Knightley announced after a thoughtful look at the sudden shadow cast over the mobile features of her younger friend. 'No, my mind is made up and I have been neglecting my duties shamefully. After all, I've managed to avoid these people until now and it's time I shared the burden. Besides, I'm intrigued; in fact I'd say that I'm *devoured* with curiosity about your naughty old Lady Buckwell and I shall be able to exchange medical symptoms with the gallant captain.'

She heaved a sigh and looked pensive for a moment. 'I shall also, with some resignation, renew my acquaintance with Mr Chettle, and I shall thank Heaven, silently but on my knees if necessary, that his monstrous mother is no more. Perhaps he will be able to have some kind of existence of his own from now onwards; I heard it on good authority – well, it was Dr Perry, you know how indiscreet he can be when it suits him – that old Mrs Chettle never allowed her son to sleep alone in his own room, even as a grown man, but always insisted that he occupy a truckle bed in her bedchamber. She was apparently afraid he would otherwise be exposed to the wiles of unscrupulous women.'

105

The atmosphere in the drawing room was not surprisingly a little subdued when the guests assembled before dinner. Subdued, indeed, as was only appropriate, but Charlotte thought she was able to detect an undercurrent of excitement; yes, excitement and something else. Glancing around the room she fancied the golden draperies and walls seemed less oppressive than they had hitherto, but that, of course, was nonsense. No, there was a lightening of tension; that was what had caused the change. She bit her lip on a gasp as she understood. It stemmed from the absence of the detective's disturbing attentions; in fact, one or two of the occupants of Waterloo House were hard put to disguise their relief.

Mrs Attwell was engaged in conversation with Lady Buckwell, her burning gaze – as usual – bent upon her son who was chatting to his hostess, with a very slight lessening of his usual tetchy manner. His mother, apart from her constant watch over him, looked almost relaxed as her companion bent her unfeasibly golden head forward, no doubt recounting some scurrilous story of royalty and ancient misdeeds.

Captain Penbury obviously felt himself to be the hero of the hour as he held forth about the shocking discovery of Mr Tibbins's body. Mr Chettle wore a slightly pained frown as if he, as the undoubted expert on death, had had his nose put out of joint, but soon he and the captain were absorbed in conversation with the newly arrived governesses, who hung on the gentlemen's every word with gratifying attention, even Dora, who was at first only too ready to offer her own opinion but then seemed to think better of it. Could Dora be competing with Melicent in the employment of some feminine wiles, Charlotte wondered? Heaven help the gentlemen if that were the case.

The two Breton counts hovered beside Elaine, and Charlotte was touched to see that Count Armel kept a protective eye on his father. The older count, however, appeared to have recovered his spirits completely and was at this moment discussing music with Mrs Knightley. The little girl, Marianne, had, as usual, taken an early supper and been despatched to bed; Charlotte had slipped into the child's room for the second evening running and had read her a bedtime story. Since yesterday afternoon at the Pump Room they had taken to spending snatched half hours together and were fast becoming good friends as Marianne unbent sufficiently to let Charlotte into her world, or rather her world before the shattering death of her mother and brother. Charlotte had walked for so long with loneliness that there was a great sympathy between the two and she found the child a delightful companion.

There could be only one topic of conversation at Waterloo House tonight, though good manners dictated that it should really be avoided. Good manners were cast summarily aside on this occasion although everyone at the dinner table made strenuous efforts to maintain a level of decorum.

'How are you recovering from your shocking ordeal, Mrs Richmond? Hey?' That was Captain Penbury amply filling the William IV mahogany dining-chair beside her, his broad shoulders edging into her own space. 'Shocking thing, hey? Shocking.' He lowered his voice to a subdued version of his quarter-deck bellow and confided, 'Can't say I took to the fellow, mind you. A sly, sneaking kind of man, always hinting and nodding, always with a smirk on his face. No, he would have made a poor shipmate, I can tell you, ma'am.' He harrumphed, looking a trifle embarrassed. 'But there, that's no reason to be glad the fellow is dead, hey?'

'No indeed.' Charlotte was somewhat startled at such a frank avowal, but she smiled and ventured to ask a question or two. 'I am quite recovered, thank you, Captain but I must confess I was most relieved to hear you call out to me as you entered the mews. M. de Kersac and I found ourselves very much shaken and it was a great consolation to know we had one of Her Majesty's gallant naval men to come to our rescue.'

The captain's weatherbeaten face increased in colour from sunrise to sunset under her compliments and he went so far as to pat her hand in his gratification. 'Why, my dear young lady,' he said, nodding in some confusion, 'I take that very kindly indeed. Mark you, I was only too glad to be of service to you and the poor old French gentleman.' He glanced across the table then nodded. 'He has a better colour on him now, I declare.'

'Indeed.' Charlotte was at her most demure and for a fleeting moment she too glanced across at the old count. He caught her eye and inclined his head very slightly, a slight warmth in the depths of his pale blue eyes. Elaine Knightley, the old man's neighbour, was looking at Charlotte with amusement and Char knew it was her own primly ladylike attitude that had sparked that quirk to the corner of her friend's expressive mouth.

She lowered her gaze modestly to her folded hands again then glanced under her lashes round the table as she tried to view her fellow diners afresh, as Elaine herself would be observing them for the first time.

She had described the naval man beside her, Captain Penbury, briefly after the first evening when she told Elaine about the other guests and now she took another look at him. A tall, heavily built man, certainly in his late fifties, perhaps even a year or so more. A fine crop of silver hair curled vigorously around a tonsure tanned to a dark mahogany; blue eyes narrowed against a lifetime of tropical suns and intemperate weather and a voice to awaken the dead from their eternal rest with its confident boom.

There was also, of course, the matter of the musket ball lodged so inconveniently somewhere in the captain's anatomy. Thank the lord, she thought, I have so far managed to avoid hearing exactly where that sharp-eyed and sharp-shooting American sailor shot him. I suspect it can only be some kind of delicate feeling that restrains him. She sighed; probably I am too young and too recently widowed to have such interesting details related to me.

'Where had you come from, Captain Penbury,' she asked suddenly, 'when you arrived so opportunely on the scene? I had only just walked up Milsom Street and along in front of Edgar Buildings and did not see you anywhere. We might have continued our journey together and I would have been spared. . . .'

She allowed an artistic falter to colour her voice and waited to see how he would react. My word, Pa – she hoped her bent head would conceal her involuntary grin – I think you were right about me. '*Sometimes, Char,*' Will had told her once, ruffling her hair with a playful, loving hand, '*sometimes I think you could be an actress, with those innocent greenish-hazel eyes of yours and a better tongue for lying than many I came across at Botany Bay. Your saving grace is that you're just too honest, my girl.*' He had heaved a mock sigh and told her that she would never make a true villain; but he had made sure that Charlotte's mother was not within earshot. Molly's hopes and dreams for her daughter's future had definitely not included either the stage or a life of crime.

Wrenching herself back to the present, Charlotte listened to the naval gentleman protesting, 'Why, ma'am,' he spluttered. 'I was just . . . I was behind you coming along George Street. Yes, that's right. Did you not hear me call out to you as you turned up the hill?'

Hmm, she cast her mind back. I did hear you shout, but as I recollect it seemed to me that you sounded a little breathless. Could you have been hurrying after me? Is that all it was? Or was it that you had recently run down the hill, dodged into the parallel street and been delighted to spot a possible alibi in me? To disguise the fact that you had just murdered a man?

CHAPTER 6

Such nonsense! Charlotte gave herself a mental shake and a severe scolding. Certainly Captain Penbury would seem to possess both the strength and the skill, as well as the experience of past battles, to stab a man, but why should he have done so? Merely because he had been in the vicinity? But M. de Kersac would surely have seen him, had that been the case. She risked another upward glance at the elderly Breton gentleman, recalling their encounter in the mews. He had looked frighteningly frail as he leaned, in an attitude of near collapse, against the wall. He was also, surely, in his eighties at least, and that meant that his eyesight might well be failing. How much time had elapsed between the actual stabbing and the count discovering the body of the American guest? Long enough for an active naval man to mingle unnoticed with the passers-by – one of whom would have been an old man lending all his concentration to climbing a steep street – and to zigzag down the hill by way of the small lanes until he reached the broad thoroughfare of George Street? And there to espy salvation, or protective colouring, in the guise of Charlotte Richmond?

No, it was of no use. Merely by repeating her hypothesis Charlotte could not make it true. Enough of this silly speculation, she concluded, but even as the rebuke formed in her mind, she found herself casting a surreptitious glance down the table towards Mr Simeon Chettle. Like Captain Penbury, Charlotte's neighbour from Hampshire had been increasingly uneasy whenever Mr Tibbins had hailed him; uneasy, too, when the American had insisted on engaging him unwillingly in one

110

of those brief, intimate huddles of private conversation that had marked out the late guest's behaviour.

Where had Mr Chettle been earlier today, she wondered? His attentions over the brief period of her stay at Waterloo House had become quite marked, as indeed had those of Captain Penbury. Elaine might tease Charlotte about her admirers but she knew very well that Charlotte had no desire for a second husband, that it was indeed quite the last thing on her mind. No, the thought was instant and definite; one husband was quite enough for me and I'm in no hurry to burden myself with another. But ... her glance strayed idly towards the younger Frenchman who raised his head and shot her an eager smile. Armel de Kersac was fulfilling Elaine's prophecy and taking a marked interest in Charlotte and, at private moments during the previous twenty-four hours, she had let herself speculate about what life might be like as chatelaine of an ancient manor house in a far away corner of France.

During the half-hour or so before dinner when it was Mrs Montgomery's pleasant custom to dispense sherry and conversation amongst her guests, Charlotte had ascertained that nearly all the residents of Waterloo House had been in the house, or in the square opposite. All of them, in fact, had been near enough to hear the shouts of consternation from the stable yard and to hasten thence to see what was afoot. Charlotte had seen every one of them milling around as she and M. de Kersac had taken refuge in the house. Mr Chettle said he had just stepped outside to take a breath of fresh air when he heard the commotion.

Surveying Mr Chettle now, Charlotte wondered if that could be true. The notion of her neighbour savouring fresh air stood at odds with his pasty complexion. No, Mr Chettle seemed more of an indoor creature; she pictured him bending enrapt over his precious funerary relics, his pale fingers stroking and cherishing pieces of terracotta pottery; his small dark eyes glinting with pride of ownership as he read aloud inscriptions copied down from obscure tombs.

But that must be nonsense too; she was struck by the sudden

111

thought. I have heard him with my own ears go on and on about the times he has spent searching among gravestones and exploring cemeteries. There were the interminable stories about the long periods he had spent assisting at archaeological excavations where, she was very much afraid, he must have been a considerable hindrance to the experts in charge. She looked at him again and frowned. He certainly possessed a swarthy but somehow pale complexion, but perhaps it was the kind that never tanned. She had come across pale-faced men and women under the Australian sun, where most of the population sported tanned or weatherbeaten features and even the fine ladies had fought a losing battle against the sun's rays under their parasols.

Mr Simeon Chettle was shorter by six inches at least than the captain but his shoulders were broad, his neck resembled a tree trunk and his hands, though pale, were large and hairy. Indeed, the wrists that protruded from his snowy linen cuffs were so thickly hirsute that he looked first cousin to the monkeys she had encountered in India. He might appear fusty and fubsy, but he was obviously possessed of enough physical strength to kill a man. She shivered a little as she recalled the fanatical glow in her Finchbourne neighbour's eyes as he described the Roman grave ornaments he had secured in the spring. Strength of body and strength of will too, she thought. But why in the world should he wish to do so?

Charlotte's morbid fancies were interrupted by an exclamation of pleasure and surprise from Mrs Montgomery. The butler had processed grandly across the golden carpet and proffered a silver tray upon which reposed one of the two letters that comprised the evening post, the second missive being handed to Charlotte with considerably less ceremony.

'Oh, what a kind attention. Ladies and gentlemen, do pray attend me, I beg of you.' Mrs Montgomery rose, gesturing to the gentlemen who had risen politely with her. 'No, gentlemen, do please be seated again. I have just this minute received an invitation, addressed to us all. A dear, dear friend of mine tells me that she has invited a private party to visit the Assembly

Rooms for tomorrow night – to attend a concert apparently, organized by the leaders of society here in Bath. There is to be a collection in aid of orphaned children in the town and I am sure it will be a delightful occasion. My friend, Mrs Smith, writes that sadly some of the friends she had invited are unable to attend owing to a sudden outbreak of illness caused alas, by some fish that was past its best, amongst the party staying at the White Hart. As you can easily imagine, Mrs Smith was most discomposed until she thought of me and Waterloo House. She writes: . . . *and so, my dear Mrs Montgomery, I was forced to lower my sights whereupon I hit upon you. I trust that none of your lodg . . .* – Ahem, she means my guests, of course – *will embarrass me and I am sure that the dreadful event which has occurred in your mews will be of interest to my more refined guests.'*

Briefly Charlotte met Elaine Knightley's dancing eyes then both women looked away. Mrs Montgomery would scarcely take kindly to laughter and mockery of her illustrious friend. Charlotte's amusement was silenced abruptly by a trill of delight from Melicent Dunwoody.

'Oh, Mrs Montgomery, how exciting. What a great delight that will be! To mingle with the upper echelons of Bath society. What an honour—'

'Nonsense.' That was Dora Benson's sharp rebuke. 'We shall certainly not be on social terms with "the upper echelons of society". That honour will be allocated to Mrs Smith's more refined guests, but at least we shall be permitted to enjoy a pleasurable diversion.'

So that had rankled with Dora, had it? Charlotte was intrigued. Miss Dora Benson was possessed of a lack of tact so entirely wholehearted that it was almost splendid. Charlotte had lived with the governess in the same house for more than a month and could not recall a single occasion upon which Dora had exercised any thought for the feelings of her companions. And yet the egregious Mrs Smith's downright rudeness had upset her, but had not apparently ruffled the feelings of the normally only too sensitive Melicent Dunwoody.

If only they had arrived here a day or so earlier I could

wonder about their part in the death of Mr Tibbins, she thought, giving herself up to a moment's idle speculation. Why could they have killed him, she mused? Sadly I can think of no convincing motive for either of them to commit murder. They are far more likely to become the victims of such a crime themselves.

Taking advantage of a discussion that did not include her, Charlotte quietly opened her own letter, having recognized the scatter of exclamation marks and the looping calligraphy of her sister-in-law Agnes Benson. It was as she had earlier suspected: Agnes had now discovered that she was with child and expressed her delight over several pages before mentioning something of interest to one of Charlotte's fellow guests: *Barnard was so interested by your mention, dearest Char, of the* Chesapeake! *He says he heard, only recently, that there is a mill at Wickham not fifteen miles from here that has some timbers from that very ship! He says, in his joking way, that he must invite the gentleman to visit us and to undertake an expedition!*

'I am so glad to see that your friend is feeling well enough to join us at dinner.' Count Armel bent to speak to her in the deep, calm voice that seemed to epitomize his character. Armel, as Charlotte had decided long ago, was a large, restful and reassuring creature and a bulwark against the attentions of the captain and the relic collector. Thrusting the letter from Agnes into her pocket she smiled assent and he continued, his slight accent adding a pleasant note, 'Mrs Knightley has a delicate beauty that reminds me of some of the legends of my home on the far west coast of Brittany.' He gave a slightly embarrassed shrug and smiled. 'When I first beheld her tonight in that pale gown I thought at once of *La Princesse Lointaine*, the unattainable lady, although that legend, indeed, is not confined to Brittany alone. My mother, who was a distant cousin on my grandfather's side, came from further inland though still in Brittany, although she was actually born in England, to *émigré* parents. Her family hailed originally from the forest of Broceliande where there abound stories of fairies and brave knights, along with enchanted caves and magic springs which guarantee eternal beauty to any woman brave enough to dabble the water on her face.'

He turned an admiring glance towards Charlotte and produced a shy smile. 'Mrs Knightley, and of course you yourself, would have no need of such spells and entrancements.'

Oh dear. Charlotte suddenly became aware that this large, friendly man could very well end up being badly hurt by her. He was clearly entertaining some serious intentions towards her and she was suddenly frightened at the prospect of making someone so congenial unhappy, and even more by the recognition of how sorely she was tempted to allow his gentle advances; to let him take care of her and carry her off to that far off stronghold on the edge of the world, where the only requirement was that she should be happy. It was too tempting, too possible, too *impossible*, so she brushed his remarks aside, taking care to do so gently. 'I fear you are a flatterer, M. Armel,' was all she said.

'Well, perhaps we must disagree upon that subject.' He smiled at her, apparently unruffled by her rebuff. 'We have fairies at home also, at Kersac.' He glanced across the table to where his father was talking eagerly with Elaine Knightley. 'I believe my father sees it too,' he said, in an aside. 'The resemblance, or rather the suggestion, I mean. She is so like a fairy princess should surely be.' He reddened, cleared his throat, then laughed at himself. 'There you are, Mrs Richmond, I, too, am caught up in her enchantment. But I was telling you of my home. The *manoir* is ancient, built of stone to withstand centuries of marauding visitors from the sea and from the land and the story goes that the house was built by a mortal man, a knight, who strayed into the circle of standing stones on our domain. There he met a fairy maiden who told him she would release him from the enchanted circle only if he built her a house and stayed with her forever.'

Charlotte was entranced. All her life she had yearned for a home of her own, for a place that took her to its heart, for roots and family and most of all to belong. And here was a man who had all of those things and more and who, with the slightest encouragement, would lay them gladly at her feet.

He smiled at the intensity visible on her charming, angular features, and went on, 'And so now we have our own fairy legend and we believe that if a man or a woman strays somehow into the stone circle the enchantment will bind him or her to Kersac for ever.'

In bed that night Charlotte put aside the memories of the shocking events of the afternoon until she could think clearly about the late Mr Tibbins and what must have been, she feared, a third and sadly successful attempt upon his life. Instead, she once more considered Count Armel and his increasingly particular attentions to her. There is nothing for it, she concluded. I must gently turn the conversation every time he ventures on one of those shy remarks that yet reveal the trend of his thoughts. Oh dear; she heaved a sigh of regret. I might be mistaken, but I really don't think so. She closed her eyes for a long, thoughtful moment. And it is so very beguiling. But no, it won't do. Perhaps I can avoid letting him come to the point; I shall have to be very busy with Elaine and – oh my goodness!

She sat bolt upright in bed aghast that something so momentous could have slipped her mind although murder, she conceded, might constitute sufficient excuse. Mrs Liddiard and her extraordinary tale of a lady from London and the baby, little Mary Wellesley. How could I possibly have forgotten about that? For Mary Wellesley and Mary, (or Molly) Wesley were surely one and the same person? They *must* be. And that person had been Charlotte's own darling mother. The details were too many and too similar and Charlotte could scarcely believe her good fortune in stumbling upon the one person in the entire world who could give her this information. She snuggled back against her pillows and counted off the coincidences on her fingers.

Mary or Molly Wesley (later Molly Glover) had been born at the end of November in 1819, in or near Bath. That was all she would ever admit to Charlotte, brushing aside Charlotte's questions with her laughing: '*It's ancient history, Char, nothing to do with us now.*'

Mary Wellesley had been born late in 1819 in a private house in Bath.

Molly Wesley had been either been born in, or sent as a baby to, an orphanage somewhere in Somerset, possibly in Bath.

Mary Wellesley had been sent as a baby to a small privately run orphanage in Bath.

Molly Wesley had been taught, she had once confided to her daughter, to speak like a gentlewoman by a friendly creature at the orphanage. Sadly for Charlotte's current investigations Molly had never mentioned the name of this well-intentioned person.

Mary Wellesley had been taught to speak like a gentlewoman by Mrs Liddiard who knew the child was quality-born.

At the age of twelve, Molly Wesley had been despatched out into service at a clergyman's house somewhere in Somerset, presumably outside the city of Bath itself. At the age of thirteen the seventeen-year-old schoolboy son of the house had fallen in love with her and his mother had taken drastic steps to nip the unsuitable affair in the bud, by the simple if ruthless means of accusing Molly of theft. This unscrupulous act had resulted in the girl, as yet quite unaware that she was with child, being shipped off to Australia as a convicted thief.

What had happened to Mary Wellesley at the age of twelve?

Charlotte chewed at her bottom lip and pondered the question. The two babies – children – had to be one and the same; it was straining coincidence too far to believe otherwise. And if that were the case then she was now in possession of something wonderful, something she had never thought to achieve. She knew something, a very little something perhaps, but far more than before, of her mother's background. Charlotte wondered about that society lady who surely was, must have been, her own grandmother. A lady who was probably already married and had 'made a mistake'; a lady who had already borne at least one child; an open-handed, impatient, hoity-toity piece, not pretty, but taking in her ways.

In the darkness Charlotte wondered again what could have gone amiss. The lady had showered money on the midwife and given her more money to find temporary respectable foster parents for the little Mary, because she planned to return at Easter to make permanent arrangements. But the day after Mary's mother returned to London the midwife had died and the child ended up in the orphanage. Had Mrs Wellesley returned that Easter? Had she been distraught at what she learned in the city? Or had she looked upon it as the hand of Providence offering a neat solution to her problem?

Charlotte cast up a fervent prayer for the soul of the lost child who had become her own mother and added a wistful hope that Mrs Wellesley had not simply abandoned her daughter. And if she is still living, she thought, does she remember that little daughter now and then, with a sigh perhaps? I wonder if I could ever trace her. Charlotte opened her eyes wide as she considered the idea. There was some suggestion that she was related somehow to the Duke of Wellington, but that might have been a joke and too late now, to ask His Grace, who had been dead for six years. Probably too delicate a matter to enquire about amongst his surviving family too, she grimaced. Oh well, I must talk to Mrs Liddiard again when Elaine goes for her treatment tomorrow.

At last she allowed herself to think of Mr Tibbins and his dreadful fate. A sob shook her slight body as she recalled the admiration in his eyes when she justified his faith in her by some intelligent deduction and she wondered, vainly, if he had recognized his attacker. But for that unlucky blow, as surmised by Inspector Nicholson, Charlotte was quite sure Mr Tibbins would have been a match for any assailant, but he must have been taken by surprise.

She spared a prayer for him, wondering if she might be his only mourner, and wondered too, if she should inform Inspector Nicholson of Jonas Tibbins's profession. Nothing had been said so she was forced to assume that no documents had been found that could identify him as anything other than the American tourist he purported to be. She wrestled uneasily with her conscience and concluded that discretion was, in this instance, the better part of valour and that Mr Tibbins would not have wished her to reveal his concerns even now.

But what a day it had been. As she drifted into sleep Charlotte was aware of momentous happenings all around. Elaine is looking so much improved in health, she whispered to herself. I have perhaps discovered something about my grandmother; and I tripped over the bloodstained corpse of a man I had begun to consider – if not a friend, then perhaps something of an ally. I wonder what tomorrow will bring.

At breakfast next morning Charlotte remained absorbed in this new and fascinating puzzle that had landed so unexpectedly in her lap. At five o'clock she had struggled awake from a tangled jumble of dreams and had merely dozed since that hour, worrying away at the ghost of an idea that she was sure might be helpful. Sadly, the notion that teased her so had proved elusive. Elaine had slept well, but was not tempting fate by rising early so she was taking her breakfast on a tray with the faithful Jackson in attendance. Later that morning the three of them, Elaine, Jackson and Charlotte would make their way on foot and by Bath chair to the consulting rooms of young Mr Radnor who would surely be delighted and gratified to hear of his patient's happy improvement.

Despite the appalling event of the previous afternoon, the even tenor of the Waterloo House breakfast-table was maintained, broken only by a small shriek from their hostess as Captain Penbury moved his cup and saucer rather abruptly out of his way.

'Oh, Captain Penbury,' she admonished him. 'Pray take more care. That breakfast china is Rockingham, you know, and came to me from my late husband's mother's cousin. It is quite irreplaceable.'

It was fortunate, Charlotte considered, that Mrs Montgomery appeared not to have heard the captain's gruff mutter of, 'If that is the case, madam, then why the devil do you put it out for use?' She shot him a smile of consolation and reached carefully for her own cup. Count Armel de Kersac was again at her side.

'I am relieved to observe, *madame*,' he murmured. 'That you seem to have recovered from yesterday's ordeal. What do you plan to do this morning?'

'Indeed I am feeling much more composed, thank you, M. Armel,' she nodded. 'This morning I propose to accompany Mrs Knightley when she goes for her electrical treatment. It seems to be doing her a great deal of good, so she is anxious to continue.'

And I propose to pump the nurse, Mrs Liddiard, she told herself. There may be more details of Ma's story that she has forgotten. It was an intriguing and exciting prospect and it would take her mind off sudden death. The former nurse might, of course, begin to suspect that she had rather more interest in the story than might be expected, bearing in mind that Charlotte had mentioned an acquaintance as the source of her knowledge; if she comes to the conclusion that I have a personal interest, I rather believe I shall give her an edited version of Ma's life history. She grinned suddenly under cover of her damask table napkin; that edited version had better not include anything to do with being transported, or with Will Glover's occupational hazards.

The morning's visit to the medical Faradist followed the same procedure as that of the previous day. Jackson stalked grimly down the length of Milsom Street in attendance on Elaine's Bath chair, keeping a minatory eye on the burly and respectable man engaged for the task of conveying the invalid to the doctor's consulting rooms. Inside those rooms Jackson dismissed the nurse with a barely disguised sniff as she firmly closed the door on the changing-room.

'Oh, it's you, ma'am.' Mrs Liddiard's door was opened by her daughter who, this morning, wore an anxious frown on her pleasantly plain face. 'Won't you come in? Mother is anxious to see you. It seems she has something on her mind.'

She led Charlotte to the room at the back but paused at the door. 'Mother is not well, today, ma'am,' she confided. 'We had the doctor to her and he believes she's had a stroke. She was bright enough when I put her to bed, most interested in her conversation with you she was, and sleeping like a baby when I settled her at ten o'clock.' A frown creased her brow. 'No, she was struck sometime just after midnight, we believe. I heard her call out and found her in distress.'

Charlotte was upset at the news and tried to suggest she should leave but the woman reached out a hand to stop her.

'If you don't mind, madam,' she ventured. 'Mother was that glad to talk to you that I reckon she might brighten up a bit if she sees you again. You won't mind her speech being slurred, I'm sure – her right side is slipped down, you see.'

It took several minutes before Charlotte was placed in a chair beside the invalid's bed and had shaken her head when offered a cup of tea. 'Oh well, ma'am, you'll call me if Mother needs me; I'm just in the kitchen nearby.'

Recognition gleamed in Mrs Liddiard's eyes as Charlotte bent over to greet her and she made some preliminary attempts at speech, growling when her visitor tried to make her rest.

'Saw her . . .' she gasped and looked her thanks as Charlotte took up a muslin cloth and wiped the spittle from her chin. 'Saw her ma . . . yes'day.'

Charlotte understood at once what she meant and she sat bolt upright in surprise.

'Molly's mother?' she gasped. 'You are telling me that you saw Molly Wesley's mother yesterday in Bath?'

'Plain 's dayligh' . . . into your house.' The words were punctuated by gasps and more pauses for the drool to be wiped away.

Again Charlotte felt she understood. 'My house? You mean Waterloo House?'

There was an attempt at a nod accompanied by a faint groan and Charlotte pressed the question. 'You saw Molly Wesley's mother at Waterloo House, yesterday? Is that what you are telling me?'

Mrs Liddiard sighed with evident relief and flapped her left hand in agreement as Charlotte bit her lip in furious thought. At last a light dawned.

'I think I see,' she faltered. 'Every day you take the same route round town in your Bath chair, do you not?' There was a mumble of assent, and she continued, 'And Mr – Mr Tibbins told

121

me that at a quarter past three precisely every weekday afternoon your Bath chair passes the front door of Waterloo House.' She saw that Mrs Liddiard was looking frail but relieved to be understood. I had better not tire her out, Charlotte decided, but I must try to find out more about this; it is too fantastical to be possible.

'You are quite certain of this, Mrs Liddiard?' Charlotte wiped the invalid's mouth and spoke with a gentle urgency. 'After all these years you are convinced that the lady you knew as Mrs Wellesley actually went into Waterloo House yesterday at three in the afternoon?'

The answer was a nod of the weary head, but then a fierce effort forced out a few difficult words. 'Yesh, her. Baby's ma. Certain. . . .'

Charlotte barely took in the sense of what the invalid was saying, momentous as it was, for she suddenly recalled that fragment of a dream, or idea, that had so teased her. At exactly quarter past three yesterday Mrs Liddiard had passed by Waterloo House in her Bath chair. And at about quarter past three yesterday Jonas Tibbins had met his untimely death in the yard of Waterloo House.

'Mrs Liddiard,' she urged, 'did you see anyone else? Someone running, perhaps? Maybe wearing bloodstained garments?'

CHAPTER 7

Murder and motherhood, thought Charlotte as she made her way back up the hill towards Waterloo House, biting her lip against the hysteria that threatened to overwhelm her. All I had in mind when I agreed to accompany Elaine to Bath was avoiding the battling governesses at home while my new house was made ready. I certainly had no expectation of becoming embroiled with detective agents and counts and dead bodies and small ladies who might, unlikely as it seems, turn out perhaps to be my grandmother. And how strange, she mused, that my own researches should coincide so exactly with such a dreadful event.

Charlotte was accustomed to examining her motives and possible choices with the clear, calm eye of reason, knowing that a wrong direction, a false step, could bring disaster down upon her head, but in this instance she felt that the danger inherent in her previous life was not a factor here in Bath. Indeed, she brushed a hand across her eyes in an attempt to marshal her thoughts; there was the ever-present fear that someone or something from her life in Australia, or that brief sojourn in India last year, might bring down her carefully constructed house of cards, but it seemed of less moment, she considered, than her present predicament.

A man had been murdered almost before her eyes. No, she had begun to correct herself but paused. That isn't an exaggeration, it's the truth. She had been present when the police inspector, Mr Nicholson, had again visited Waterloo House. Pressed to take tea he had become expansive, directing his conversation more towards Charlotte than towards her hostess.

'Indeed, Mrs Montgomery, Mrs Richmond,' – he had nodded, with what Charlotte devoutly hoped was merely an avuncular smile, in her direction – 'I fancy I am correct in my conclusions and so, I am gratified to say, does my superior. It is my considered belief that the poor American gentleman's untimely death was the unfortunate result of an attempted robbery.' He nodded again, with that very particular smile aimed at Charlotte and she was sure that for two pins he would have patted her upon her chestnut poplin-covered knee had they been alone in the room. What? Another of 'em? Was no young widow safe from gentlemen's attentions in this historic city? She stifled a sigh and tried to concentrate upon the inspector's remarks. 'Yes,' he said, sagely, 'the villainous perpetrator was most fortuitously interrupted firstly by the arrival in the mews of the elderly Count de Kersac, and almost immediately following that, by your own appearance on the scene, dear lady.'

There was more of the same as the genial policeman repeated his conclusions several times but while Charlotte had bowed her head in apparent meek acceptance of this edict, a rebellious small voice in her head said: *there was no time for anyone to run away*. M. de Kersac says he saw nobody and I'm certain he was telling the truth; I saw nobody either. I don't believe anyone could possibly have escaped from the mews without M. de Kersac or me seeing them. And there was no one, I would swear to that.

She sat up straight, all trace of incipient hysteria vanished. I looked in vain into the stable so if nobody came out of the mews or could have escaped over those very high walls covered in broken glass, she mused, they must have run into Waterloo House through the basement. The indignant face of Mrs Montgomery's cook swam before her mind's eye, swearing, 'On my Bible oath, Inspector!' that there had certainly not been any intruder in her kitchen at the time the inspector was talking about or indeed at any other. 'I keep a respectable kitchen, I'll have you know,' she had stormed, breathing hard, her broad face assuming an alarming tinge of crimson.

As far as Charlotte could make out that meant there was only one escape route left for the murderer and that was by way of the gravelled path along the side of Waterloo House leading to the paved area beneath the front door. There was a narrow set of steps up to the street from the lower level, by which an assailant might have escaped, but this theory too received a check. According to the statements the inspector had gathered, the only persons who had been observed to use the side path were those persons who had every right to do so and Mrs Liddiard had managed to convey the intelligence that she had seen no suspicious person running away. In other words, the only persons observed to use that path, upon that occasion, were guests at Waterloo House.

She shook her head and set the conundrum aside. It is not my problem, she told herself. Inspector Nicholson is an able and efficient officer of the law and I have every confidence in his discovering the murderer. The words rang hollow in her head even as she articulated them. Inspector Nicholson, competent and hardworking as he might well be, had already come to his decision. The villain was either a cut-purse who had been interrupted in his dastardly work, or else it was a gypsy bent also upon theft. In either case it would almost certainly prove impossible to bring the culprit to justice; even in a city as famously genteel as Bath there was an underworld into which a man could disappear, while gypsies were famously clever at vanishing overnight.

Relinquishing her theories into the murder, Charlotte allowed herself to consider the lady glimpsed so tantalizingly by Mrs Liddiard whose judgement, she felt on reflection, was trustworthy. A small, fair-haired lady who had entered the front door of Waterloo House yesterday afternoon. Charlotte had already made discreet enquiries among the maids and the footmen and ascertained that there had been no visitor answering that description on the previous afternoon, so she ran her eye down a mental list of ladies currently residing within doors.

The two governesses? Thankfully Charlotte was able to dismiss them at once from her speculations; to be forced to claim either as a parent would be intolerable, she felt. Dora Benson was blessed with an abundance of very light brown hair, but she had not arrived at Waterloo House until much later in the day and besides, she was still somewhere under forty, about the same age, indeed, as Molly Glover would have been now. Melicent Dunwoody was older, to be sure, but by no means old enough to be Charlotte's grandmother and the nurse would not have mistaken Melicent's pasty face and lankly dark and drooping locks for the woman she had described. Anyway, she shrugged, although Miss Dunwoody could qualify as a small woman that description could certainly not apply to Dora Benson. No indeed. Charlotte pictured the other woman; Dora is at least as tall as I am and probably taller, and she is splendidly built, rather on the lines of Boadicea. For a moment she slipped back into her earlier wishful thinking. It really is a pity that dear, sanctimonious Dora has so perfect an alibi for the murder, she sighed. I can so readily imagine her stabbing someone with a sharp pen nib in a fit of righteous anger, perhaps over a misplaced apostrophe, or because of a profusion of ink blots scattered across an ill-written essay, while a breach of schoolroom decorum would almost certainly precipitate a public flogging.

Who else then? Lady Buckwell was small, certainly, but her hair was so improbably golden that surely Mrs Liddiard, even in her incapacitated condition, would have remarked upon it. Then again her age was difficult to determine. Charlotte grinned as she recalled the face the lady presented to the world, immaculately lacquered and quite impossible to tell if she were fifty or as much as seventy-five years old.

Dismissing the cook and the maids – Mrs Liddiard had described the so-called Mrs Wellesley as a lady, even if she were suspected of being no better than she should be – Charlotte pursed her lips. Who was left? Mrs Attwell, the vicar's mother might, like Lady Buckwell, be almost any age between fifty and seventy odd; she could certainly be described as small in stature if not in girth. Charlotte knitted her brows. I suppose Mrs Liddiard could have forgotten to mention that Mrs Attwell is as fat as a suet dumpling. It seemed unlikely; Mrs Liddiard had been urgent in her attempt to enlighten Charlotte and in spite of her infirmity it had been plain to see that she still retained her intense interest in the topic. Mrs Liddiard, Charlotte recalled, had said something during the course of their first conversation about the mysterious Mrs Wellesley having sandy hair. Well, what hair Mrs Attwell allows to be seen is more rusty than sandy but that is not conclusive evidence. I am not so naïve as to suppose a lady's hair need always remain the same colour. Charlotte bit her lip at the memory of one of Will's parishioners. *'I swear to God, Molly my love, I truly thought the woman had a ginger tom cat perched on her head as she walked down the aisle,'* he had crowed once, when later describing the startling effect of the lady's hair dye.

That left . . . she broke off her deliberations in surprise. The only lady who had been in and about Waterloo House on the previous afternoon, and who seemed exactly to fit Mrs Liddiard's description, was Mrs Montgomery herself. Charlotte reviewed what she had been told. A little lady: Mrs Montgomery was slightly built and very small, shorter even than Melicent Dunwoody who drooped around somewhere beneath Charlotte's shoulder. A light-haired lady: Mrs Montgomery's hair might be a little faded nowadays but she could definitely be described as 'light' in colour, with those fiddly curls and rings of ash-pale hair, the gold fading into silver, on her forehead, with fussy little puffed curls that sprouted at the sides of her head in far too girlish a manner for a woman who must certainly be somewhere approaching sixty, if not more. Mrs Liddiard had made no mention of the colour of Mrs Wellesley's eyes but those protuberant pale-blue eyes that took account of every transgression by her guests would fit Mrs Montgomery comfortably into the picture.

I must observe Mrs Montgomery much more closely, she told herself, as she made her way back slowly to meet Elaine after her electrical session. But I don't *like* Mrs Montgomery very much, the thought insinuated itself into her consciousness and was dismissed with a guilty shake of her head. That's nonsense, Char, she snapped. What did you expect?

The truth refused to go away, Mrs Montgomery was far from the grandmother of her dreams. It was pointless to fall prey to regret; she had observed from the sidelines too many families whose members tore at each other's throats to hope for a fairy godmother of a grandmother to wave her wand and make all well. It may be true, she reflected. Perhaps Ma's mother did come back for her and perhaps she was sent distracted by the news that met her, of a woman dead, a child fostered and lost. If it turns out to be Mrs Montgomery perhaps her fussy manner and constant nagging about her wretched heirlooms stems from that time and masks a broken heart? There's certainly nothing nowadays that could be described as 'taking' or even 'hoity toity'. But I don't like Mrs Attwell either, she sighed. Or her bad-tempered son.

'What *is* the matter, Char?' Elaine turned her head to look at the tall girl walking along beside the Bath chair on their way back to Waterloo House. 'You are frowning so ferociously that I'm almost afraid to address a remark to you!'

Contrite, Charlotte reached out and clasped the slim, pale hand held out to her. 'Oh, goodness, Elaine. I'm so sorry. I was lost in thought.'

'So I observed,' came the reply, with a slight note of relief. 'I hope you're not worrying about your experience of yesterday, Char? It must have shaken you far more than you will admit, tripping over that poor American gentleman.'

'Perhaps.' Charlotte took refuge in a half truth. 'I confess I had rather come to like him and it's very sad, but I promise you I am quite recovered. It was unpleasant and upsetting but I am going on very well. But what of you, Elaine? I was surprised that you were not dispatched off to the hot bath again today.'

'Mr Radnor considers that as my electrical treatment today was more intense I might be spared the rigours of the bath.' Elaine darted a mischievous grin at her friend. 'Besides, had I gone to the baths I might have tired myself out and Jackson would never have granted permission for tonight's dissipation, our outing to attend the concert at the Assembly Rooms. And that would never do.'

'Heavens, I had completely forgotten about that excitement.' Charlotte opened her eyes wide. 'How does Mrs Montgomery propose to convey her household to the Assembly Rooms, I wonder? It's not very far, so I doubt if she has it in mind to hire a fleet of carriages. Shall you retain this Bath chair, Elaine?'

'I have already made sure of it,' Mrs Knightley smiled up at the chair-man. 'I expect you are right, Char, the distance is quite short and the weather is glorious today. There is less of that enervating heat so a walk in the early evening will be most pleasurable for those of you who possess workable legs!'

'Legs? Good gracious,' Charlotte exclaimed, with a startled glance at Elaine. 'What about the weeping willow, I wonder? Melicent can't walk very far, with her false leg.' She broke off with a rueful laugh. 'How foolish I am that I must assume every problem will be brought to me for a solution. It is Mrs Montgomery's quandary and I have nothing to do but enjoy myself tonight. I wonder what is considered suitable attire for an evening with Bath high society.'

A state occasion such as this, Charlotte realized suddenly, would provide her with an excellent opportunity to stare at her fellow residents without being suspected of undue curiosity. She caught herself up with a gasp. Of course, Mr Tibbins had told her something very similar when he hinted that a party could put what he called his 'quarry' off their guard. This is not merely a party then, she told herself, but a chance to find out whatever I can about the people here and to calculate whether any of them was responsible for murder.

After an early dinner the guests at Waterloo House assembled in the drawing room so that Mrs Montgomery could marshal them towards the Assembly Rooms. Charlotte was amused to see that even the serenely complacent Dora Benson was casting surreptitious glances at herself in the great circular mirror with its ornate gilt frame. You may admire yourself as much as you please, dear Dora, Charlotte addressed the governess silently, but when all is said and done I'm afraid you will still resemble a well-bred horse. At least, she conceded, Dora was a well-*dressed* horse, in a plain but perfectly acceptable gown of dull purple-grey silk over a crinoline that was neither unsuitably wide nor niggardly skimpy. Unlike Melicent Dunwoody who, draped in rusty black with nothing at all in the way of a hoop, however small, drooped around the room – *like the skeleton at the feast* – as Lady Meg, Charlotte's beloved godmother, would have commented, her judgement accompanied by a disdainful sniff.

Charlotte refrained from peering and preening in the round mirror, 'a keepsake from my dear late sister-in-law's aunt' as Mrs Montgomery had informed her guests a night or so previously. She had inspected herself from head to toe before dinner in the looking-glass in Elaine's room.

'I wonder how old this mirror is?' she had observed, reaching out a careful finger to touch the fragile pale gold leaf that adorned the frame. 'The glass is wavy and difficult to look into.'

'I know,' agreed Elaine. 'When I look at myself in it I feel I'm looking at my drowning soul, in a magical lake.' She gave a snort of laughter. 'What a pretentious flight of fancy! Now then . . .' She glanced complacently at her own silvery grey satin then looked Charlotte up and down. 'You look very fine, my dear. That amber silk gives you some colour and suits you very well. What a pity, though, that you can't wear your lovely black silk shawl with the pink embroidered roses, but the plain black wrap looks very stylish.'

She had turned to speak to her maid at that moment so did not observe the colour she had admired drain suddenly from Charlotte's face. The pink silk roses would certainly not have gone with the amber of the dress but that was not the only reason Charlotte had hesitated to wear the Chinese shawl that had been her mother's. She had, in the face of all unreason and when all else was lost, clung to the shawl during her perilous journey across India during the Mutiny and there were more recent, more painful, associations with the shawl that she was not yet ready to confront.

The rest of the company were also arrayed in their finery. Mrs Montgomery was dressed in pale blue, her widowhood presumably of such duration that the late Mr Montgomery no longer merited the gloom of widow's weeds. Could the diminutive landlady be on the catch for another husband, Charlotte wondered, observing with a cynical eye the manner in which Mrs Montgomery fluttered up at the tall, bluff naval man and the brawny funeral chaser alike? She was also, Charlotte noted, paying attention to the elderly French count, but even as Charlotte peeped under her lashes across the drawing room, the old man directed a swift glance in her own direction, betraying a glimpse of the chilly amusement that he had shared with her before. No, she thought with a sudden rush of gladness, the lady will never catch that particular Frenchman.

Mrs Attwell was, as usual, arrayed in black, but although nothing could enhance her unfortunate figure, her gown was of the finest quality; there was manifestly no lack of funds in that quarter. The clergyman son had so far not come very much within Charlotte's orbit, for which she had been grateful as his rage seemed permanently aroused, but tonight he seemed to gravitate towards her at every given moment. They had been neighbours at dinner and Mr Attwell had been surprisingly attentive though Charlotte had been glad to make her escape as soon as possible.

'I inherited my father's parish,' he explained, holding his temper in check as he edged closer to her and ignored a beady glare from his maternal parent, as they partook of the excellent beef quenelles being served to everyone except Captain Penbury who sighed over his gruel. 'There have been Attwell parsons incumbent since the Ark, but I have higher ambitions.' She realized that his small dark eyes were fixed hotly upon the low neck of her dress and she tightened her lips, hitching her shawl higher to cover her bare skin. Ugh, she managed not to shiver, but he persisted, breathing heavily through his open mouth and essaying several clumsy pleasantries. It was all too plain to see that The Revd Decimus Attwell had decided Charlotte was worthy of his advances. Had he, she wondered, made enquiries of their hostess about her position and fortune? Well, she gave a small shrug as she made her escape, he won't have discovered much, though I suppose I must present a fairly prosperous appearance. A smile glimmered in her hazel eyes as she recalled her situation less than twelve months since; fleeing across the Indian countryside during the Mutiny, with nothing but what she had managed to beg, borrow or steal.

She wondered if Mr Attwell had indeed decided that young Mrs Richmond was a suitable wife for the bishopric he had hinted to be within his grasp, subject only to the present incumbent's gross dereliction of duty in refusing still to die when all his doctors had predicted such an outcome some weeks previously. The ginger eyebrows had bristled at the very recollection of this ailing prelate and Charlotte could have sworn she heard the gnashing of his teeth. His temper alone, she reflected, would be enough to put her off matrimony with him, apart from all other considerations. She had noticed that his conversations took the form of a series of ill-natured barks and that most of the time he sat in simmering silence.

The short journey to the Bath Assembly Rooms was accomplished with surprising efficiency with Mrs Montgomery acting the part of whipper-in among those of her guests who chose to walk, while Captain Penbury accompanied Lady Buckwell and Miss Dunwoody in a cab, the captain confiding in his booming whisper that he was 'suffering from the old trouble amidships, don't y'know.' The elder governess cast a languishing glance at him as he spoke and tried to insinuate herself between the captain and Lady Buckwell as they mounted the steps of the cab.

'Out of the way, madam,' ordered the elder lady with a peremptory wave of the fan she had assumed for the occasion. 'You may be old and infirm, as indeed I observe that you are, but I am senior to you in rank and it ill becomes you to jostle a lady of my quality and my years.'

Over the top of the depressing black bonnet whose brim was shaped like an upside down spoon, Charlotte met the flashing twinkle in the old lady's green eyes. Her answering grin was swiftly disguised as she helped the captain give Melicent Dunwoody, now making plaintive protests of her abject humility, a shove up the step into the interior. God help us all, she panted – noting that either Miss Dunwoody, or perhaps her wooden leg, weighed considerably more than seemed reasonable – if the captain overdoes it and his trouble shifts from amidships to somewhere even more distressing.

As Elaine had prophesied the early evening was glorious indeed, the light glowed golden and heartening and Charlotte felt an insensible lift to her spirits as she strolled along beside her friend, accompanied by the indispensable Jackson who had insisted on attending, 'just in case. . . .' as she had darkly declaimed.

I have so much to be thankful for, Charlotte reminded herself, with an inward smile. Last year I was in despair and sorrow, and in desperate straits, alone and penniless in a foreign country with not a penny to my name and look at me now: I am respectably dressed, I have an income, money in the bank besides, and in my purse too. I have a home, a very impressive and ancient home, and I have a family who love me and are loved by me in return. Probably by the time we return to Hampshire I shall have a house of my own which I will share with the dearest, most surprising old lady I have ever met, who happens by a great stroke of good fortune to be my grandmother-in-law and at the moment I am on holiday here in Bath, a place I dreamed of visiting all my life.

Yes, replied the inner Charlotte, sermonizing is all very well, my girl, but Bath has turned out somewhat different from those daydreams, has it not? You pictured the city to be thronged with characters from your favourite novels: you thought of encountering Captain Wentworth and his quietly elegant wife, and you imagined Mr Knightley . . . A sigh halted her wandering reverie at that point as Mrs Montgomery hove in sight, bent on her sheepdog duties, so Charlotte gave her a friendly smile in greeting.

'This is a great treat you have arranged for us, Mrs Montgomery,' she began, hoping that she was not ladling too much honey on to the bread. 'I believe you have travelled around England quite extensively. Do you enjoy good music? You must have visited many other grand assembly rooms in your journeyings.'

Her landlady's response surprised her. With a frowning look of suspicion Mrs Montgomery flapped a small hand, clad in a fingerless mitten, and delved into the bag suspended by a silken cord from her wrist. 'What's that? Music? I have no time for such nonsense,' she said. With this repressive reply she swished forward to the head of the straggle of guests and began to line them up at the entrance to the Assembly Rooms.

All through dinner that night, all the way up the hill and under the grateful shade of the trees, Charlotte had been aware of something wrong, something different about the party. The relief from tension this morning had been palpable and she had attributed this to the dramatic removal of the inquisitive American gentleman. But now . . . the atmosphere was no longer light-hearted and the tension had returned in greater strength than before.

All of those guests whom she had observed to be under some duress from the late detective's intimate and unsettling nods and winks – Mrs Attwell and her son, Captain Penbury, Mr Chettle, M. de Kersac – were wearing frowns and holding themselves a little stiffly as if under a great strain. That too, she concluded, must be the reason for Mrs Montgomery's strange inattention.

The American detective, Mr Tibbins, might well be dead but his legacy lived on. The guests at Waterloo house had been frightened when he was alive. Now they were frightened again.

CHAPTER 8

Charlotte stood at Elaine's side and gazed round the lofty, elegant room in awe. 'Imagine,' she bent down to whisper in her friend's ear, 'my godmother came to assemblies here and loved to tell me all about them. She was in this very room.' With a little laugh of excitement she bestowed a kiss on Elaine Knightley's luminous cheek, a rare gesture of affection from Charlotte whose reserve was seldom breached. 'There, that's for being so kind as to invite me to accompany you to Bath, my dear. I never dreamed of coming to the Assembly Rooms as well, it's almost too much!'

'Go and sit down, Char.' Elaine smiled and reached up to squeeze the younger woman's hand; such a long, strong and tanned hand in contrast to her own delicate one. 'I shall do very well with Lady Buckwell to keep me company over here on the dowagers' bench and there is Captain Penbury to run my errands. Oh,' she broke off with a suppressed laugh. 'I should have said Captain Penbury and Miss Dunwoody to run my errands for me, for here he comes with the lady in tow.'

She looked up in surprise at a choked off exclamation from Charlotte. 'Why, Char? You surely do not grudge his defection? It may be a little sudden, but he seems very much taken with Finchbourne's former governess; it seems excessively suitable, do not you think so?'

'Yes, I suppose so,' Charlotte sighed. 'But I had other ideas for him. And for her, too. Oh well. . . .'

She was amused to see that their hostess for the evening, Mrs Montgomery's friend, was as cavalier in her treatment of 'the

135

Waterloo House lodgers' as Charlotte had anticipated. The lady had unerringly targeted Elaine Knightley as a lady of wealth and breeding, but Mrs Attwell and the two governesses were dismissed with a curt greeting and a sniff of disdain from a nose well suited to such pursuits, as it was immensely long and bony and dangled a small icicle in the shape of a constant drip. Charlotte, in Elaine Knightley's train, received a more gracious welcome and was even offered two chill, bony fingers, but found herself able to conceal her transports at this honour under a cloak of well-bred indifference.

Mrs Knightley, quite as alive to the situation as Charlotte, stirred the pot by saying: 'Mrs Richmond was just telling me that her godmother, Lady Margaret, came often to Bath, visiting the Assembly Rooms many times.'

Charlotte's head swivelled as she gazed in astonishment at her friend, but Mrs Smith had stopped in her tracks, even as she turned in search of bigger fry.

'Lady Margaret, you say?' she enquired in a suddenly conciliatory voice.

A barely concealed grin on Elaine's face alerted Charlotte and she bestowed a chill nod on her hostess for the evening. 'Oh yes,' she said carelessly. 'Lady Margaret Fenton; she spent much of her youth in Bath and was often here with her mother, the countess, about thirty years ago.'

No attempt had been made to introduce the two parties and Charlotte was heartily thankful for this dispensation for Mrs Smith's guests looked as disagreeable as their hostess, but she did note that the gentlemen from Waterloo House were received considerably more graciously than the ladies, and that they were treated to a smile from a mouth surely more full of teeth than was customary. However, on hearing of Charlotte's grand connections, Mrs Smith changed tack and made strenuous efforts to engage Charlotte's interest, all of which were dashed by her victim's studied indifference.

Unmistakable signs and sounds indicated that the concert was about to begin so Charlotte made a hasty escape while Mrs Montgomery slunk submissively away from their hostess as she and her party were dismissed to their inferior seats, well away from their fellow guests.

As the lights in the main part of the room were dimmed, Charlotte checked on Elaine's comfort once more and hastened to take her place in the audience, nodding gratefully to little Marianne de Kersac who, given special permission to stay up late, had begged to be allowed to reserve a place beside her for Charlotte, her favourite among the grown-ups.

Less welcome to Charlotte was the presence on her other side of The Revd Decimus Attwell whose hot porcine eyes now seemed to her to brighten whenever they beheld her. It was becoming only too plain to her that since dinner Mr Attwell seemed to have decided that she would indeed grace a bishop's palace and had begun to take even more particular notice of her. Oh dear, she sighed; why must men always complicate matters so? Besides, even in the unlikely event that I *did* find Mr Attwell companionable, his mother would never allow him to make advances to me.

Ah well, she was cheered by a sudden recollection: at least Mr Chettle and Captain Penbury seem to have transferred their attentions effortlessly from me to Dora and to Melicent. Alas, I must have been but the plaything of an idle moment and am now cast aside like the proverbial worn glove. Her mouth twisted in a grin. I must not repine, however, as I am pretty confident that I still have admirers in abundance, and how I wish I had not. It was not vain self-delusion she knew, for even as she sat quietly waiting for the opening strains of the concert, she was aware that Armel de Kersac was smiling at her from his seat next to his daughter and there – oh lord, how ironic given her adventurous life story – a police inspector with an interest in music – for clearly visible on the other side of the room, a large, broad man was waving at her with a great deal of pleasure reflected on his genial countenance.

'Are you quite comfortable, Mrs Richmond?' It was Mr Attwell, bending his newly solicitous head towards her and speaking in a confidential growl as the audience began to rustle in anticipation as the hands of the clock reached the hour. 'I could change seats with you if you would prefer?'

There was time only for a smiling shake of her head before an elderly gentleman creaked to his feet, mumbled some inaudible remarks and took his place again as a much younger gentleman bounded on to the stage to introduce the participants.

The first half of the proceedings could only have taken an hour at the most, Charlotte decided, when the master of ceremonies at last raised his hand and announced that there would now be a short intermission for rest and refreshment, but it had seemed far, far longer. Charlotte could only thank the mercies of Providence which had placed her at a safe distance from Elaine Knightley. Had they been seated side by side she considered, one or both of them would surely have disgraced herself with an outburst of uncontrollable laughter.

The young gentleman who was in charge had announced each successive act in such glowing terms that anticipation rose to a peak and the first performer received a storm of applause as she tripped daintily on to the stage.

Charlotte, as she had laughingly told Elaine that morning, had few ladylike accomplishments at all. 'I cannot sing,' she had said. 'I cannot draw, I cannot play the pianoforte or the harp, and I cannot produce delicately beautiful embroideries; sadly the ability to do quantities of mending, to cook a good plain dinner and to shoot a marauding crocodile as I once did, are not appreciated in Polite Society.'

When the young lady on the stage opened her mouth to sing it was soon clearly borne in upon Charlotte that this was a concert of amateur performers. How singular, she thought, raising her eyebrows at the uncertain soprano; I somehow expected the cream of Bath society to stage something a little more professional. She settled down to listen politely, but, as so often happened, a memory of her stepfather flashed into her mind.

The darkened splendour of the room vanished and once more she and her mother made up part of the audience in a dry and scorching little township somewhere north of Brisbane. Boxes and crates were arranged as seating and the performers made their stage on a bluff with the glorious blue of the Pacific behind them. All went well, with Will Glover standing in as master of ceremonies when the original was discovered drunk under a cart; but disaster struck when Will announced a quartet of husky Scotsmen who began to dance the Highland Fling.

Faster and faster they danced, louder and louder rang out the shouts of 'Och aye!' and wilder and wilder came the applause from the audience until, with a deafening crack, the stage and the dancers disappeared from sight.

Charlotte came back to the present to discover a pair of youngsters singing a sentimental ballad, accompanied by coy smiles and bashful glances and when the unfortunate youth's voice cracked on the top note and swooped to a gruff baritone, Charlotte found herself wishing for a present-day landslip to rescue him from his embarrassment. Nobody had suffered serious injury in that ancient calamity; the section of cliff had only slid twenty feet or so and the dancers soon scrambled up, to be plied with strong drink by their sympathetic friends, including Charlotte and her mother, who tended to their sprains and abrasions, though Will had been precious little use, she recalled, as he lay on the ground crowing with helpless laughter.

Her eyes darkened as she recalled that the next day had come the usual summons to a deathbed, usually Will's mother (chosen for dramatic effect) and off they had gone, along with the proceeds of the concert party. Why did we let him get away with it, Charlotte wondered now? He led Ma a merry dance and me along with her, always up to some shady or saucy lark or other and always on the verge of riches or ruin. Why? She gave the tiniest of shrugs. Because Will Glover had the devil's own charm and at heart he was the kindest of men; he adored us and we adored him right back. But as she stared back down the years Charlotte realized her views had changed. Charm, adventure, adoration and an insouciant kindness, these were good qualities even in a man who had never been able to resist a gamble, a dare, a romp, but Charlotte knew in her heart that her mother had yearned always for peace and quiet, for solvency and safety, for respectability and a little settled home of her own. Molly, like

Charlotte, had been suspicious of too much charm in the end, though she had never ceased from loving Will.

Charlotte gave a quiet sigh. I prize honesty high above all other attributes, she thought. Only a man of the utmost probity could ever win me now; charm is not enough; it will never be enough. In her mind's eye she had a glimpse, swiftly extinguished, of a man whose charm was rooted in his honesty and who had pressed her hand with warm and affectionate friendship as he bade farewell to her and to his wife on their journey to Bath.

This would never do. Charlotte raised her eyes to the stage and tried to concentrate, banishing her innermost thoughts.

A harpist was followed by a pianist who strummed inexpertly at a mournful passage, and in turn was succeeded by what was announced as 'a charming troupe of dancers', which turned out to be several ladies who pranced across the stage in slippered feet, taking turns to perform solo pirouettes while their fellows rested in attitudes of graceful admiration on benches to the side. Judged on the quality of the preceding acts, Charlotte was not surprised to see that the dancers ranged in age from about twelve to the shady side of forty, or that every size and shape of female seemed to be represented. Nor was she unduly surprised when a bench gave way with a loud crack, taking its occupants by surprise so that the audience was treated to a view of upended crinolines with feet waving frantically among the petticoats, accompanied by much wailing.

Charlotte was snorting almost uncontrollably at the end of the first half of the performance. The only consolation, she concluded as she blew her nose and hastily mopped her eyes, was that she was not distinguishable in the darkness, nor when the lights rose, was she alone. A glance showed Elaine Knightley, slender shoulders heaving and her face buried in her hands while Charlotte's favourite fellow guest, cynical old Lady Buckwell, was busy applying a dainty lace edged handkerchief to her usually sardonic green eyes, their sparkle discreetly concealed for once.

Mr Attwell seemed, unfortunately, to be bent upon making up

for his late entry into the courtship stakes and was offering the full range of intimate whispers, significant glances and heartfelt sighs, schooling his ferocious features into a semblance of *politesse* and now he was at her elbow with his mouth open to speak when he was forestalled, very skilfully, by the younger Comte de Kersac who bowed and asked if she would like him to fetch her a cup of tea or coffee.

'You need not scruple to make use of me, Mrs Richmond,' he smiled at her, with a politely dismissive nod to her other neighbour. 'My father has requested a cup of coffee, though to be truthful he holds out no great hope of the coffee being drinkable. This being the case it would be my pleasure to obtain refreshment for you at the same time.' He smiled down at her with marked affection in his expression. 'To be sure, I hardly need ask. I am quite sure your answer will be that a cup of tea would be most welcome. Am I correct?'

'Indeed you are, M. Armel,' she laughed. 'What a predictable creature of habit I must be. I confess though that a cup of tea is just what I should enjoy above all things.' She rose from her seat and shook her head at Mr Attwell who rose eagerly with her. 'No, no, Mr Attwell, you should attend to your mother while I must go to talk to Mrs Knightley and discover how she is enjoying this wonderful treat.'

Ignoring the volcanic rumblings that arose from this treatment of the fiery cleric, and seeing from afar that Mrs Smith was headed in her direction, crocodile teeth all agleam, Charlotte took Marianne by the hand and escaped to the side of the room where she ascertained that Elaine Knightley was quite comfortable and being waited upon by Captain Penbury and a very tall young man with curly brown hair who had attached himself to their party. He smiled at Marianne de Kersac and bent to speak to her while the captain explained that his new friend was a mathematical lecturer at Oxford and here in pursuit of his new hobby of photography. Charlotte was intrigued.

'I only wish I could have had photographs of my mother and stepfather,' she sighed as she admired the photographic *cartes de visites* their new acquaintance was showing to her and

Marianne. 'As it is, they live on only in my memory.'

To her surprise the normally timid little French girl was chattering with great animation to the tall young man, but when Captain Penbury bent down also to engage her in ponderous conversation, she became dumb and he turned away looking downcast.

'I am so sorry, *madame*,' the child whispered to Charlotte. 'But I never can think of anything to say to gentlemen.'

'Never mind, my dear,' Charlotte comforted her. 'Just do as my godmother and my stepfather both advised me. When you are feeling very shy you should curtsy while you are thinking what to say. Something will usually occur to you while you are bobbing up and down.'

'What good advice,' the young Oxford scholar remarked, his grey-blue eyes alight with amusement. 'I must make a note of that.' To Charlotte's amusement he took out a small writing tablet and held his pencil in readiness. 'What was it you said?' He raised a quizzical eyebrow at her. 'Curtsy while you are thinking. . . .'

Across the handsome room Charlotte espied Armel de Kersac carefully carrying a tray. 'Come, Marianne, we must say goodbye for the moment. I see your papa with my cup of tea and your glass of lemonade.'

They nodded to their new friend and took their places again and as she drank her tea Charlotte's gaze flickered round the room as she recalled once more the late detective's advice. Here she was at a party indeed, and surrounded by Mr Tibbins's quarry; could she use those powers of observation that he had admired in her, to discover something about his death?

Had she been mistaken about the change of atmosphere? But no, there was Mrs Montgomery deep in conversation with Mr Chettle and both of them wearing prodigious scowls. Goodness me, how intriguing; a frown creased her own brow as she tried to imagine the topic of their discussion. And who else? Lady Buckwell and Mrs Attwell were now engaged in some unexceptionable talk, along with Captain Penbury who had somehow, Charlotte was thankful to note, become detached from the clinging attentions of the drooping Melicent Dunwoody. Lady Buckwell wore her usual air but Mrs Attwell and the captain both sported abstracted frowns.

The two French gentlemen were in attendance on herself and appeared at first glance to have not a care in the world other than making sure that she was enjoying her cup of tea. At second glance however, it was plain to see that the elder count had withdrawn into himself again while his son, determined upon charming Charlotte herself, was shooting frequent surreptitious glances at his father, and frowning anxiously each time that he did so.

There was no doubt about it, she told herself, whatever had frightened them all so much when the detective was alive, was still giving rise to considerable unease even now. I wish so much, Mr Tibbins, she sighed, that you were here with me. I can see, just as you told me, that they seem disturbed away from their usual places, but what am I to make of that? Is it merely a fading of the first excitement of being so near to something shocking, or is there something new that makes them so uneasy?

After the enthralling disasters of the first half of the concert, Charlotte settled down to enjoy the remainder of the evening which was apparently to consist of recitations and playlets, commencing with a series of tableaux taken from history. There was a dramatic swish of the curtain to reveal several stout Roman soldiers who seemed to resemble the troupe of dancing girls and were clad in sundry draperies, with papier mâché helmets as they stood, allegedly on the shores of Britain, and made threatening gestures at a couple of dispirited ancient Britons who shook their fists with obvious reluctance.

This stirring episode in British history was succeeded by a despondent King Harold lying on the floor, quite failing to convince the audience that the point of the arrow he clutched in his fist was actually in his eye, rather than concealed down the side of his head. The Conqueror gloated realistically in front of him.

Queen Elizabeth and Raleigh, Cromwell and Charles I, all appeared before the audience and Charlotte was congratulating

143

herself that she was managing very creditably not to laugh when the curtains were drawn back with a flourish upon the next scene which was not to be a mere tableau, but a dramatic rendering.

A rough scaffold had been raised and was surrounded by what Charlotte recognized as the former Roman soldiers who, in later incarnations had appeared as Normans, Tudor courtiers, Royalists and Roundheads alike. This time they purported to be an angry mob, shaking their fists at a woman clad in gaudy finery presumably denoting her status as an aristocrat and trampler of the poor.

Charlotte was a trifle uncertain, at first, as to which particular episode in history this scene represented but a roll of drums soon informed her and she drew a sharp breath as the woman knelt and placed her head on a block, to the accompaniment of jeers from the spectators and a denunciation of her alleged crimes by a fiery orator. The lights were dimmed even further, one of the musicians played a swooshing downward note on his violin to denote the fall of the guillotine; there was a clash of cymbals, a gasp, and a burly man in black held up a papier mâché head clad in a powdered wig. The chastened mob now wept and wailed but Queen Marie Antoinette had met her untimely end.

Charlotte had felt a momentary amusement at the dreadful, stilted performance, but was immediately aware of a sudden stillness in the elder Comte de Kersac, sitting next but one to her, beside his granddaughter, Marianne. Oh my God, she bit her lip, recalling the brief nuggets of information about his childhood that the old man had let slip. He told me his mother was guillotined, I remember now. What an unfortunate subject to hit upon. On an impulse she slipped an unobtrusive arm behind the little girl and gave a gentle squeeze to the dark-clad shoulder held in so upright and rigid a posture. As if returning from that icy wilderness of the past that seemed to be both refuge and torment, M. de Kersac slowly turned his head to her. His pale-blue eyes glistened with unaccustomed dew and it was clear to Charlotte that he was considerably discomposed but he rallied and summoned up a smile as he thanked her with a slight inclination of his head.

The rest of the performance was quickly over, with bows and smiles from the performers and repeated cheers from an audience whose unbridled delight must surely betoken close acquaintance and possibly even closer relationship; and sooner than she thought possible Charlotte was retracing her steps from the Assembly Rooms and back to Waterloo House, walking as before in attendance upon Elaine Knightley's Bath chair.

'Pray do not fuss, Charlotte,' Elaine remonstrated. 'I am tired, I confess, but that's quite natural, you know. I rarely go out at night and I shall go straight to bed. But make no mistake, I found this evening's entertainment so unexpectedly delightful and I'm only too sorry that Kit could not have been here too. He would so much have enjoyed the dancing troupe and poor King Harold.'

Knowing how stubborn Elaine could be where her health was concerned Charlotte let the topic alone. The slight improvement in her friend's health still appeared to be in force but Charlotte had not been unaware, during the period of that improvement, of the occasional sharp intake of breath that was so hastily concealed. During the sole gem of the evening, an unexpectedly touching song from a short stout woman of uncertain age whose appearance was against her but who sang like a nightingale, a glance across the assembly room had revealed Elaine looking drained for a moment, her eyes screwed shut against an obvious spasm of discomfort. No use, Charlotte knew, to mention that glimpse; Elaine would laugh and disclaim all knowledge of it, but was it her heart, weak from childhood, or something else that lay unseen and deadly?

To distract her anxious thoughts, Charlotte managed an elaborately casual glance around such members of the group from Waterloo House as were nearby. There was no question, something was concerning several of her fellow guests and there were frowns and drawn-down mouths a-plenty.

As Mrs Montgomery was assembling her party before leaving the Rooms, Charlotte noticed what seemed to be an altercation, conducted in furious undertones, between the simmering and resentful Mr Attwell and his dominant mother, but Mr Attwell, she realized, spent most of his days on the edge of an angry outburst and in any case they broke off their conversation when she drifted closer and were now stalking silently down the hill, their large feet carrying them ahead of the pack. M. de Kersac was looking pale and old, but surely it was nothing more than the natural fatigue of a man, already elderly, who, during an expedition that extended late into the evening, had been reminded of the unimaginable tragedies of his youth? If that were solely the case, though, why did the old man stare at his son with so anxious a regard? M. Armel de Kersac had never appeared to be disturbed by the late Mr Tibbins; it was rather the case that the detective's attentions had been directed at the elder French gentleman. But she could not be mistaken; it was the younger count who was now frowning and the elder who watched him with anxiety in those chill, pale eyes.

Mr Simeon Chettle, her funereal neighbour from Hampshire, was walking down the hill in animated and, it had to be admitted, intimate conversation with the other governess, Dora Benson. Charlotte sighed and thought of her poor sister-in-law, Agnes, so newly married to Dora's own brother. I don't want Mr Chettle to propose to Dora, she shuddered. Imagine her living a mere half mile up the road from Agnes and Percy at the vicarage; why, it would never do. Tomorrow, she decided, she would try to detach Dora from Mr Chettle and push her under the large and rubicund nose of Captain Penbury who lived somewhere in Kent or Sussex, she believed, but wherever it was it was certainly at a safe distance from Hampshire.

As they reached the square in which Waterloo House was situated Charlotte observed Mr Chettle from under the tilted brim of her frivolous little straw hat. A hasty movement had attracted her gaze and she saw him turn to stare at the group thronged about the cab which had drawn up at their destination. His expression startled her, that heavy, beetling brow loomed darkly enough at any time, nature had already seen to that, but just at this moment there was something angry and brooding about his glare, then the moment passed and he returned to his conversation with Dora Benson.

Curious to discover who was the recipient of that lowering stare Charlotte craned her neck to observe the party, only to be baffled even further. Mrs Montgomery was there, as was only fitting; it was her house and her party after all. Captain Penbury was leaning out of the carriage to hand down Lady Buckwell who, displaying not a scrap of exhaustion, looked most ungrateful for his attention bestowing her hand upon a surprised Mr Attwell as he reached up to assist her. The clergyman then turned to perform the same office for Melicent Dunwoody only to be surprised by a tirade from the gallant naval gentleman, his normally bluff features suffused with an angry flush.

'How dare you, sir. Unhand Miss Dunwoody this instant. Do you think I have not noticed, sir, how you have pressed your unwelcome attentions upon the lady? Hey? Hey? Enticing her to sit beside you for the second half of tonight's performance when you were very well aware that the lady was engaged to sit beside me? Hey? Hey?'

Before Decimus Attwell could do more than open his mouth in complete astonishment at this attack upon him, Captain Penbury gathered more steam and continued to upbraid his fellow guest.

'Aye, I thought that would make you take notice, sir. It is all the same with you sneaking fellows with your mealy-mouthed manners. Do not think that your cloth will protect you, it does not, sir. Most assuredly it does not.'

Knowing that Elaine was in the safe hands of her own maid and with the additional assistance, if required, of the solicitous chair-man, Charlotte hesitated on the pavement outside Waterloo House. Had the captain run mad? She was not the only person present to come to that conclusion.

'How dare you impugn my son, sir,' burst out Mrs Attwell, in furious support of her son who, Charlotte was not surprised to observe, did not appear at all grateful. 'How can you suppose that he would harbour pretensions to that whey-faced little

147

nobody. He would not lower himself, I can assure you.'

'Mother!' With a furious reddening of his face The Revd Mr Attwell turned on his strong-minded parent. 'Hold your tongue. Have you not done enough to ruin my happiness in the past? Do you wish me to instance the number of occasions upon which your meddling and jumping to unwarranted conclusions has caused nothing but embarrassment and heartache to me? Shame upon you, madam, this is the last straw. You will do me the honour of making arrangements to move out of the vicarage when we return home. The Glebe cottage will make a very suitable residence and I will, of course, provide for you and a limited household appropriate to your position. I . . .' His pause was quite sufficiently theatrical as to make his audience aware that something of moment was about to occur. 'I should inform you that I am considering setting up an establishment of my own.'

With this dramatic, and all too public, announcement, the beleaguered clergyman turned on his heel, even his balding dome glowing with temper, and stalked up the short flight of steps to the front door leaving his mother and Charlotte alone on the pavement, Captain Penbury having marched indoors with the shrinking governess limping beside him. And clinging possessively to his arm, Charlotte had observed with a wry smile; it was becoming plain that not only did the bluff naval captain harbour intentions towards Miss Dunwoody but that the lady was only too determined to bring him to the point of proposal. Only Lady Buckwell lingered in the lighted doorway as if reluctant to abandon so promising a drama; however, she caught Charlotte's eye, shooting her a grin of that mingled commiseration with pure mischief, and shrugged her way into the house.

Oh heavens, now what? Charlotte sighed as she put an arm round Mrs Attwell whose squat, shapeless body was shaken with sobs intermingled with strangled yelps of misery. A suspicion rose in Charlotte's mind as she caught an unmistakable whiff of alcohol. Had Mrs Attwell been indulging in secret, she wondered? If that were the case, several circumstances became clear – the lady's occasional uneven gait and florid face. I suppose I can hardly abandon the poor foolish creature in the street and she is in no case to go peacefully to bed. A medicinal measure of brandy is probably called for, she decided. For both of us, that is, even if she is already under the influence.

'Come, Mrs Attwell.' She spoke in a brisk tone. 'Let me take you into the dining room where it is quiet and we will pour ourselves a glass of brandy to calm our nerves.'

'How can he speak so to me?' Mrs Attwell's hands were tensed into fists but she accompanied Charlotte to the dining-room in quite a docile manner. 'When everything I have ever done has been for him. Only for him.' She gulped down the brandy in quite an accustomed manner and held out the glass for more. 'I have lied for him. I have perjured myself in a court of law and only for him. I have blackened characters and written secret letters – all for him. And I told him long ago that if the need ever arose, I would kill for him.'

CHAPTER 9

Unseen by the distraught lady, Charlotte made a face. Oh Lord, she sighed inwardly; here I go again. Why must I assume that it is I who need sort out every predicament? Straighten every tangle? And I'm so tired tonight, heaven knows why; it must be all the dramas I've stumbled upon since we arrived in Bath. She opened her eyes wide as Mrs Attwell reached out blindly, evidently demanding that her glass be refilled for a third time. Oh well, Charlotte shrugged, obediently upending the bottle. If she is drunk at least she will sleep tonight and whether she and her son reconcile their differences is tomorrow's problem. And it is not mine. With a slight shiver she recalled Decimus Attwell's declaration of his impending marriage and prayed that he had not talked himself into thinking she would fill the position of bride.

'The things I have done for him.' It was a low mutter and Charlotte steeled herself to sit across the polished mahogany and listen patiently until Mrs Attwell had talked herself out of her gloom, or into a stupor. 'You have no notion, have you?' In the angry red face the pale eyes glittered as she rounded on Charlotte. 'No, neither you nor any other. Nobody could.' The muttering voice sank low and it was impossible to make out more than an infrequent word until she pulled herself upright and addressed her unwilling audience as if she were at a public parish meeting.

'That man accused me, you know. The American gentleman, or at least – hah! He was certainly no gentleman in his manner to me. He had some cock-and-bull tale about Decimus's time at

Oxford and those nonsensical examinations as well as the other
. . . but he did not have it right, that was a friend of Decimus's,
not my son and besides, who cares for a piece of paper? As for
the other rumour I scotched that long ago and those who put it
about were soon dealt with. Decimus did not know then and he
still has no idea that it was I who rescued his reputation. And
how mistaken in any case . . . ha!' Her laugh ended in a sob but
she wiped her eyes and rambled on. 'Far from what was
implied, here have I been hard put, more than once, to find
homes and foster parents for his little – indiscretions. A far cry
from what they . . .' She blew her nose loudly. 'He has always
been a high-spirited lad,' she sniffed proudly. 'But to have him
turn upon me like this, and all for the sake of that pasty little
drab. . . .'

'I'm sure Mr Attwell has no thought of Miss Dunwoody in
that way,' Charlotte ventured, hiding a surprised grin as she
hastily reappraised the bad-tempered and unprepossessing Mr
Attwell. Little indiscretions indeed. It appeared that he was, as
Will had once remarked about a notorious Irish priest – *bent upon
increasing his congregation by his own Herculean exertions.* 'He was
merely being polite and offering assistance to a lady who is not
able to clamber easily in and out of a carriage. He offered the
same assistance to Lady Buckwell. And it was not his idea that
Miss Dunwoody should change her seat after the interval. I
know that, because I heard her complain that she could not see
the dancing properly from her original place, so I pointed out to
her the vacant chair beside your son. Indeed it was not from any
desire of his that the change took place.'

She could not be sure that the lady had either heard or taken
in the explanation. The grumbling monotone continued until
Mrs Attwell sat up again, her face twisted in a sudden drunken
smile.

'His father had to buy off the keeper's son when Decimus was
only ten; such a fuss about a leg wound and saying it was
temper. Why, it was only gunshot and the boy recovered all but
a limp. And what's a limp, pray?' She held out her glass and
Charlotte hastily looked round for another bottle. 'The first time

I myself rescued him was when he was a mere boy,' she announced in a slurred voice. 'My husband said I should have guessed that a lad of Decimus's age would fall for a pretty face, but he was a child in my eyes still and she a grown woman and a governess. My little high-spirited boy.' She hiccupped and clapped a genteel hand to her mouth. 'What was she about? To seduce a lad of fourteen and then to wail and moan and claim he had hit her and forced himself upon her? Well' – Mrs Attwell's voice took on a note of congratulation – 'I helped her employer, my neighbour, to send her to Ireland out of the way so all ended well.'

'What happened to her, Mrs Attwell?' Charlotte's own voice was faltering now as she contemplated the fate of the governess.

'What happened?' Mrs Attwell raised her ravaged face and stared haughtily at Charlotte. 'How should I know? It was no concern of mine. I believe she was married off to some worthy farmer who gave her brat a name; it was more than she deserved, the scheming hussy.'

It was too much. Too many violent incidents had begun to take their toll and Charlotte was exhausted, vowing that if she had to hear any more confidences about the high-spirited Decimus – a description that made her shudder in sympathy with his victims – or if she had to speak another word herself she would collapse into hysterics. Stiffly she rose from her chair taking Mrs Attwell by the arm in a gentle but firm grasp, and led her upstairs to her room. There she pushed the older woman on to the half-tester bed and removed her shoes, pulled a blanket over her, then as an afterthought occasioned by the recollection of all that brandy together with the lady's sudden unaccustomed pallor, found a slop bucket and placed it strategically beside the bed. She hesitated for a moment but, turning to the door, left the room in darkness.

As she headed for her room Charlotte jumped nearly out of her skin at the sound of sobs. She opened the door to the backstairs and saw a wretched little face looking up at her. One of the young maids was huddled there and when she beheld Charlotte her mouth opened in an O of horror.

'Don't run away.' Charlotte's weariness vanished and she slipped down to sit beside the girl on the top stair. 'Now then, tell me what is wrong. I'm sure I can help put everything right.'

The sobs continued for some moments then the sorry tale came spilling out.

'I didn't mean to take it, ma'am,' the girl hiccupped, 'but it was so pretty.' Charlotte made soothing noises and the little maid carried on, 'Missus had me strip the bed, that poor gentleman, you know?' Charlotte gave her an encouraging nod. 'Well, it was when I emptied out the chest of drawers that I found it, slipped down the back somehow, it was.'

She let out a subdued wail and her hands writhed together in shame. 'It was so pretty and I thought nobody would miss it. But now I daren't keep it for fear Missus finds out, or my mam when I go home.'

'Would you like me to take care of it?' Charlotte asked kindly, wondering what the 'pretty thing' might be. 'I promise not to tell Mrs Montgomery.' The suggestion was received with fulsome gratitude and in a very few moments the girl had mopped herself up and gone to bed, leaving Charlotte in possession of a little bundle wrapped in blue velvet.

It did look dainty, she thought wearily as she reached her own room and untied the cloth to reveal a gold locket that opened upon two miniature portraits, but it was late and she was too tired to examine it tonight so she slipped the pretty trifle into a drawer. Charlotte removed her clothing mechanically, unpinned her hair and replaited it for the night, then splashed her face with water that had long grown cold since the maid had brought in the brass can. Sleepily she climbed into bed and blew out her candle before dropping off into a sound sleep.

Breakfast next morning was a subdued affair reflecting the general level of exhaustion among the residents after the dissipation of the previous evening. Elaine had greeted Charlotte with a tired smile and a mild complaint about the heat, even at an early hour. 'I shall be quite content to go and sit quietly in Mr Radnor's buckets and basins of water to cool down,' she said. 'And you look weary too, dearest Char, so I beg you will not dance attendance upon me today.'

It came as no surprise to Charlotte to discover that Mrs Attwell was not one of the breakfast party, but she was intrigued to witness a stiff encounter between Captain Penbury and The Reverend Decimus Attwell each of whom was eagerly intent upon apology. Captain Penbury carried the day by sheer weight of bluster and an outright refusal to listen to the other man.

'No, sir, I must insist,' he boomed, holding out a large red hand to the clergyman. 'I owe you an apology for my behaviour last night and I insist that you shake hands upon it. Hey? Hey? I was overcome by my sentiments towards the lady in question and I completely misunderstood your kind attentions to her. My apologies, sir. My most sincere apologies.'

'Thank you, Captain.' Decimus Attwell had clearly been practising the benign but stern expression fitting to a bishop as he shook the ham-like hand, with a slight but gracious smile that sat uneasily upon a face designed for rage and bluster. 'I must proffer apologies upon my mother's behalf also. She was not feeling well last night. The heat, you understand, coupled with the excitements of the evening's entertainment, led her to a misreading of the circumstance. I trust we may say no more about it.'

Charlotte managed to avoid having to sit next to Mr Attwell at breakfast by the simple expedient of whisking out of his eye-line until he had taken his place. I must choke him off as politely as possible, she resolved, managing a cool half bow as she greeted his eager gaze and moved along the table to a vacant chair beside the gallant captain.

'And how are you feeling this morning, Captain?' she enquired, as she partook of kedgeree. 'No further trouble amidships, I do trust?'

'Not at all, thank you kindly for asking, ma'am.' Captain Penbury leaned closer, his manner confidential. Charlotte was aware of a gimlet glare directed at her from somewhere close by and looked up to observe Melicent Dunwoody presently being seated further down the table. Oh well, wherever I look, she told herself with a philosophical shrug, I shall probably give offence to someone. She blinked as the naval man bent even closer and assumed a slightly embarrassed undertone.

'I believe I heard you mention that you had studied native medicines during your visit to Australia?'

She nodded, her eyes gleaming at that interpretation of her Antipodean experiences. 'To a degree, I suppose that is correct. Had you some particular reason for your enquiry, sir?'

The weatherbeaten countenance assumed an even deeper mahogany hue and he dragged out a large purple silk handkerchief and mopped his manly brow. He nodded and his voice sank even lower, to a booming whisper. 'The doctors at the Mineral Water Hospital have professed themselves baffled, ma'am, by my latest symptom. Baffled, I say.' He looked smug till he remembered his ailment. 'A trifle of skin trouble, you understand. A rash that is causing me some discomfort.' He harrumphed into his handkerchief again and shot a furtive glance across the table to Miss Dunwoody. 'I can confide in you, dear lady,' he hissed. 'As a widowed lady, that is. Not like an unmarried. . . .' His voice tailed off.

'Oh dear.' Charlotte strove for gravity. 'I'm afraid that nothing springs to mind, Captain. The only instance I recall is something my stepfather mentioned.' Her neighbour brightened and bent towards her once more. 'I believe he observed an aboriginal chief placing a man suffering from a skin disease in a . . .' Charlotte too lowered her voice as she glanced round the room. 'It was a – a heap of cow manure,' she concluded, hoping her translation was sufficiently genteel. 'The patient was buried up to his chin and remained there steaming, for about twenty-four hours. Several days later his skin lesions had begun to heal and I believe there was no recurrence of the condition.' She gazed innocently at him. 'I confess I don't feel this is something you should attempt while you are in Bath, Captain.'

'Good God no,' he looked ludicrously disappointed. 'Oh well, did your stepfather have any other miracle cures that you know of? The sort that might offer relief to my – er – my trouble amidships?'

'Only one, and I suspect that might kill you, Captain, so you must promise not to try it,' she told him firmly. 'I don't know if this was something Will encountered in Australia or in England before he ... before he travelled abroad. Apparently a patient who was believed to have misplaced some internal organ was taken to a barn where his clothes were removed. He was then hung by his feet from a cross beam and the healer beat him with stinging nettles. In his frantic efforts to twist and turn away from the pain the abdominal obstruction shifted and he was cured.'

She bit her lip at the broad crestfallen face turned towards her. Poor man, she thought guiltily; he's in pain and I shouldn't tease him about it, but I do trust, most fervently, that he will refrain from giving me chapter and verse about this rash of his, and most particularly its location.

Mercifully the captain left off his quest for medical advice and disconsolately addressed his bowl of gruel so she was able to turn to her other neighbour, Mrs Montgomery, who was seated as usual at the head of the table.

'I must thank you again, Mrs Montgomery,' Charlotte said, with an ingratiating smile, 'for arranging such a pleasant evening's entertainment last night. I do trust that you also enjoyed the treat?'

She received a polite nod in reply and tried not to become distracted by the bobbing grey-blonde puffs and curls at either side of the lady's face as they bounced in time to her response. There was no warmth in the glance her hostess directed towards her and Charlotte wondered if her own antipathy was returned. She persevered; mutual dislike must not prove a barrier to discovering the truth about her mother's birth.

'Had you visited Bath at an earlier time, Mrs Montgomery?' she asked, summoning up a smile. 'Perhaps that was why you decided to open up Waterloo House to your fortunate guests.'

No doubt about it, Mrs Montgomery was far from delighted to be thus engaged in such a conversation. Charlotte received a pale and distinctly hostile stare, accompanied by a furrowing of the brow and a pursing of the lips.

'No, I had not been here before,' she said brusquely. 'I came here because I inherited the house from a connection of my husband.'

And that was that. Charlotte acknowledged her dismissal with a polite smile and watched under her lashes as Mrs Montgomery, turning pointedly to Mr Chettle who was seated at her other hand, addressed him graciously in low tones, manifestly designed to indicate to Charlotte that she was not included in the conversation.

Oh dear, Charlotte bit her lip. She really does not like me, does she? Or is it that she does not wish to discuss her past? After all, if she does indeed turn out to be the lady formerly known as Mrs Wellesley, the last thing she is going to want is to have someone asking questions about such an irregular time in her history.

With a furrowed brow Charlotte returned to her room, but heard the chime of the hall clock so instead of examining the young maid's 'pretty little locket', she tucked it, on an impulse, into her reticule and headed for Elaine Knightley's room where, breakfast being over, the maid had dressed her mistress and settled her in an easy chair beside the window where she was frowning over a letter.

'Dear Charlotte.' Smiling as always Elaine put down the brief note and held out her hand to the younger girl. 'How were they all at breakfast? Recovered from the gaieties of last night's outing I trust?' She listened to Charlotte's tale of poor Captain Penbury and the nautical delicacy with which he was wont to describe his various complaints but Charlotte could tell that her mind was otherwise occupied. 'Oh, I'm sorry,' Elaine exclaimed, looking contrite. 'But I'm in a quandary. Here is a note from Kit to tell me that the bailiff is now recovering, the harvest is being brought in splendidly, in record time, because of the delightful weather, and that he proposes to take a leave of absence and come on a visit to Bath the day after tomorrow.'

Charlotte looked at her friend in astonishment. 'But that . . . that's good news, isn't it? Why, then, do you look so perturbed?'

'I don't *want* Kit to come here,' sighed Elaine, then she hastened to explain. 'Oh, don't look so worried, Char. In other circumstances I should wish for nothing better but in spite of

157

what he writes here I know he should not really contemplate leaving the place. He has certainly never done so before; we always make a point of remaining at the hall until the harvest is home and all the tenants satisfied. I know perfectly well that he is only doing this because of me and I don't want him to. Besides, I know only too well that he'll start haranguing young Mr Radnor about my treatment and wanting me to undertake more and more of it, and generally bustling around like a . . . like a. . . .'

'Like a flea on a blanket,' Charlotte supplied as Elaine searched for a simile. 'It's what an old woman in Melbourne used to say to me,' she explained, as Elaine stared then went off into a peal of giggles at the expression. 'Ma used to employ her sometimes – Bessie was her name. She used to come and look after me now and then. It means what you said, buzzing and bustling around.' She opened her mouth to speak but a knock at the door silenced her.

'That will be my good and reliable chair-man,' Elaine announced firmly. 'Even Kit could not quibble about the service he provides.' She reached out and squeezed Charlotte's hand. 'Don't fret, Char. I've made up my mind in any case and have a letter here for Kit, already written. I shall post it on the way to my incarceration in Mr Radnor's baths and bowls and basins. I've told Kit that the treatment is progressing well, that my medical Faradist is pleased with my progress and that we have taken happily to city life and are enjoying a life of pleasure and dissipation.'

She tied the ribbons on her bonnet and suffered her maid and the chair-man to help her out to the pavement. 'I mean it, Char,' she spoke over her shoulder as she left. 'I've told Kit he is not to come to Bath and I do not propose to discuss it any further, either with him, or with you. Now, be off with you on another of your explorations of Bath, you cannot have exhausted its delights yet – and take that worried frown off your face this instant.'

Charlotte spent a restless day. Elaine departed for her morning session with Mr Radnor her face alight with smiling courage and her head held high, but Charlotte was filled with foreboding. Was Elaine just a little too bright and cheerful? Did she brush aside Charlotte's concerns a little too abruptly? There was no question but that she looked better, and it was unquestionable too that she seemed to have more power of movement of her limbs, though she had so far refrained from walking more than a few steps in public, but Charlotte was not convinced that the improvement would prove lasting. Elaine herself had cautioned against undue optimism, and Charlotte sighed with no confidence in the existence of medical miracles.

The little Marianne was engaged with her father and grandfather to go on a river trip and had left early, or Charlotte thought she might have joined them. Balked of their company she walked briskly towards the Downs in search of a breeze and some relief from the relentless heat of the city. Charlotte recalled Will Glover's deathbed in India. The fever that took him had struck with no warning and had raged for two days until, less than a week after their arrival in the sub-continent, there had been a short period of lucidity.

'*Damn and blast it, Char,*' Will had panted, scandalizing the Presbyterian minister who was their prop and mainstay in this dire need. '*If I'm going to die, I'll die with a loved one's hand in mine, a brandy in my belly and a laugh on my lips.*' Brushing aside the clergyman's protests Charlotte, dry-eyed and at that moment shocked beyond emotion, had held a large dose of cognac to the lips of the man who had been husband to her mother and – in spite of his erratic behaviour – never less than a loving and adored stepfather to her, and helped him to sip at the drink.

'*Dearest Char,*' he had murmured, apparently refreshed. '*Don't forget, spare the lies and remember to try the truth now and then . . .*' And with those words of advice on his lips he had died. If he had not quite managed the laugh he had aspired to it was none the less so typical of Will that the tears had begun to flow at once as she lovingly laid down his hand. The upright non-conformist minister had given her some very searching glances in the days that followed, and which preceded her hasty marriage of convenience to Frampton Richmond, but Char had known what

Will meant. *Lies*, he used to say, *were all very well, but were apt to trip you up*. The truth, on the other hand, or at least, as close an approximation to the truth as might be deemed expedient, could only enhance your story.

Elaine, who had never known Will and would never, under any circumstances, have been allowed by her careful parents to meet a man like him, was even now employing his principles, such as they were. No pretence. Such a subterfuge would be foreign to her, but an edited version of the truth, that was what Elaine Knightley was offering to her anxious husband who, far away in Hampshire, could not give her the lie. And I am colluding with her, sighed Charlotte, pausing to gaze down at Bath, spread out below her. But what could I tell him? That I believe she is dying? She shook her head sadly. Kit knows that; Elaine knows that; and I know it too, that something is eating away at her and killing her, but we are all locked in this pretence because Elaine cannot bear Kit to give up hope.

During the light luncheon back at Waterloo House, Mrs Montgomery looked subdued but determined as she greeted her guests at the dining room door. She pressed each hand and murmured a word in each ear, and the result seemed to exacerbate the atmosphere of unease, rather than to relieve it. Charlotte received no word, merely a curt nod of greeting, which came as a relief, rather than otherwise.

Captain Penbury frowned heavily at his hostess's murmured words and granted her a barely courteous nod in return as he barged into the seat next to Melicent Dunwoody. Mr Chettle purpled with what looked like suppressed rage as he stalked into the room but he restrained himself and placed himself beside Dora Benson who cast an anxious glance at him and made haste to distract him by talking about the memorial tablets in the Abbey. Charlotte had strained her ears to hear what Mrs Montgomery had said but all she heard was some murmur about Egyptian relics, surely nothing to enrage her neighbour.

Sitting opposite Dora, Charlotte encouraged her in her discussion with Mr Chettle because a brief conclave with Elaine Knightley earlier that morning had made her think again about

160

her distaste for this union.

'No, listen to me, Char.' Elaine had held up an urgent hand to forestall her friend's complaint. 'You have not fully considered this circumstance. Yes, I understand you feel that to have Dora Benson living a mere half mile away from you at Finchbourne would be insupportable, but have you not considered that whoever marries Mr Chettle will be required to spend large parts of every year abroad, on a quest for funereal artefacts?'

Encouraged by Charlotte's suddenly arrested expression, Elaine had pressed home her case. 'You see? If, as I suspect you have been hoping, Mr Chettle should fix his attentions upon Miss Dunwoody, you should remember that she is frail and disabled, as well as a wet blanket and would be a hindrance to his explorations and to his sociable activities, with the result that they would reside the year round in Hampshire, confining their attentions to a limited circle, that of their neighbours in the village. Only steer Mr Chettle's thoughts in the direction of, say, Egypt or Pompeii, and he will trot off happily with Miss Dora Benson in tow, always on the alert for ways and means to improve the shining hour.'

The common sense of this argument had struck home and Charlotte was no longer disposed to promote the other match, which had at first seemed so much more desirable. Besides, she sighed, casting a covert glance at the two couples in question, they have proved to be such fast workers. Mr Chettle is clearly besotted with Dora and as for Captain Penbury, he seems to have found his heart's desire in that mangy, droopy, irritating little scrat in her everlasting old black dress with its unaccountable greenish tinge. Charlotte had, she reflected, often been in such dire financial straits that one black dress made up the whole of her wardrobe but she had never, she was proud to recollect, allowed that solitary garment to become moth eaten, or positively mouldy, in appearance. No, hissed the voice of conscience, that was because you stole another one to replace it.

Besides, a further recollection cheered her considerably: Captain Penbury lived miles away from Finchbourne and depend upon it, Melicent would not allow him to travel far from home once she had netted him. Charlotte addressed Dora Benson with a smile of approval that had that lady looking startled and Mr Chettle bridling with pleasure. I must remember, Charlotte told herself with an inward grin at the irony, that the Richmonds are the great family in Finchbourne and that a nod from the manor house will always give satisfaction; how that will grate upon dear Dora.

'I have always dreamed of visiting Italy, have you not, Miss Dora?' she smiled with deliberate and unfeigned interest. 'What a wonderful opportunity it would surely be to make a pilgrimage to Pompeii, to those haunted ruins in the company of an expert such as Mr Chettle whose learned discourse would bring so much to the experience. I believe that many thousands perished in the volcanic disaster and how sad it is to recall their tragic deaths, is it not?'

Dora picked up this hint at once and set about asking Mr Chettle if he had visited the ruins so, satisfied that Dora's immediate accession of interest had sparked her Hampshire neighbour's curiosity and inflamed his passion – as evinced by the high colour and the increased activity of his single heavy eyebrow which waggled furiously with excitement – Charlotte, complacent at the accomplishment of a satisfactory piece of work, sat back in her chair and took a surreptitious look around the table at the rest of the guests.

She remained baffled. Mrs Montgomery, who might, or might not, prove to be her own maternal grandmother, sat brooding at the head of the table. To her left sat Mrs Attwell, squat and brooding and looking to be suffering from a well-deserved headache. The Reverend Decimus Attwell brooded also, with an abstracted air, alternately shot darkling looks at his errant parent, and angrily disappointed glances in her own direction. Thank the Lord, she breathed a silent sigh; he has not renewed his tentative advances and at least his interest in me seems to have died a natural death. He has manifestly realized that I am not a suitable wife to a bishop.

The two French counts, refreshed by their morning on the river, both worked their way silently through the cold mutton upon their plates, but Charlotte was a little anxious when she observed that M. Armel de Kersac had nearly drained a second glass of claret, a most unusual indulgence at this time of day; he was usually the most abstemious of drinkers. His father maintained his customary air of being somewhere in another place, but none the less Charlotte noticed that the old man shot frequent anxious glances at his son.

The only person at the table apparently quite at her ease was Lady Buckwell and she tucked in heartily to her cold meat and bread and butter while casting bright-eyed, curious glances around the table. As Charlotte was looking at her the old lady raised her own green eyes and stared openly at Charlotte, her customary cynicism for once in abeyance so that only curiosity remained. Realizing that she was under observation Lady Buckwell merely raised her eyebrows, cast a glance around the table, and gave an infinitesimal nod to Charlotte before returning to her plate.

Charlotte puzzled over what Lady Buckwell's quizzical nod might have suggested but dismissed it and instead she allowed her thoughts to roil round and round in her head as she strode down Milsom Street in the early afternoon.

The atmosphere at Waterloo House was still poisoned by fear; there was no doubt of that. She could sense it the moment she walked into the building and to a young woman who had lived her entire life in the shadow of discovery and disgrace, the smell of fear was a palpable thing. No, they were almost all afraid. But what did they fear? Or should that be *whom* did they fear?

She wandered blindly up and down the elegant shopping thoroughfares of the city and saw nothing until, realizing her feet were painful and the heat becoming unbearable, she fetched up outside an old curio shop in a side street somewhere near the Pump Room.

'Gran,' she exclaimed aloud. 'I ought to find her a little memento of my visit. I wonder if there is anything suitable in here?'

The interior of the shop was cool and shadowy and much cleaner than she had expected. She nodded to the proprietor who evidently saw no cause for alarm in the person of a respectable young matron and so retreated to continue reading his week-old copy of *The Times*.

Charlotte's eye lit upon a piece of ancient glass that glowed in the shaft of sunlight breaking through the window into the gloom. She coveted its sensuous curves but smiled regretfully when the shop's owner, observing her interest, informed her that it was a Roman piece and very expensive. She also liked the look of a small rosewood writing desk inlaid with mother of pearl, which was quite cheap, although the shop proprietor told her it was French and dated to the turn of the century, because there was a large splay-shaped blot of ink disfiguring the inner drawer. Charlotte hesitated but Lady Frampton had no need of such a thing so she bought the old lady a string of beads in carved and polished jet instead.

At the door she had a sudden recollection and made her way back to the counter.

'I beg your pardon, sir,' she addressed the proprietor as she opened her bag. 'But I wonder if I might trouble you for some advice?' She took out the small velvet bundle that had been in Mr Tibbins's possession and opened out the locket to display the two miniatures. 'I am ... I am making enquiries about these paintings,' she told him, with a frank smile. 'And I wondered if you might be so kind as to tell me about them?'

He nodded kindly and picked it up, reaching for a magnifying glass. 'This is very fine work, very fine work indeed,' he remarked, looking up at her in surprise. 'And these are diamonds of the first water.' He pointed to the glittering stones on the inner edge of the gold cover. Charlotte gasped; she had assumed that they were paste. The shopkeeper eyed her with interest then turned to the picture of a woman. 'Do you have particular interest in the turbulent history of our Gallic cousins across the water, my dear lady?' He gave a hearty guffaw and nodded sagely at his own passing wit.

Charlotte shot him a quick glance and looked again at the little portrait of a woman in old-fashioned dress. 'They are French then, sir?'

'This portrait here is that of the late unfortunate Queen of France, Marie Antoinette. Poor lady.' He gave a philosophical sigh. 'A sad end and a violent one, but it is good to recall that a wax death mask was taken of her severed head, so we know that her portraits did indeed show a true resemblance of the living queen.' He turned the locket over and stared again at the delicate tracery engraved on the cover. 'These are initials, but I cannot make them out,' he said thoughtfully but shook his head. 'I wonder who owned it originally. It is a particularly fine specimen.'

He turned his attention to the other portrait. 'And this? Ah, but of course.' There was a gleam of satisfaction in his eyes as he looked down at the painted face of a little boy. 'Such a sad and romantic history,' he said, displaying an unexpected streak of sentiment. 'This is the Lost Dauphin, of course, the son and heir of King Louis XVI and Queen Marie Antoinette of France who were, as of course you must know, cruelly murdered on the guillotine. This little boy was the second son, the elder boy died, but this child's inheritance was a hollow throne along with death and disgrace. He was otherwise known as King Louis the XVII; poor little princeling, his reign was negligible, unacknowledged except by fanatical royalist supporters. He had a sad, tragic life, so cruelly incarcerated and then to die unloved in the Temple prison and to end his short, unhappy life in an unknown pauper's grave.' He shook his head at the wicked ways of the past and returned the locket to her, his eyes gleaming with a sudden thought. 'Do you think of selling it, by any chance? I would certainly give you a very fair price and such trifles are popular in France these days, particularly of this quality.'

'Thank you,' she said, stowing the miniatures safely back into her bag. 'I am most obliged to you for your kind assistance, but they are not mine to sell.'

As she entered her bedroom at Waterloo House later on, she was startled to see a small white envelope lying on the floor where it had obviously been pushed under the door.

She turned it in her hand. No postmark and no address,

merely her name, so it had not arrived in the post. She had been happily delayed in the gardens opposite Waterloo House by little Marianne de Kersac who was bubbling with excitement about her boat trip and a subsequent visit to a toyshop, so Charlotte laid the note on her side table while she changed for dinner into her favourite dark green silk gown. Once her hair was tidily arranged and topped by a tiny black lace confection which represented a widow's cap, she reached idly for the letter.

The handwriting was unknown to her and indeed it looked very odd, as though, she later realized, the writer had written it with his or her unpractised left hand. That deduction came later though, after the sharply inhaled breath with which she greeted the contents of the letter. It was brief enough:

Ask no more questions or it will be the worse for you.

Her hand flew to her mouth and she froze in her seat, transfixed by the threat – a threat made directly to me, she whispered aloud, and that means that someone in this house is feeling afraid; afraid of me and what I might do. But what on earth does anyone think I can do to them? Exposure, of course, but I don't know anything anyway and besides, it is unlikely that I, of all the people currently residing in this house, would expose another. Not after the upbringing I have had.

A tap at her door roused her from her momentary introspection and she opened it to find the little housemaid looking apologetic.

'If you please, ma'am, Mrs Knightley said to tell you she has gone to the drawing room and she sent me to remind you that it's almost time for dinner. Oh yes, and here's the evening post for you.'

Smiling her thanks, Charlotte picked up her shawl, dropped the letters on to a small occasional table in the bay window, and hid the anonymous note in her pocket as she followed the maid down the hall.

'I do apologize, Mrs Montgomery,' she said to her hostess as she hastened into the drawing room and realized she was almost the last of the diners to arrive. 'I was reading and quite forgot the time.'

A polite but chilly nod was her only response so Charlotte half turned away then spun back on her heel as she overheard Mrs Montgomery resume the conversation she had broken off to greet her tardy guest.

'Oh yes, Mrs Attwell,' she said, with a much warmer note to her voice. 'That is a most interesting little writing desk. It was a gift to my late grandmother from her younger brother and if you open up the lid you will observe a large blot of ink. To an uninitiated observer that might appear to be a disfigurement but it is not so. In my family history it is a mark of great significance, commemorating as it does the moment when my grandmother heard of her brother's unfortunate demise at Waterloo. She was in the very act of writing to him, you see, and the grievous shock at hearing the news caused her to upturn her ink bottle.' Mrs Montgomery smiled with manifest satisfaction at this touching tale. 'That makes it, as you will readily comprehend, a most sacred relic to me.'

Concealing a grimace at this flowery tribute Charlotte thought she had better join the little throng around the holy relic. Fortunately there was a buzz of admiration, particularly from an eager, heavy-breathing Mr Chettle, manifestly excited at the mention of a sudden death, that masked her own intake of breath as she gazed down at the very same little writing desk she had admired only that afternoon in the curio shop. There could be no mistake, the ink blot that so memorably recalled Mrs Montgomery's grandmother's distress was identical to the ink blot that had disfigured the box in the shop.

What a mercy I have been schooled to keep a straight face, Charlotte thought. I must not show Mrs Montgomery by any sign that I have seen that box before. But what audacity! Charlotte assumed an expression of mild interest and gazed around the room, noting once again the vases that must not be moved because of their associations; the chair that must remain empty; the cushion that summoned up the wraith of yet another long lost loved one. Were they *all* without provenance after all?

167

And if so, what could be the story behind Mrs Montgomery's affectation of family and friends?

As she mulled over this new and astonishing revelation Charlotte missed the murmur of greeting that welcomed the last comer to the drawing-room, even as their hostess had begun to look anxiously at the handsome grandfather clock near the door. 'A relic of my early childhood,' she had sighed a day or so ago when questioned about it. As the guests collected at the door to the dining room Charlotte heard a startled gasp and looked round to find the usually cool and collected Lady Buckwell staring, unmistakably, straight at her, green eyes dilated and her face perfectly white with shock.

CHAPTER 10

All through the meal that followed Charlotte was aware that Lady Buckwell was making a determined effort not to look in her direction; picking at her food and making determined small talk in a bright voice and sprightly manner with The Reverend Decimus Attwell who looked more than a little surprised. His mother, Charlotte had observed, had seemed taken aback also, but her habitual bridling should any female make the mistake of engaging Mr Attwell in conversation, subsided before the onslaught of Lady Buckwell's camouflage and her years. But why, mused Charlotte, taking care not to stare overtly down the table, why should the lady need to mask her emotions? And what had given rise to such a punishing shock? For two pins, Charlotte frowned, I almost thought she was going to faint when she saw me. But why? I thought she had rather taken a liking to me.

It was very puzzling and to distract herself she turned to Captain Penbury beside her. 'I have not had an opportunity of telling you this, Captain,' she addressed him, 'but I have heard from my sister-in-law in Hampshire that there is a relic of the ship most near to your heart – I refer of course to the *Chesapeake*.'

He was all eager attention as she told him the little she knew and when, rather reluctantly, she passed on the suggestion that Barnard might invite the captain to visit, his face lit up and he cast a very significant glance towards his left where Melicent Dunwoody was engaged in a laboured discussion on Breton customs with the younger Comte de Kersac.

'That is a most gratifying attention,' exclaimed Captain

Penbury, his large red face deepening to a darker mahogany. 'Most gratifying indeed. And I must tell you, dear lady . . .' He leaned closer and spoke in a confidential whisper. 'I shall very much welcome such an invitation as Miss Dunwoody has consented to make me the happiest of men. It has been a whirlwind romance.' He haw-hawed with hearty laughter at his own audacity in such an undertaking. 'A veritable whirlwind, has it not, hey? So if your brother-in-law will indeed invite me to Finchbourne, I can combine celebrating my nuptials along with a visit to that very mill.'

Good God! So it was true after all. As a result of her discussion with Elaine, Charlotte had been expecting some such announcement for Melicent had been lately showing unmistakable signs of complacency. A pity her smugness doesn't go as far as to splash out on a new dress, Charlotte grumbled inwardly, but was instantly contrite as her conscience nudged her yet again. I shouldn't be so horrid, the poor creature probably has no savings and cannot afford anything new. It's not so long ago, she reflected with a rueful frown, that I was reduced to stealing garments from unsuspecting ladies all across the sub-continent of India, so I should display more charity; maybe I should buy her a new dress as a betrothal gift?

It was another beautiful evening so after dinner the guests dispersed either, like Elaine, to their rooms, or like Captain Penbury and Melicent, and Mr Chettle and Dora, out for a stroll or else over the road to the gardens opposite the house.

Charlotte helped to settle Elaine and then wondered what to do; it was far too early to go to bed herself. Play gooseberry with the two attached couples? I think not, she decided firmly, but what shall I do instead. The air was so still and warm and her room so hot and stuffy that the decision was made for her and she made her way down the hall towards the front entrance. As she approached Mrs Montgomery's tiny private sitting-room she realized that the door was slightly ajar and that she could hear her hostess quite clearly. Mrs Montgomery was speaking quietly but there was a carrying quality about her tone, along with an almost imperceptible flattening of her vowels that Elaine had explained was a sign that the lady was originally from the north of England and spoke with a trace of a Yorkshire accent.

'You see, M. Armel' – the words were soft – 'I had occasion to be in the uppermost attic on the day of Mr Tibbins's death and I saw – something.'

'Well?' Armel de Kersac's reply was indifferent, Charlotte thought. Or was there a touch of wary attention there? 'I cannot imagine, *madame*, what it is that you think you saw or indeed why you should be so gracious as to inform me of such a circumstance.'

Yes, the listener decided, the younger count had an excellent grasp of English and spoke the language fluently, yet that reply was stilted and his accent much more pronounced than usual. He doesn't like her questioning him, but why? Please God, don't let *him* be the murderer.

At this point Charlotte realized that she was eavesdropping on a most intriguing conversation. Of course, she told herself, no lady would ever dream of listening to someone else's secrets. If I had the instincts of a gentlewoman, her face twisted in a wry grin, I would either march straight past this door or I would cough, shuffle my feet to alert them to my presence and walk into the room. But then, I'm hardly a real lady and besides, she shrugged, I have it on the authority of a real lady, that eavesdropping can be providential.

'Never be constrained by bourgeois notions of gentility, Char,' had been the advice of her godmother, Lady Margaret Fenton. *'Listening at doors is the action of a sensible woman and you should never forget that other people's secrets can be extremely useful.'* Meg had laughed and wagged her finger at the long-legged, sun-tanned urchin perched on a boulder along a southern shore. *'Why, if I had not overheard my papa when he was engaged in rather too close a conversation with my mother's dearest friend, I should have been married off in disgrace to a man nearly fifty years my senior. As it was, my papa was persuaded to pack me off to Australia with a generous allowance and my faithful and heartfelt promise never to darken his door again.'* Meg had sobered for a moment then she brightened. *'And even at our lowest point – and we've had some*

pretty low points, have we not, dearest Char? Even then I never
regretted that poor old husband; he had a fortunate escape!'

No; Charlotte stiffened her resolve and bent her head closer to
the narrow aperture. This was no time to worry about behaving
like a lady.

'I saw Mr Tibbins enter the mews,' came the startling
announcement. There was a pause but Armel de Kersac made no
response. 'I looked away for a moment but when I returned to
the window I observed that another person had approached
him. Unfortunately, from my upstairs viewpoint, I was looking
straight down and could only see the newcomer's shoulders. I
had only the briefest of glimpses and I could not discern
whether this was a man or a woman, but I was able to take note
that this person wore a dark-blue coat or cloak along with
something dark on his or her head.' Charlotte heard a tut-tut and
pictured Mrs Montgomery's puckered brow. 'At that moment I
was distracted by a noise from downstairs and when I returned
to the window I could see nothing.'

'If you truly believe that you saw something appertaining to
the death of your late guest, *madame*,' Armel de Kersac
addressed his hostess in a stern voice, 'You should at once
inform the policeman, Inspector Nicholson. I advise you to do so
immediately.' There was a pause and he continued, 'And if it is
you, *madame*, who has posted anonymous notes under my door,
I request that you refrain henceforth from doing so. I am not to
be swayed by hints and scandals.'

'I cannot agree,' was Mrs Montgomery's reply, completely
ignoring his latter words. 'I am unable to say with any certainty
who it was that I saw, but I am quite sure that it was one of the
guests here at Waterloo House. If any stranger had been in the
vicinity he or she would have been remarked upon. Besides, it is
undeniably the case that Mrs Richmond and your own father
stumbled upon Mr Tibbins's body shortly afterwards.'

There was a pause and Charlotte felt a sudden unease.

Mrs Montgomery coughed slightly then resumed her quietly
conversational manner. 'You yourself were wearing a dark blue
coat that afternoon, were you not, M. Armel?'

'What? But that is nonsense.' To the listener Armel de Kersac's protest had a ring of truth but then, she bit her lip, just so had Will Glover been wont to protest his innocence and time and again he had been telling an untruth. 'I was in the gardens across the road from the front of the house. I was watching my daughter playing with another child.'

'Indeed you were, *monsieur*,' came the response still in that quiet voice, but this time surely there was something else? A hint of triumph? 'But I should have explained: before I saw Mr Tibbins from the upper window at the back of the house I had occasion to look out from the front landing window on the floor below. I observed your daughter, M. Armel, but I also observed you in the act of crossing the road, whereupon you entered the side gate. Only residents at Waterloo House have a key to the area gate so pray do not try to tell me that I was mistaken. I saw you quite clearly as you entered the gate and from there the passageway leads only down the side of this house and into the back yard, and thence to the mews.'

'Mrs Montgomery.' Charlotte heard movement within the sitting-room and hastily turned on her heel so that she would appear to be walking in the opposite direction if she were apprehended. 'I do not understand your purpose in telling me all of this. As you say, I left Marianne in the square and entered the side passage. If you had continued your observations you would have noticed that I emerged from that same gateway a very few moments later. I had undertaken to search for the doll's coat that Marianne was certain she had dropped somewhere along the side path. She was correct. I retrieved the garment and returned, without delay, to the square.'

Discretion being by far the better part of valour, Charlotte hastened to make herself scarce but Mrs Montgomery's final thrust was audible.

'So you say, *monsieur*. So you say.'

There was a sound of movement within the room and Charlotte whisked round the corner and headed blindly for the safety of the drawing room as she tried to make sense of what she had just overheard. Never mind *what* you heard, her inner voice told her; what about Mrs Montgomery? *She* wrote the notes? If she wasn't trying to blackmail Armel de Kersac I'll eat my best Sunday bonnet. But Armel isn't a murderer, Charlotte was quite sure of that. Wasn't she? Perhaps he did own a dark-blue coat, he was certainly not alone in that; in fact, now she came to review the guests and their wardrobes, practically everyone currently residing at Waterloo House seemed to be in possession of such a garment. Dark blue, she reflected, covered a multitude of social situations as her sister-in-law, Lily Richmond, had pronounced only the previous month when she forced Barnard, her sartorially careless husband, into the reluctant purchase of a smart new coat.

Mrs Attwell, for example, had an imposing dark blue shawl made in a heavy silk, which she liked to swirl rather theatrically around her shoulders when waddling out and about in the town. Her son, too, was not invariably faithful to his clerical black and Charlotte had certainly seen him looking spruce in blue and with a hat concealing his domed pate.

Who else? Charlotte paused outside the drawing room door and ran down the mental list. Captain Penbury, as befitted a naval gentleman, rarely wore anything *but* blue and even Mr Chettle sported a dark grey-blue coat on occasion. In fact dark blue was apparently the colour of choice of most of her fellow guests. And, yes, Armel's broad shoulders were clad either in dark blue or a dark grey, to denote his half-mourning. As were his father's.

An unwelcome thought struck her as she opened the door, but before she could develop her idea further she discovered that the large golden room was not empty. Seated in the bay window was Lady Buckwell who, on Charlotte's entrance, raised her head and, after a moment's silent staring, addressed the newcomer.

'Where had you that shawl?' she demanded, with no polite greeting or preamble, and in a harsh voice strangely unlike her own clear, confident tones. 'That shawl; yes, the one you are wearing now. How did you come by it?'

'It was Molly's. My mother's,' Charlotte answered, so

shocked that she entertained no thought of how peculiar was such an interrogation; instead she let out a sigh that she recognized, hours later, as relief. She had known, somehow, within her heart, that this moment would come. With the Chinese shawl of black silk draped over her shoulders, displaying to advantage the embroidered pink roses, she walked slowly across the thick, golden carpet that absorbed sound and had on occasion caused the room to seem suffocating. Her answer was as bald as the lady's question but then she elaborated, 'It was the only thing that was left with her when she was sent to an orphanage as a baby.'

All colour drained from the older lady's face leaving patches of carefully applied rouge only too visible. Her eyes never left Charlotte's face as she clutched a hand to her breast and tried to speak.

'When?'

'My mother was born in Bath on the 10 November, 1819,' Charlotte told her, gripping her hands so tightly together that her nails left dents in the flesh though she scarcely realized it at the time. 'Since I have been in Bath I have met the nurse who was present at her birth and who, much later, looked after her in the orphanage.'

The other woman gave a great, gasping sigh and leaned back in her chair, her eyes closed. It seemed to Charlotte that Lady Buckwell had aged ten years in as many seconds. She herself could feel nothing; her thoughts were stilled and she felt numb both in body and mind as she stared in silence at the other occupant of the drawing-room.

'Mary Amelia.' It was a thread of a voice and Charlotte had to move closer to catch the words. 'That's what she was baptized. And Wellesley, well, that was a joke. The duke was a friend, nothing more. I have always been fond of a good joke. . . .' As her voice faltered her eyes snapped open and she looked straight at Charlotte.

'I came back,' she said loudly. 'I *did*. I came back for her, just as I promised, but she was nowhere to be found.' She bent her head and looked at the small elegant hands in her lap, their fingers – heavy with rings – interlaced. 'The woman had died and they said the baby, Mary, had been fostered out but nobody knew where.' Her voice was still ragged with an excess of emotion Charlotte thought must be alien to a woman of such control, and tears began to slide down the rose-painted cheeks. 'I think I went mad. I *know* I went mad.'

Charlotte felt that all-encompassing numbness begin to thaw and, shaking all over, she knelt beside the window seat and held out a tentative hand to the other woman. Ma, she breathed to herself, think of Ma and how she would have reacted to this; don't think of yourself. She needed no reminder. Molly had been a loving creature whose ready compassion would have been stirred by this harsh, difficult grief.

'The nurse, Mrs Liddiard, she told me what happened.' Charlotte swallowed her own tears and told the sad little story in as calm and collected a manner as she could manage. 'She said that Ma's mother – you, ma'am – had asked the lady in charge to find good, respectable foster parents to look after the baby and that you would certainly return before Easter. And she told me you left a great deal of money and said no expense was to be spared. It wasn't your fault that the lady died the day after you left, or that Mrs Liddiard had already been sent for to her ailing mother.'

She squeezed the hand that lay passively in hers and said: 'Ma never blamed you, not ever. And if she could have known all this, she would have understood.'

'She's . . . dead? Mary?' Lady Buckwell gave a shudder and she reached into her tiny reticule for a handkerchief. 'Oh God, I came to Bath in the hope of finding some trace of her, some clue as to her whereabouts. I hadn't been back here since that time when I came back for her. I hated the place when I was at school here and that's why I chose it for my confinement. I knew nobody would dream that I would come back to Bath. And now it's too late; it was always going to be too late.'

'No it's not,' Charlotte urged her. 'You've told me about it and I can promise you that Ma – Molly – would have been so happy to know that you didn't abandon her. She would have loved you. Yes, really,' as the older lady raised a sceptical eyebrow. 'She was like that, never bearing a grudge and loving everyone. And everyone loved her, so dearly.' She gulped and mopped her eyes on her sleeve. 'But please, I don't understand why you came here in the first place. The nurse thought that you must have "made a mistake", that's how she put it, but she knew you had already had a child and that you had all the hallmarks of a lady in high society. Is that what happened?' She put the question very tentatively. In spite of the intimacy induced by this revelation she felt a distinct unease at making such a delicate enquiry.

'Yes, or rather no, as it turns out.' Lady Buckwell's voice had regained its strength but now carried a suggestion of uncertainty, very foreign to her usual manner. 'We lived a very rackety life, you see. My first husband was an army officer and a great gambler and we lived from hand to mouth, dodging creditors all the time. At first it was a great game, but then we had a little boy and the game became less amusing and in the end I was forced to take measures that I regret now though at the time it seemed the sensible thing to do.'

She fell silent for a moment and Charlotte waited, still kneeling beside her, her thoughts in a turmoil, but above it all she felt a surge of triumphant homecoming. I have a grandmother, she thought, I have a family of my own! And hard upon that thought came a moment's great relief: thank God it isn't Mrs Montgomery. Or Mrs Attwell. . . .

Lady Buckwell continued, speaking very low, 'I was much admired, you know. Men liked my saucy ways and my sharp wit, but I was always careful to draw the line, until Lord St—' Again she sighed. 'No, better keep quiet about him, even now. All you need to know is that there was a man who kept us solvent, handing out money to pay the rent, money to pay for food – all of the best quality, of course – and all for no apparent return.

'I thought I could handle him.' She pouted and gave a slight toss of her head. 'But I was a fool. My husband was away at the time and had barely returned by the time I realized I was with child again.'

'Couldn't you have pretended the baby was your husband's?' asked Charlotte, enthralled. 'It's hardly unusual, after all.'

She was amused at the initial expression of surprise on the lady's face, but they exchanged smiles of wry sympathy.

'Perhaps, but I chose to go away. It could have been managed satisfactorily; I could pretend I'd had a premature child as long as nobody actually saw the baby, but there were, I thought, at least six weeks to be accounted for, possibly more, though I was never sure of my dates. Unlikely as it might seem, I had scruples about cuckolding my husband. Besides, shortly afterwards my husband was sent abroad for several months so I took my son down to his aunt and uncle's home in Hampshire . . . What?' She had spotted Charlotte's look of eager surprise and upon hearing that 'home' to Charlotte was now also in Hampshire, she bit her lip. 'Oh well, later on, perhaps, when we have come to know each other better. Then I'll tell you the whole story.'

Charlotte's curiosity was roused but she kept her tongue between her teeth until a look of weariness crossed the older lady's face.

'May I get you a glass of wine, ma'am? Or brandy?' She rose and, at Lady Buckwell's nod, crossed over to the double doors to the dining-room and Mrs Montgomery's precious array of bottles. 'Here we are, I've poured us both a large brandy.' She grinned at her newly discovered grandmother in whom she now recognized a fleeting likeness to Molly in the liveliness of her expression, the twinkle in her eyes and the shape of her face. 'I don't know about you, ma'am, but I'm sadly in need of a restorative after all this revelation and emotion.'

An answering light danced in the green eyes and Lady Buckwell raised her glass in a toast to her granddaughter. For a few minutes the two women sat peaceably side by side on the cushioned window seat, drinking their brandy and openly assessing each other. Charlotte suddenly remembered something that had puzzled her.

'Why did you look at me so strangely, ma'am?' she asked tentatively. 'When we were first introduced?'

'Did I? Oh yes, I do recall that. Why? Because, my dear, you have a distinct resemblance to . . . to my first husband.' She frowned and slid her fingers up and down the stem of her brandy glass before setting it down on the wide window sill. 'It unsettled me, but now I begin to think . . . to wonder . . .' She glanced at Charlotte, looking up from under her carefully darkened lashes. 'You see, Molly . . .' She looked uncharacteristically timid as she came out with the name. 'The baby was late in arriving; in fact she was three weeks overdue, calculating from the time that I. . . .'

'I understand, I believe.' Charlotte reached out a gentle hand. 'You began to suspect, perhaps to hope, that the child might be your husband's after all?'

The hand she held began to tremble violently and she realized that Lady Buckwell was shaken by a storm of tears, wrenched from inside herself.

'Dear God.' The whisper was almost inaudible. 'I have done so many things in my life and regretted so very few of them, but this . . . believe me, Charlotte, this is the one action of mine for which I have never . . . can never forgive myself.'

Half an hour later Charlotte let herself quietly into her room, feeling shattered by all that had happened lately. She had seen Lady Buckwell to her room and into the hands of her competent maid, with a promise that they would talk again the next morning. Fortunately there had been no sound from Mrs Montgomery's sitting-room as Charlotte passed it on her way to bed though she shivered at the thought that her hostess might have caught a glimpse of Charlotte hastening into the drawing-room.

Dear God, what a day, she sighed as she took down her hair and unbuttoned her dress. To think I came to Bath hoping for some peace and quiet away from Dora and Melicent and here I am, not only trapped in the same house as the pair of them, but with so much else happening that I can barely catch my breath. Bodies and blackmail; now a grandmother and my mother's history; blackmail and bodies; tall tales and short shrift.

As she folded the Chinese shawl that had, yet again, proved a catalyst in her life, and prepared to lay it on the small table, her gaze fell upon the two letters she had dropped there before dinner. I'll read them in bed, she decided and clambered wearily into the comfortable half-tester bed with a sigh of relief.

The first letter was from her sister-in-law, Lily, now complacently settled as Lady of the Manor of Finchbourne and contained, besides several pages of local gossip, a request that Charlotte visit the Bath shops in pursuit of patterns for new curtains, particularly for the drawing-room at home. *I have heard that Her Majesty has introduced tartans and plaids and that they are all the rage in London*, wrote Lily. *Pray look out particularly for these, Char.*

A simple enough request, she decided, and something she would be glad enough to undertake. To be sure, the notion of tartan curtains and hangings draped around the drawing-room at Finchbourne was not a happy one, but with any luck Lily would soon be darting off on another tack. And in any case, she nodded complacently, I shan't have to live with it.

She folded the letter and set it to one side as she reached for the other one. Sleepily she slit open the envelope and started to scan the contents. After a moment she sat up, her attention arrested.

My dear Mr Tibbins
    Report on subject: Montgomery, as requested. . . .

Tibbins? Montgomery? She turned over the envelope and read: *Mr Jonas Tibbins, Waterloo House. . . .* After a moment's bemused contemplation of the letter the explanation struck her. The maid must have delivered the letter by accident, caught up perhaps with the communication from Lily Richmond, in Hampshire. There was no address and no signature, which accorded only too well with the detective's cautious habits.

So, dear Meg? And Will? Do we have any precepts from the past about reading correspondence wrongly delivered into our hands? She pursed her lips and stared at the envelope. No, she decided; I don't think there was anything in my youthful training that precludes me from taking a look at this and, if anything, they would be urging me not to be so missish and to read it. Besides, Mr Tibbins is dead so who can possibly object? In fact, she concluded, Mr Tibbins would certainly expect her to read this letter and find out anything that might lead her to discover his assassin.

The letter was brief and to the point, containing as it did a list of addresses at which the 'subject under enquiry, Letitia Montgomery,' had served either as housekeeper or companion to a varied assortment of elderly ladies and gentlemen. The detective's agent had done his work well, she told herself. Dates, names, streets, counties, they were all there together with the dates of death of the various employers and, far more interestingly, the particulars of their wills. She gave a low whistle as she read the list and then read it through once more.

My word, she thought, Mrs Montgomery has been busy. And fortunate. There were at least fifteen different names and directions on the list, spread over the last thirty years, and the latest of these mentioned an elderly lady who had lived in Brighton. According to Mr Tibbins's correspondent, Mrs Montgomery had been named the major beneficiary in her will and by the time the lady's disaffected relatives realized what was afoot, their quarry had removed herself from Brighton, together with her sizeable inheritance, and no forwarding address.

Charlotte opened her eyes wide as she read the final paragraph in which the agent reported that *as Mr Tibbins was already aware*, there were rumours afoot that, like many of her predecessors, the old lady had been helped on her way to Paradise by the ministrations of her faithful housekeeper, Letitia Montgomery, but that nothing concrete had ever come to light.

Oh Lord, she sighed. Too much has happened to me today; too many snippets of information have come into my possession; too many people have confided in me. Now I'm weary and confused, but I know only too well that I'll never sleep until I have considered all of this.

First of all, she counted off on her fingers, there is this

astonishing revelation from Lady Buckwell. She refused to dwell too deeply on her own emotions, time enough for that, she decided, when I have an hour or so of peace, but underneath the tears and shock and *surprise* of it all, Charlotte was aware of a feeling of deep and joyful satisfaction bubbling away within her. Lady Buckwell was an adventuress, there could be no two minds about that, but does that matter, Charlotte asked herself? The response was instant: of course not, we are alike, she and I, although I suspect we have differing moral standards. I have lied, I have stolen, I have run away, I have chosen the course of expedience. But I have never deceived a man and since arriving in Hampshire I have striven to deal honestly with everyone I encounter.

So, a grandmother after my own heart, to a degree, she pondered.

Chuckling, she turned her thoughts from her newly discovered relative and considered the situation she found herself in at Waterloo House. The detective was gone but in his place reigned Letitia Montgomery who, it seemed reasonable to deduce from the conversation Charlotte had overheard, was dabbling in a spot of blackmail on her own account which must indicate that she now possessed some of Mr Tibbins's information. Surely, Charlotte reasoned, it must have been Mrs Montgomery who slipped that anonymous letter under my door. To be sure she did not answer M. Armel when he accused her of such, but she did not deny it either. And if that is the case, am I in some kind of danger? And is that even more the case if I was observed eavesdropping this evening?

Physical danger was a consideration indeed, but Charlotte was getting on for forty years younger than her hostess and was, besides, a strong, healthy young woman. No, there were other kinds of danger, the threat of exposure – that was what frightened Charlotte. If, somehow, Mrs Montgomery should come into possession of any hint of Charlotte's history, Charlotte's recent happiness and comfort would be destroyed. Certainly Elaine Knightley knew a good deal about that history and Charlotte was sure that Kit Knightley, as well as her brother-in-law, Barnard Richmond, would see no reason to treat her differently. But the rest of the family? Barnard's wife, Lily, would be horrified, excited and gleeful and ultimately would use it as a lever to try to make Charlotte her slave. The rest of the family would suffer from an intolerable degree of exposure and humiliation.

Hmm, she yawned. Even though Mr Tibbins had not possessed this proof of Mrs Montgomery's misdemeanours, even the hint of a rumour would be enough to have her on the defensive if it threatened her standing and livelihood here in Bath. Is that what the detective did? Dropped hints, mentioned friends in Brighton? (Yes, he had, hadn't he?) Just enough to unsettle her?

There was no further information in the letter, but it was enough to give Charlotte food for thought. If Mr Tibbins was employed by someone who entertained suspicions of Mrs Montgomery, what did he know about the other guests? M. de Kersac had certainly looked uneasy in the detective's presence, as had Mr Chettle and Captain Penbury. And there was surely some uneasy connection between him and the Attwells, mother and son.

But . . . she tried to stay awake. Jonas Tibbins was dead now but there was still that sense of unease in the house and it seemed to emanate from Mrs Montgomery. Had she somehow come into possession of some of his secrets? For she was the person causing the unrest, that much was sure, although what hints Charlotte had overheard sounded harmless enough to the untutored ear. I must tread even more warily, she resolved; no more questions about the lady's travels and sojourns in other towns. And when she exhibits yet another of her treasured heirlooms I must make sure to ooh and aah as admiringly as everyone else.

Her own brief and tantalizing conversations with the detective came back to her. He had certainly not been blackmailing anyone at Waterloo House, not as such, but he had indubitably been playing on their nerves in an attempt to trap them – but into what? Some admission of guilt of some kind?

Presumably Mr Tibbins would have waited until he had definite proof of whatever he was after and would then have contacted his principals to ascertain their instructions.

But, she pursed her lips. If he had played such a game with me, wouldn't I have taken it that he was blackmailing me? That it was a veiled demand for money? That he would expose me if money was not forthcoming? And if I had no money, or refused to consider paying this supposititious blackmailer, what then would I do, if I were desperate?

The answer, cold and stark, slipped into her mind. I might warn him off, she sighed; throw a brick at him as a warning shot and then, when he still persisted in his nods and hints and smiles, I might very well let loose a heavy cart in his direction and if it killed him, so much the better, but if it missed, well then – that would be another warning.

And if all else failed to make him leave me alone and my secret weighed heavily on me, I might very well come upon him unexpectedly and stab him with his own sword.

CHAPTER 11

'Dearest Char,' Elaine's voice bore an unusual note of diffidence. 'If we were to cut short our visit to Bath, would it distress you greatly?' As Charlotte opened her mouth to respond, Elaine went on, 'I have to confess that although I have truly derived some benefit from this electrical treatment I'm bored to tears with being away from home. Oh don't pout at me like that, my dear; you know perfectly well I don't refer to you, but there are so many things I could and should be attending to at home. I'm not at all certain I've persuaded Kit he must not come rushing to Bath until after the harvest is in, which would never do. And besides' – her smile was rueful – 'I miss Kit so much.'

'Then we must go home at once,' was Charlotte's prompt reply, accompanied by a sympathetic grin. 'Shall I run down to the station now and buy tickets, or will you allow me have my breakfast first?'

'Foolish girl.' There was a suspicion of relief in Elaine's answering laugh. 'The day after tomorrow will give us ample time. I'll give our notice to Mrs Montgomery, write to Kit to meet us at Salisbury Station and arrange for me to have two more sessions with Mr Radnor so that I can prove to Kit that I have taken every advantage of the electrical Faradism. And it will afford you two more days, including this one, to go on a final expedition to explore the city.'

Before making her way to the breakfast table Charlotte slipped once more into her room to compose herself. So soon . . . It would, she admitted, remove her from the temptation of probing and spying and putting her in Mrs Montgomery's way, but how frustrating if she should have to leave Bath without finding out what it was all about. There is no use disguising it, she sighed, as she pinned her godmother's golden acanthus leaf brooch to the collar of her morning dress in golden-brown poplin. The fact is that I am the most inquisitive of creatures and I shall be wondering what happens next.

An idea occurred to her. I suppose I could confide in Lady Buckwell? She is a strong-minded old lady who must have relished a thousand intrigues in her time; perhaps she would let me know the end of the story? If there is an end at all. There was no doubt in her mind that she and this newly discovered grandmother would remain in touch, there was a spark of kinship between them that would see to that.

'Here you are, Mrs Richmond, here you are.' Captain Penbury was in splendid form this morning, loud and cheerful and beaming at all and sundry as he bounded around the table to settle Charlotte into her place. 'Will this do, my dear? Opposite Mr Attwell and next to Mounseer Armel, lucky dogs that they are, hey?'

Charlotte blinked at this laboured pleasantry and accorded the clergyman a polite nod but greeted the younger Breton much more warmly. Decimus Attwell's gingery brows beetled hopefully at her, but on finding her politely unresponsive he growled and reddened, and addressed the plate of beef steak in front of him. That's right, Mr Attwell, she chuckled to herself, remembering Mrs Attwell's remarks about his little mishaps; be sure to take plenty of red meat to keep up your strength for your parochial duties. She bit her lip and turned hastily to Armel de Kersac.

'I was wondering, M. Armel,' she began, 'how it is that you speak such excellent English? Your father is quite fluent, but you have almost no accent at all, and neither does Marianne.'

He looked pleased at this manifestation of interest. 'Did I not mention it before? There is no mystery, it is just that my mother was born to royalist *émigré* parents and brought up in England. After the Battle of Waterloo when it became clear that France was once again safe her family returned to their château in Broceliande.

186

'Brittany,' he explained. 'is not like the rest of France. For many centuries it was a separate country and we still strongly value our independence. The royalist cause was never entirely defeated in the region and both my parents were fortunate in that their homes were not destroyed in the Revolution.' He wiped his mouth on his napkin. 'One of the many benefits of living on the edge of the world.'

'Of course.' She was stricken with contrition. 'I believe you did tell me, in the Pump Room, but – oh dear – that seems so long ago!' She shot a guilty smile at him and was relieved when he laughed at her. 'And did, pray forgive me, did your wife also speak English?' She was intrigued at the notion of exiles returning to their homeland. That will never be my own fate, she surmised, though, of course so many of the settlers in Australia spoke of England as Home, and here I am after all.

'Only a little.' Armel de Kersac looked encouraged by her interest. 'But my mother taught Marianne until her death only two years ago. *Maman* made a point of speaking only in English to the . . .' He hesitated, his pleasant features suddenly bleak. 'To the children, and *petit* Armel spoke the language very well for his age.'

She was moved by the distress manifest on his large, tanned face and on impulse laid her hand on his sleeve. At his look of delight she drew a breath, cursing herself inwardly. Oh no, this will never do. He must not think of me in that way, but she knew that it was too late. Armel de Kersac was already thinking of her in that way and clearly his intentions towards her were strictly honourable. She was going to have to do something about that and sooner rather than later.

For the rest of the meal Charlotte maintained a flow of light, bright chatter and turned as often as she could towards her other neighbour, Dora Benson whom ordinarily she would have avoided like the plague.

'Do you not agree, Miss Dora,' she enquired, still in that slightly artificial, social tone, 'that Mr Chettle would enjoy visiting the ruins at Pompeii? We discussed it the other day, did we not? I wonder if he has had any further thoughts on the

187

subject. I'm sure he would find artefacts and funerary objects there to satisfy even his tastes.' She cast around for something else to say about her Hampshire neighbour. 'Did you chance to observe his house at Finchbourne? The large red-brick place on the left hand side of the road to Winchester?'

To her astonishment the usually staid and commanding Dora Benson actually simpered in reply. 'I do recall admiring that house,' she admitted, directing an unpractised fluttering of her lashes at Mr Chettle who was seated opposite. 'Very handsome indeed. And to answer your question, I believe Mr Chettle has quite resolved to undertake a protracted tour to southern Italy very shortly. As you are aware he has but recently returned from Rome, but I think I can say, with some certainty . . .' At this point she electrified Charlotte by giving vent to what, in a less stately personage, could only be called a giggle. 'As I was saying,' she continued, 'a trip to Pompeii is very much on Mr Chettle's proposed itinerary when we . . .' Her hand flew to her mouth in confusion and she blushed a fiery scarlet. 'Oh my goodness,' she hissed in Charlotte's ear. 'It's a secret, but I'm sure I can trust you. Mr Chettle and I are to be married and Pompeii is to be the destination for our wedding trip.'

Charlotte gave complete satisfaction by gasping in admiration, squeezing her hand in womanly sympathy and nodding in a significant manner to Mr Chettle who was gazing across at his intended bride with a smile that could only be described as besotted. He looks like a mooncalf was Charlotte's uncharitable conclusion, but Elaine is right, they'll spend most of their time traipsing around the world digging up unfortunate dead people who would much prefer to rest in peace, so I can afford to be tolerant. Besides, she sighed, I can only sympathize and rejoice in her good fortune as a woman with no money but what she can earn and no home unless she takes up residence with poor Agnes. And that would never do.

Elaine's favourite chair attendant appeared at his allotted hour and Charlotte walked down Milsom Street and as far as Mr Radnor's consulting rooms. I'll go to see Mrs Liddiard tomorrow, to say goodbye, determined Charlotte. Perhaps I might confess to the truth, some of the truth, or at least let her know that I have identified and talked to the lady she recognized the other day. But not today, I need time to digest it all myself.

'I'll make my own way back,' she told Elaine, who nodded, preoccupied with the nurse who was settling her and making sure her arms and feet were placed correctly in their pans and buckets of water, ready for treatment. At the door, Charlotte was accosted politely by the medical Faradist himself who wore a slightly furtive air.

'Mrs Richmond,' he murmured, drawing her into his office, 'might I trespass upon your good nature for a moment? Thank you,' he said, as she nodded, looking mystified. 'I have not liked to ask Mrs Knightley but there have been rumours flying round the city. Is it true that the American gentleman from Waterloo House was actually murdered?'

She nodded and waited.

'Ah.' He bit his lip and looked perturbed. 'I wonder who . . . I had seen him, you know, a year or so ago when I was practising in Paris. I know nothing of him except that after I had observed my employer's junior partner in conversation with that gentleman, he, the junior partner, disappeared along with all the money he had withdrawn under some pretext from my employer's bank. What Mr Tibbins's dealings with the man may have been, I have no idea and cannot speculate without slanderous supposition, but I had no desire to have any association with him. It was a considerable shock to me when I encountered him here, but I trust he did not recognize me.'

'Oh dear,' was all Charlotte, who knew that he had indeed been recognized, could think of saying, inadequate though it was, and then, without pausing to consider her words, 'Where were you, Mr Radnor, on the afternoon of his death?'

There was a shocked hiss of breath as he realized what she was asking but he quickly recovered himself and looked down his nose at her pompously. 'I am shocked that you could even think of asking such a thing, Mrs Richmond,' he announced. 'But as it happens I was visiting a patient up on Claverton Down and was with her from noon until her evening dinner which she graciously invited me to share.'

He turned on his heel with a curt nod of dismissal and Charlotte gave a philosophical shrug. Oh dear, I've offended him, but no matter, I'll never need to speak to him again. What shall I do? I've visited quantities of the places named in my guide book and I have said my prayers in the Abbey, so perhaps a walk along the river would be pleasant in this heat.

First, however, she strolled along to the station to look at the timetable and discovered that the train would leave just after noon the day after tomorrow. That errand completed, she hesitated – the seats overlooking the river failed to attract her; she was reluctant to sit alone, afraid of the thoughts that crowded into her mind so she gladly let herself be distracted by the sight of several ladies eating and drinking in what was evidently a coffee room, just along North Parade Passage. As she was ushered to a small table, Charlotte noticed that the other customers all seemed to be eating buttered buns.

'Those are Sally Lunns, madam,' said the waiter. 'This is Sally Lunn's house, and our buns are famous.'

'Then I must certainly try one,' Charlotte nodded. 'Who is Sally Lunn?'

'Some say she was a French lady who escaped those blood-thirsty Frenchies,' came the reply. 'Others say 'twas not her name, but nowadays they still make her special buns which nobody has ever been able to copy.'

'Really?' Charlotte was intrigued. 'Did she come over during the Revolution, then?'

'No, indeed, madam. It was hundreds of years ago; them foreigners are always fighting and chopping people's heads off. Nasty place it must be, abroad.'

In the end Charlotte decided on a brisk walk up past the Royal Crescent, taking in a rest on a bench in Victoria Park where she stared unseeing at the ducks on the pond, barely conscious of a refreshing breeze. Foremost of her anxieties was Mrs

Montgomery. What should I do, she fretted? Should I stand up in the drawing room and announce that I suspect she is blackmailing some of the guests at Waterloo House? And should I then expose her as being less than the driven snow herself? That would be the simplest way to put a stop to her activities, but what then? Those people are staying in the house, she is their hostess; what are they to do? How are they to look each other in the eye if I have announced that each has a guilty secret? And how is Mrs Montgomery to continue in her role as landlady, provider of meals and beds, if they all know she has a shady past and that she has not scrupled to make use of stolen knowledge? And that's a consideration, she realized. Just how did Mrs Montgomery discover the secrets that Mr Tibbins was aware of, or has she her own sources of information so that blackmail is simply another 'service' that she offers?

No explanation occurred to her and she chewed reflectively at her thumb. Besides, there was the unsigned letter: *It will be the worse for you.* Is that an empty threat? Or should I be constantly on my guard against some kind of attack by her? What could she do anyway? I've already considered that a physical assault seems unlikely. I suppose she could poison me if she really wanted to, but she must be aware that the police inspector, whatever his name was – Mr Nicholson, that was it – that he would be exceedingly interested in a house that was the scene of two suspicious deaths in so short a time.

Mrs Montgomery also seemed an unlikely candidate when considered as a potential murderer, Charlotte sighed. It was impossible to picture the small, elderly woman punching the sturdy American so vigorously that he fell to the ground and even less likely that Mrs Montgomery would have picked up a naked blade and stabbed him where he lay.

Her thoughts flew to the other occupants of Waterloo House who apparently had something to hide. Captain Penbury, she thought. He was badly disturbed by Mr Tibbins and has looked dismayed when Mrs Montgomery hove in sight. Could I have been hasty in dismissing him so easily? He is prone to attacks of discomfort from his musket ball, but for the most part he is a large, strongly built man with experience of warfare. Her mouth twisted at the thought. That's the sticking point, she told herself; the captain is a trained warrior and surely the very method of Mr Tibbins's death seems to indicate a spur of the moment attack. Not a planned, disciplined campaign.

Simeon Chettle was another whom she had not seriously considered as a murderer, but he too had simmered with anger and resentment whenever the Pinkerton's detective engaged him in conversation. Since the murder Mr Chettle had gone from initial relief to evident discomfort, notwithstanding his transports of delight at his speedy romance with Dora Benson. Have I been too urgent in my desire to ship Dora off to Italy, Charlotte wondered? She shook her head. Mr Chettle was no trained military man but neither did he fit the bill as an opportunist assailant. His habit of monopolizing conversations and of standing much too close to one might be irritating, but he showed no sign of rancour when his reluctant audience managed to sidle away. Surely a man who would kill in so unpremeditated a manner would have revealed earlier signs of unbridled anger?

The kind of unbridled anger that characterized Decimus Attwell, perhaps. Charlotte gave a gasp. If Captain Penbury were too disciplined and Mr Chettle too unnoticing, who among the occupants of Waterloo House had consistently displayed a temperament given to outbursts of rage and sudden thunderous glowering?

A hopeful duck pecked about her feet and eventually gave up in disgust upon receiving no crumbs, but Charlotte scarcely noticed it as she examined her theory. With her own eyes she had observed Decimus Attwell's explosive outbursts and his barely concealed resentful muttering when thwarted. Beside that she had the testimony of his own doting mother that The Revd Decimus had been prone to violence from an early age; that glancing mention of an injured boy, together with the history of the unfortunate governess who, it was only too plain, had been raped by Mrs Attwell's 'high-spirited' schoolboy son.

She pressed her hand to her eyes. It seemed to fit so well, but conjecture alone was of no use. What can I do, she asked herself? I can hardly drop a hint to the police inspector, for what could *he* do about it? Mr Attwell would meet any accusation with a growl of rage at such impertinence and in the absence of any proof, the police could not proceed. In fact, she made a wry face, if such a charge was made, Mrs Attwell would make it her business to have the inspector removed from his post, or at least subjected to strict discipline.

Could she have done the murder herself, Charlotte wondered, suddenly distracted by the notion? She is a veritable tiger when her cub is even mildly criticized, let alone threatened with whatever it was that Mr Tibbins knew. And what was it that he knew, anyway?

She rose reluctantly from her bench, smoothed down her dress and headed back towards Waterloo House. I must behave with circumspection, she told herself, for the short time I am still a guest. Mrs Montgomery must be persuaded that I am far too dull and demure to excite her suspicions and I must maintain my aloof manner with Decimus. His mother has avoided me since her outburst after the concert so all I have to do is keep out of her way; after all, neither she nor her son has any reason to think I suspect him of attacking a man in a fit of madness so I am in no danger from them. She shuddered and consoled herself. It's not for much more than twenty-four hours and then I'll be safely away from Bath and I can leave it in the lap of the gods.

Despite her brave words her feet dragged a little and she made a detour back down to the bustling shops; anything to distract her from the anxieties that weighed so heavily upon her. Pat upon her musing in the park it was suddenly borne in upon her that the large figure some fifty yards ahead of her was in fact that of The Revd Decimus Attwell. Oh my God, she faltered, I cannot speak to him now, surely he would deduce my thoughts as he glared into my face?

She slowed her pace, keeping a weather eye on the burly cleric who seemed, to her feverish conjecture, to be looking more irate than ever. Even at this distance and glimpsed only from behind any barrier that offered, Charlotte could see that Mr Attwell was muttering to himself and that, now and then, he punched the air with a fist the size of a ham. Oh dear, Mr Attwell looked to have worked himself up into a fine old fury. She grimaced. This is certainly my cue to keep out of his way. What could have aroused his ire so badly, she wondered? But with a shudder she cast the thought aside. Never mind why, she determined, all that matters is that he does not let his eye fall upon me.

Keeping at a discreet distance from him, Charlotte rounded the corner and made her way up the steep incline towards Waterloo House. Across the square she could see Armel de Kersac teaching his little daughter to catch a ball while his father seemed bent on mending something, possibly a doll.

Just as she felt safe to heave a sigh of relief at reaching the house in safety, Charlotte was startled at the abrupt appearance on the pavement of Mrs Montgomery herself. In spite of her earlier resolution Charlotte felt a pang of alarm as she realized the other woman not only looked *distrait*, but was glaring directly at her.

'G-good afternoon,' she faltered, hoping to avoid any kind of confrontation. After all, what could the woman accuse her of? I've done nothing, the thought flashed through her mind. Nothing to threaten her and the questions I've asked have been quite innocent, not really intrusive, so why does she glower at me so furiously?

'Mrs Richmond, you are a nuisance.' It was a bald statement and Charlotte was stopped in her tracks by the malevolence in the older woman's voice. 'I am tired of your looks and glances, your questions and your meddling; interviewing my servants, of all things, and eavesdropping upon private conversations that are no concern of yours.'

'But I haven't *done* anything,' Charlotte protested, putting out both her hands, palms up, in a gesture characteristic to her, a kind of supplication. 'You wrote that note, I suppose, but I don't know what you mean by it.' At the same time she was aware that The Revd Decimus Attwell had halted in his tracks and was looming behind the other woman, a reddish glint evident in his choleric eye.

'What's that?' he bellowed. '*You* are the author of those damnable notes, madam? You'll pay for that just as that other did. I silenced him, by God.' Charlotte let out a gasp at this confirmation of her suspicion, but she had no time for further consideration.

'Why, I'll. . . .' He gobbled with rage, his face contorted, and lunged with outstretched hands at Mrs Montgomery who ignored him as she continued to harangue the girl who shrank from her. His face crimson with passion, the maddened cleric cannoned into the older woman, pushing her quite off balance so that in turn she stumbled heavily against Charlotte, elbowing her into the road.

Charlotte gasped and cried out as she tried to right herself but Mrs Montgomery was falling and Charlotte along with her. Something . . . someone . . . heavy and roaring barrelled past her, propelling her and the landlady into the path of a smart little equipage, a dowager's britzka and pair, so that the terrified horses snorted and started to rear, accompanied by warning shouts from the coachman.

Just as she knew that all was lost, something or someone grabbed sharply at her arm and she was pulled back to the kerb, where she collapsed in a trembling heap, her modest crinoline billowing around her. Panting and gasping, she raised her head to see Lady Buckwell unhooking the handle of her parasol from where she had caught at Charlotte's arm and tugged with all her strength.

As she collapsed on to the safety of the pavement a series of terrible screams rent the air, the more dreadful because the sound was suddenly cut off. When she raised her eyes she saw that both Mr Attwell and Mrs Montgomery were no longer on the pavement and that the wheels of the carriage were splashed and stained with blood, with something fearful lying beneath.

The noise was intolerable. Passers-by were screaming, horses neighed in terror, the coachman was letting fly with terrible oaths and Lady Buckwell knelt beside Charlotte, holding her tightly in her arms and begging her to speak. The occupant of the britzka had her venerable head out of the carriage window and was demanding to be told what was going on, falling into a dead faint when she beheld what lay below her own wheels; bystanders were converging upon the entrance to the house from all corners of the square.

Suddenly, above the racket, came another dreadful echoing scream and, as Charlotte dragged herself up on to her knees, she saw that Mrs Attwell was hastening down the steps of Waterloo House in a gasping, ungainly frenzy as she staggered towards the appalling carnage. A ragged cry rose from her own lips as she watched the woman collapse to her knees, a thin wail of desolation escaping her as she held out her hands towards her only son.

Several stout young men rushed to offer their assistance, but it was too late. One young man bravely crawled under the britzka now that others were helping the afflicted coachman and holding still his trembling horses, but his voice was soon heard announcing that 'the poor lady was certainly dead, and the gentleman too.' A great groan of dismay went up and one or two women in the crowd began to wail again, aghast at the speed of events and their dreadful conclusion. One of the men, recovering from his shock more quickly than the rest, urged the women gathered on the pavement to remove to the shelter of the trees in the square, while another ran for medical assistance, fruitless as it might prove.

Charlotte scrambled to her feet, ignoring the nagging ache in her arm where the parasol had wrenched her to safety; nothing else mattered now but she was filled with a deep and painful longing that could not be denied. She helped her rescuer up and stood in front of her, shuddering from head to toe. Her grandmother took her into a fiercely possessive embrace.

'There, there, my pet, you're safe now, it's all over.' Lady Buckwell's voice was shaking as she patted Charlotte's heaving shoulders and if the endearment sounded unpractised Charlotte cared nothing for that. For just a moment, when she had most need of it, she could feel herself held in the safety and comfort of loving arms, no matter that she and the lady were barely acquainted.

All around them the noise and excitement continued unabated until Armel de Kersac pushed his way through the throng.

'Charlotte, Mrs Richmond . . .' The words spilled out of him in his anxiety for her well-being. 'You are unhurt? Allow me to escort you into the house, and you too, my lady, if you will be so kind. It is not fitting that you should stay out here.'

'Can you walk, child?' That was Lady Buckwell who was already looking on the way to recovery, her colour improved and her breathing back to normal.

They were interrupted by Mr Chettle and the captain, both vying for the right to assume command of the situation. The captain won by virtue of a lifetime of bellowing orders against wind and weather.

'Silence!' He looked gratified when he was obeyed and hastened to take advantage of the lull. 'Has a doctor been called for?' He elbowed past the young man who had announced the fatal outcome of the accident and was now recovering and ready to tell his tale. Ignoring his efforts to speak, the captain peered under the carriage; what he saw clearly made him pause for thought and he nodded slowly, the colour draining from his weatherbeaten face. 'Dear God, what a dreadful thing. Yes, well, nevertheless a doctor must still be summoned. Already sent for? Then someone must help this poor lady to her room. Good. Now, can anyone tell us what happened here? Mrs Richmond?'

As Charlotte shuddered but made an effort to pull herself together, she was forestalled by Lady Buckwell who pushed forward and addressed Captain Penbury, holding his attention with a steely expression.

'I saw it all,' she proclaimed and, as Charlotte tried to speak, directed a severe frown in her direction. 'No, my dear, you are too shaken, pray allow me to explain what happened.' She turned back to the captain. 'It was very sudden and most tragic. Mrs Richmond here had just reached the entrance to Waterloo House when Mrs Montgomery, our hostess, stepped out to speak to her, no doubt in welcome, at the same time as both ladies were greeted by poor Mr Attwell. I believe Mrs

197

Montgomery tripped, possibly on that uneven flagstone there…'
The crowd turned as one man and stared accusingly at the
offending stone. 'In trying to regain her balance, the unfortunate
lady lurched forward and took poor Mrs Richmond by surprise.
By some unknown means Mr Attwell stumbled too and they all
staggered into the street, straight into the path of this carriage.'

She closed her eyes for a moment's dramatic effect and the
audience gasped and sighed in sympathy, then her green eyes
snapped open as she continued. 'Indeed, but for one merciful
circumstance, I believe Mrs Richmond must have perished also.
The moment of good fortune was when I myself bethought me
of my parasol and, by some instinct, reached out and pulled the
young lady back from the jaws of death.'

Enthralling as this narrative was proving Charlotte felt
impelled to make some kind of protest, but was halted as her
mouth opened, by a sharp pinch on the back of her hand as the
orator turned to her.

'Hush,' Lady Buckwell's whisper was urgent and not to be
denied. 'We'll discuss this later.'

To the immense gratification of the onlookers the lady then
raised a handkerchief to her face evidently quite overcome with
emotion. So much so, in fact, that the crowd made no demur
when Lady Buckwell braced herself and took control by taking
Charlotte by the arm and with a nod to Captain Penbury made
her way up the front steps and into Waterloo House.

'Quickly,' she hissed. 'Into the drawing room and let's both
have a very large brandy before the rest of them come in and
drive us to distraction.'

There was nobody in the large, golden reception room so she
gave Charlotte a gentle push into a commodious and
comfortable chair and after a few moments busy work with the
decanter both ladies were sitting close together partaking of a
medicinal cognac.

'Are you certain you are quite recovered, Charlotte?' she
asked urgently, scanning the pale face. 'Yes? Sit quietly then
while I go and see after Mrs Attwell, poor creature.'

She left the room while Charlotte slumped into her chair

feeling she must be in a nightmare.

Ten minutes later Lady Buckwell returned looking pale and strained. She refilled their glasses without a word and sat down heavily while she took a long sip of brandy.

'That poor woman,' she sighed. 'What a dreadful thing to happen. Did you know he was her tenth child, hence his name, and the only one to live beyond infancy? The doctor is with her and her maid seems competent so I felt I could come away; I am not good at offering condolences in any case. They have sent for a clergyman too, to bring her comfort though I doubt she'll find any.'

She set her glass down on a small table and looked at her granddaughter. 'Are you feeling stronger, child? Then let us take this moment to ascertain what really happened and after that I propose, very strongly, that we never mention this event again.'

Charlotte, shrugged, dumb with shock and exhaustion so Lady Buckwell continued.

'I had just come up the stairs from the side path and was a couple of paces behind Mrs Montgomery when she encountered you, my dear Charlotte, so I could not see her face but yours was clearly visible to me. I observed that when she accosted you, your expression altered to one of considerable dismay, which shortly turned to some distress. I was about to interrupt what, to you, was clearly an unwelcome conversation, when I realized that Mr Attwell had entered the fray and was bellowing at the woman. To my astonishment he then turned upon her with upraised fists and the force of his attack sent her stumbling into you and thence into the road, into the way of a carriage which was approaching rapidly.

'For a moment I confess I was rooted to the spot in surprise; after all, it is hardly every day that one witnesses an attempt at murder, for Mr Attwell certainly looked murderous, in broad daylight! Fortunately I collected my senses and thought of my parasol which has, as you no doubt felt very painfully, a handle shaped like a shepherd's crook. I could think of no other course of action than to lunge forward and hook the parasol around your arm and pull you back with all my strength. That action mercifully broke Mrs Montgomery's frantic hold on you and I was able to reach out and seize you with both hands, which made it possible to drag you back.'

Charlotte felt the shrewd green eyes upon her and roused herself to make some response, but they were distracted by the sound of voices and heavy footsteps in the hall that made them raise their heads and look at each other.

'Oh dear,' sighed Lady Buckwell, picking up her brandy and taking another sip. 'Here they come, the vultures. My dear, it has been delightful that we have had this quiet time together and I think you are looking a little restored. Leave all the talking to me; I will explain that I witnessed poor Mrs Montgomery and Mr Attwell meet their sad end in the distressing manner I described earlier, having fortunately been in a position to observe the entire catastrophe.'

She stood up and addressed Mr Chettle who had elbowed his way to the front of the clutch of guests who now entered.

'I suggest that the butler be questioned as to the name and whereabouts of Mrs Montgomery's lawyer,' she said, before turning to Charlotte and, to that young lady's relief, brushing aside the attempted ministrations of the two governesses. 'In the meantime, I think Mrs Richmond should retire to her room to compose herself and I suggest further that someone should see about tea for us all. Immediately. Followed,' she threw over her shoulder as she left the room, 'followed by arrangements for dinner tonight. We will all be in need of sustenance by then.'

She insisted upon escorting Charlotte to her bedroom door.

'Do as I said, Charlotte, and compose yourself. Wash your face and lie down upon your bed. I will see that someone brings you a cup of tea and you need have no anxiety.' Her smile was tired. 'I will also make sure that Mrs Knightley is not alarmed by disturbing rumours.'

When Charlotte's eyelids fluttered open again she became aware that Elaine Knightley was sitting beside the bed placidly reading.

'Oh good, you are awake, dearest Char.' Elaine smiled and

rang a small bell, replacing it on the bedside table along with her book. 'Jackson will bring you some tea directly, I'm sure you must be ready for it.' Then, as Charlotte struggled to sit up, Elaine reached out to take her hand. 'Pray be calm, my dear. Lady Buckwell has told me everything that happened and I can't tell you how sorry I am that you were embroiled in such a dreadful accident, or how thankful I am that you seem to be unharmed.'

Accident? Charlotte shook her muzzy head and tried to recall the dreadful accident but at first all she could hear and see and feel was the frantic neighing of the horses, the creak of harness as the britzka bore down on her, and the terrible feeling of falling.

'Oh God!' She put a hand to her head. 'I remember now. The parasol.' She rubbed her arm as a dull ache reminded her of that dramatic rescue. 'She saved me, Lady Buckwell; did I thank her properly? And then . . . Oh!' She turned anxiously to Elaine. 'Mrs Montgomery. She fell, did she not? And Mr Attwell said . . . he said . . . Did he. . . ? Are they. . . ?'

'Mrs Montgomery must have died instantly, Char,' Elaine told her gently, squeezing her hand in sympathy. 'She can have felt very little pain, the doctor assured us of that. Mr Attwell also.'

'Us?' Charlotte still felt some confusion, but the clouds were gradually clearing.

'Lady Buckwell has taken charge of the household for the moment and has most kindly included me in the discussions, as your representative, I imagine. The doctor spoke to both of us an hour ago when they . . . when Mrs Attwell was taken away to stay with the local vicar who thought it best she should not stay here with such dreadful associations.'

Jackson entered at that moment bearing a tray of tea and bread and butter and helped Charlotte sit up before passing the cup to her. She appraised the patient and gave a nod of satisfaction. 'You'll do, Miss Char,' she said before turning her attentions to her mistress. 'And you too, my dear.' She sounded surprised. 'I suppose you'll be wanting to go in to dinner tonight to catch all the latest gossip, for gossip there'll be, no matter how grim the day.'

201

'Dinner?' Charlotte drained her cup and returned it to Jackson with a faint smile. 'How long is it till dinner? I am quite rested and I – I would rather not stay on my own.'

'You have about three-quarters of an hour, Char,' Elaine told her, waving aside the maid's protest. 'Nonsense, Jackson. It will do Charlotte good to see other people, and better as she says that she should not dwell on events. You said yourself that we are both quite able and this will be our last appearance at the Waterloo House dining-table, for I have telegraphed to Kit that we will be leaving Bath tomorrow and that he is to meet us at Salisbury a day earlier than planned.'

Charlotte opened her mouth and then shut it again. Elaine was right; it was time to go home.

CHAPTER 12

Half an hour later Charlotte was up, dressed and feeling hungry; she was also bruised from head to toe with a particularly painful ache to her upper arm and shoulder. As this was caused by Lady Buckwell's parasol she felt almost thankful for the discomfort, reminding her as it did how miraculous had been her rescue. She had brushed aside Jackson's determination to assist in her dressing, sending the maid back flying to her mistress upon Charlotte's frowning suggestion that Elaine was probably putting a brave face on things and that she must have been considerably disturbed by all the drama.

As she tied tapes and fastened buttons Charlotte forced herself to consider recent events. Mrs Montgomery had been out of her senses with rage and Mr Attwell had attacked the landlady with what had certainly appeared to be murderous intent. I saw her face, Charlotte told herself, staring in the looking glass as she pinned up her plaits and tucked them tidily into a netted snood. She was crazed with anger at me, but why? All I did was ask a few questions, all of them innocuous. And yes, I was eavesdropping at her door, but she can't have known for certain that I heard anything incriminating; the most she can possibly have seen was my back view retreating along the hall to the drawing room. It was a mystery and she could only conclude that the other woman had been living with the fear of discovery and danger for so many years that Charlotte's questions coming so pat upon Mr Tibbins's unsettling hints had tipped her over the edge of sanity.

It would be a long time, Charlotte gave a shuddering sigh,

before she could forget the woman's breath on her face as they fell together towards the kerb. As for Mr Attwell's part in the horror, she had only an impression of violence and anger and noise and no recollection of what had become of him. The only thing that remained with her was his ferocious voice bellowing out the words she could not forget: 'You'll pay for that, as did that other ... I silenced him.' There could be no other interpretation put upon it. The conclusion she had formed in the park was in fact the true one: The Revd Decimus Attwell had killed Jonas Tibbins. Charlotte suffered a moment's faintness and recovered to shudder with horror, thrusting the intelligence away from her, but then her attention was arrested by a different thought.

Had Mr Tibbins after all maintained some kind of record of the intelligence received from his agents, in a notebook perhaps? And had Mrs Montgomery discovered this record? It would explain so much. Excitement sparked in her tired thoughts as she considered the idea. Mrs Montgomery must have found something in the detective's room when she had turned it out after his death. It was surely the only means by which she was able to implement her blackmailing attempts. I wonder what. . . .

Mrs Montgomery had caused Mr Tibbins's body to be carried into the scullery and there she must have run through his pockets; initially, no doubt, to look for information of his next of kin. If there had been such a notebook, taking it must have been a mere impulse, but what a treasure for such a woman to lay her hands upon. And if there had indeed been such a record, where was it now and what intelligence could it have contained about her fellow guests?

Useless to speculate, she sighed, but speculated all the same. Captain Penbury for instance; there had been some mention of a naval battle and he had been upset for some reason and surely ... she knitted her brow as she strove to recollect. Mr Tibbins had made some comment to the effect that even if the captain had not been engaged in that battle, perhaps a relative had been there. Some scandal perhaps but lost now, she thought.

Her neighbour from Hampshire had been discomposed by a

hint about Egyptian relics, but why? Again, she racked her brains; some mention of artefacts, she thought, that had set Mr Chettle frowning.

Mr Tibbins himself had told her that he had a client who sought someone staying at Waterloo House. Yes, and he was pleased, wasn't he, she remembered, because it was all going according to plan, and he had said something about another case involving a different guest and another client.

She shuddered at the thought of Mrs Attwell and her maudlin rambling on the evening of the concert. Could that be one of Mr Tibbins's cases, she wondered? Mr Attwell's ungovernable temper would have been only too familiar to his parishioners and if he entertained real hope of a bishopric, might someone in the diocese have doubts regarding his suitability? A wealthy citizen or fellow churchman could have heard rumours of those little indiscretions, and might well consider the detective's fee money well spent if it eliminated a potentially embarrassing appointment. Another shudder shook her as she recalled the air of barely suppressed violence about the man. It took little imagination to picture him turning on the detective in a fury and landing a lucky punch, and it was sadly only too easy to think of him seizing the fallen sword-stick and using it in a frenzy of rage.

But she had not seen him in the yard until Captain Penbury had given the alarm and spectators thronged the cobbled mews so where. . . ? She was struck by a memory, of herself giving a cursory glance into the stable where the old pony chomped placidly at his feed. Could Mr Attwell have secreted himself in there somehow? The stable was large and its corners shadowy and dark; a desperate man might well have flattened himself against the wall not daring to breathe until he heard the sound of many voices outside. It would have been simple enough then to saunter out and join the mêlée and if anyone had remarked his presence at the stable door, why, he could simply have claimed to be calming the pony.

I'll never know, she sighed, but it could have happened that way; in any case, he has paid the price now. She turned her thoughts away in distress, only to wonder what Mr Tibbins had found so interesting about the two Breton gentlemen but she was too tired, too affected by events, to speculate further.

In the drawing-room the remaining residents of the house huddled together round the imposing fireplace as if warding off any further disasters, but Charlotte was instantly aware that once again there was an inappropriate air of relaxation, of tension dissipated and even departed. It was uncannily like the assembly after the stabbing of the Pinkerton's detective.

As she entered the room there was a flurry of activity as several of the women surged towards her, crinolines billowing and hands fluttering as they hastened to express their shock, their horror and their relief at her delivery from danger. She nodded and thanked them and pressed their eager hands, was intrigued to notice that the female guests had all taken the same route as she herself had done, and were wearing gowns in sober hues but that not one of them had specifically arrayed herself in mourning.

Melicent Dunwoody was, indeed, wearing her shabby black dress, but that was an instance of necessity, while Dora Benson was arrayed in a dull purple silk. Charlotte and Elaine had merely refrained from bright colours. At least we're not hypocrites, Charlotte thought and glanced at her own dark green silk and hid a smile, but sobered instantly as she thought: no, I would not wear mourning for a woman who tried her damnedest to murder me.

The gentlemen were equally urgent in their expressions of relief at her miraculous survival and of good wishes, and glasses of sherry were thrust under her nose from several quarters. She tried to answer with a universal smile of thanks and took the glass from the nearest hand. To her hastily concealed dismay the hand belonged to Armel de Kersac who loomed over her with an anxious frown creasing his brow and with a dawning smile as he realized she had chosen to accept his proffered sherry above all the others.

Oh Lord, her sigh was weary but she disguised it gallantly and smiled again. I'd forgotten all about Armel. I suppose I shall have to allow him to speak and then let him down very gently. I shan't be able to leave Bath without doing that. Her glance shot beyond Armel to where his father stood beside the mantelpiece, watching her with an expression of studied blankness. He caught her eye and she saw an involuntary warmth lighten his features; he nodded, smiled very slightly and raised his glass to her.

Dinner was a testament to Mrs Montgomery's careful management and to the skills of her excellent cook. Insensibly too, as the meal went on, the atmosphere grew warmer and lighter, possibly assisted by the liberality with which the wine belonging to the late mistress of the house was served to all the guests. Charlotte suspected that the wine would be served in equally generous measures below stairs, and why not? The servants would soon find themselves out of a job as the household was broken up; let them make the most of it.

The gentlemen did not linger over their port this evening but made their way to the drawing room hard upon the heels of the ladies, as if unwilling to forego any moment of this final evening.

Charlotte found herself sitting beside Lady Buckwell on a small spindle-legged sofa to one side of the room. The lacquered little lady of the previous day was now returned in full fig, with no trace of the grandmother who had, with unaccustomed tenderness, held in her arms a trembling, shocked young woman.

'I hope you are quite recovered, Charlotte?' That was Lady Buckwell, demanding her attention and looking pleased at Charlotte's reply in the affirmative. 'I am glad to hear it but to be honest, I expected no less. You are indeed my granddaughter!' She lowered her voice to a discreet pitch. 'We will not say goodbye, my dear, but *au revoir*. My son's estate is in Hampshire and when I go to visit him next I shall write to invite you to stay with me there. Your company will provide me with a welcome leaven from that sanctimonious wife of his.' Her mischievous smile lit her face. 'However, I fear we cannot have you calling me Grandmama, can we? And Lady Buckwell is far too formal.

Shall we tell everyone that we have discovered relatives in common – perhaps on my father's side of the family? He was an artist and that is quite obscure enough to excite no interest. I suggest we settle on it that you should call me Aunt Becky. How does that suit?'

'I shall be honoured and delighted, Aunt Becky.' Charlotte smiled in reply and unseen by the rest of the assembly, their hands joined under cover of their flowing skirts.

Elaine Knightley had gone to her room soon after dinner, assuring Charlotte that she was perfectly well but wanted to be sure of a good night's sleep before the next day's long journey. When she returned from accompanying Elaine to her room, Charlotte's heart sank as she observed Armel de Kersac approaching her, determination writ large on his amiable countenance.

'It is a beautiful evening,' he began and with some skill shepherded her towards the drawing-room door. 'Won't you take one last look at Bath by moonlight?'

There was no escape; Armel was going to propose to her and she was going to refuse him, so she summoned up a smile and allowed him to drape her rose-patterned shawl around her shoulders. As he did so she caught Lady Buckwell's eye and looked away, only to see that the elder Count de Kersac was also observing her. She turned her head aside to hide her distress but was unable to avoid seeing that the old man was regarding his son with affection but also with pity.

Armel held out his arm and she slipped her hand into it as they strolled over into the square. She said nothing and indeed she could think of no words that would alter what was to come. Better let it happen, she sighed.

'Mrs Richmond ... Charlotte,' he began, pressing her hand with urgent affection. 'You cannot be in ignorance of what I am about to say to you.' He shook his head as she opened her mouth. 'No, pray let me speak. I have told you something of my home, of Brittany and of the magical stories that abound. I also told you about the legend of the fairies that inhabit our land. I know that I am not mistaken in saying that you were intrigued at those tales, and that you would find the Manoir de Kersac to your taste.' He took a deep breath and Charlotte remained silent.

'You know also that my wife and son died last year and that it was a great grief to me, but I have my little Marianne still and I flatter myself that you have come to love the child during our short acquaintance.' He led her to a bench under the trees and sat beside her. 'Oh, do not be apprehensive.' He gave a short, embarrassed laugh. 'I have no intention of kneeling down to say this, but say it I will and must. Could you, dearest Charlotte, extend your love for my daughter to include myself? And would you do me the very great honour of becoming my wife?'

Hot tears sprang to her eyes and she found herself unable to speak for the surge of emotion that rose within her breast. He was such a good man and he deserved so much more.

She gulped and found her handkerchief.

'Oh, Armel,' she faltered, keeping her eyes downcast and looking at her lap. 'I – I can't, I simply can't. You are quite correct; I do love Marianne and I love your father and I love you too, but not in the way you want me to love you. Not in the way you *should* be loved. I should never be the wife you deserve because I should never be able to give you the love you need and besides, it's not . . .' She hesitated. 'It's not suitable, it really is not. No.' She put a gentle finger to his lips. 'Don't, please don't. I've . . . I've been married before, as you are aware, and it wasn't a success. It is not an experiment I anticipate repeating for a long time, if indeed I ever do. Please don't make me hurt you any more.' She rose and held out her hand to hold him off. 'No, don't come in with me. I must go . . . I can't. . . .'

As the clock in the hall struck midnight Charlotte was still awake, curled up in the comfortable upholstered chair provided by her deceased, but thoughtful, landlady. She had been unable to restrain a storm of painful tears as a result of her refusal of Armel de Kersac's offer of marriage. I know I hurt him, she thought, gulping down one of the sobs that still threatened to overwhelm her. Dear God, if I had met him a year ago, six months even, how I would have leapt at such a chance and done all I could to make him happy. But now? I know that I cannot marry him, it wouldn't be fair. He is too good, too true and I cannot offer him less than he deserves and no, it would never do. She shied away from the emotions that the episode had stirred and forced herself to turn her attention to the other events of the evening.

No mention had been made of any notebook being found on either of the victims of the carriage accident and her own swift search of Mrs Montgomery's apartment after dinner had revealed nothing, if indeed there had been anything to find. I know nothing at all, she sighed, it is all speculation so I shall keep my mouth firmly closed. No good can come of my raking up old embers that I don't understand, and I have lived long enough with secrets of my own so why should I expose those of other people? Mr Chettle can rest easy as can Captain Penbury. I have no need to hold them up to public scrutiny, let them marry their willing governesses and go off to dig for funeral urns in Italy or reminisce about old naval campaigns in some snug little town along the coast.

Mrs Montgomery is beyond exposure now and no useful purpose can be obtained by telling anyone about her activities either in Bath and recently, or long ago and all across the country. As for Decimus Attwell, his mother, poor woman, has her own hell to inhabit and I will not make it worse by hinting at secrets and suspicions.

She remembered her last brief conversation with Jonas Tibbins when he had mentioned the two cases which concerned him at Waterloo House and a third which looked promising. I suspect that Mr Tibbins was investigating the proposed bishop, she mused, employed to do so by someone who had heard about Mr Attwell's scattering of bonny little bastards and perhaps also his episodes of violent temper. Mr Chettle and Captain Penbury looked angry and disturbed by the detective's hints but surely they came under his heading of minor misdemeanours that were not his concern. As for the commission he was hoping to acquire, that must have concerned Mrs Montgomery, which leads me to what I suspect was his primary business here.

She came at last to the greatest mystery of them all: something she had returned to over and over again in the few quiet moments she had been granted lately. Reaching into her reticule she stared at the tiny bundle before her and, with a hesitant delicacy of touch, untied the cord and opened up the piece of blue velvet cloth to reveal the locket so that the two miniatures lay face up in front of her while she gazed at them with something like awe.

As the last chime of midnight died away Charlotte cast one more searching glance at the two portraits and sighed. It could not be true, she thought, biting her lip, but the more she assured herself of the impossibility of her deduction, the more the two painted faces stared back at her and she could no longer deny the resemblance. If one were to substitute white hair for fair. . . .

No, she said firmly, as she restored the locket to its velvet wrapping. It cannot possibly be true and yet, how can it be otherwise? And if it is true, if this one astounding circumstance is indeed proven, everything will change.

Next day Lady Buckwell and Elaine Knightley joined together in making Charlotte breakfast in her room so that she was only just dressed when, at ten o'clock, Lady Buckwell tapped on her door.

'I think you should not go downstairs yet, Charlotte,' she announced without ceremony and carried on, cutting short Charlotte's enquiry as she closed the door firmly behind her, 'an employee of the late Mr Tibbins has just called, having only yesterday learned of his principal's death. Fortunately he was brought to me in the drawing room where I was alone so I was able to help him conclude his business with dispatch. In short, I referred him to Inspector Nicholson of the local constabulary and told him that depositions had been taken regarding the discovery of the body.

'He was naturally distressed, but when I informed him of yesterday's sad "accident" and the subsequent deaths of Mrs Montgomery and Mr Attwell, he gave me a very straight look particularly when I was able to give him an eye-witness account of the tragedy. After several minutes of deliberation he thanked me for my assistance and said he was confident that no guest remaining at Waterloo House would now be an object of his organization's attention. Whereupon he left to go and see the inspector.'

Charlotte listened in silence and Lady Buckwell ended by saying, 'I did not ask the man about Mr Tibbins's profession, nor did he volunteer any information, but I can draw conclusions as well as the next man or woman.' She raised an eyebrow and smiled slightly. 'I see you either know what he was, or have come to the same conclusion, so we will say no more. I believe we may rest easy that we shall have no further communication upon the subject.'

'M. de Kersac?' Ever since she had lain in bed at dawn, cataloguing her bruises, Charlotte had wondered how she was to broach the subject that was to occupy her every waking moment so far that day, and here he was, the elder Breton gentleman, about to make his way across the road evidently bent on a short rest under the shade of the beech trees. She had observed his progress from an upstairs window and had paused only long enough to hurry into her own room and take a small packet from the leather valise that had been Will Glover's.

'Mrs Richmond? You will not, I feel sure, object if I call you Charlotte?' There was a familiar wariness in those pale-blue eyes but there was pleasure and yes, affection too, while a smile of welcome softened the austerity of his features as she smiled and nodded permission. 'Are you also bound for a few moments' peace and quiet? Pray do me the honour of bestowing your company upon me. We shall have no more opportunity for our little discussions.'

'As long as I do not disturb you, *monsieur*?' She hesitated, but he held out his arm in a courtly gesture so she walked with him, suiting her pace to his own.

'I am glad of an opportunity of talking to you, my dear young lady,' he began, as they made themselves comfortable on a bench some distance from the road and barely visible from Waterloo

House and any inquisitive eyes.

She opened her mouth to speak but bit her lip instead. The old man had something on his mind, better let him relieve his anxieties. She could guess what he was going to say.

'My son is very unhappy at your decision, my dear,' he said gently and, as she raised her eyes to meet his gaze, he took her hand in a cool, but friendly clasp. 'He had told me of his intention; that he hoped to make you his wife and I had assured him that if he was sufficiently fortunate to win your love, nothing would give me greater pleasure.'

She tried to speak but he raised his hand to silence her. 'No, *ma chère* Charlotte, do not tell me anything. I saw from the outset that your relations with Armel were mere friendship and liking, however much I, as well as he, tried to delude ourselves that you felt otherwise. You must not reproach yourself, you were honest and open and not once have I observed anything in your conduct either with Armel or with any other gentleman in this house, that could give rise to any other interpretation.'

He sighed and squeezed her hand. 'Like my son I could indeed have wished for a different, happier, outcome. He has suffered so much grief in this last twelve months that your acceptance of his offer would have been a beacon of hope to us all. Marianne, also, is more than half in love with you and in no time at all would have been your own loving little daughter.'

Charlotte's head was bent, but she was aware of his eyes on her and of his affectionate sympathy. 'I have said nothing of this to Armel, my dear, but I have come to suspect that your heart is not your own.'

'Oh *no*.' She lifted her head in dismay. 'M. de Kersac, pray do not say so. There is nothing, no one. It is merely that having had no reason to look back upon my late marriage with any pleasure I am reluctant to try again so soon. I do assure you. . . .'

His smile deepened and he patted her hand again. 'Assure me of nothing, my dear Charlotte, for I should not believe you.' The smile vanished and he gave her a searching glance. 'I think I can guess your fate, my child, but rest tranquil, I shall say nothing, either to my son, Armel, or to any other living soul.'

For a moment hot tears stung her eyelids and she had to bite her lips to prevent a sob escaping them. Sympathy was not something Charlotte had experienced very often of late and that it should come from this man, of all men, touched her heart.

'Thank you, *monsieur*,' she said gravely, as she took her hand from his and reached into her pocket. Her thoughts were in turmoil. Should I do this, she demanded of herself? Must I tackle him at such a time? But time was running out and there was no real question, no dilemma, and no option but to continue with what she had begun.

She took the blue velvet bundle out of the bag, untied the cord and placed the beautiful little locket, still in its wrapping, carefully upon his knee.

'I suspect . . . that is I have come to believe that this should be in your keeping, M. de Kersac,' she told him quietly and watched as, almost fearfully, the old man folded back the cloth covering, his hands – slightly gnarled with rheumatism – shaking a little as he did so.

She observed him closely as he opened the locket and looked down at the tiny portraits and she was aware of a long shuddering sigh that shook his frail body. He reached out a finger and touched the face of the young woman whose white powdered hair was piled high and adorned with ostrich plumes and strands of pearls. Through a mist of tears Charlotte was aware that the old man's pale-blue eyes, also glistening, were just the same as the eyes of the woman whose portrait he held so reverently.

Not a word was spoken and she reached over and pointed to the other miniature, that of the small boy staring out from the painted ivory. Did he have a haunted look about him? A sense that his life would not, in any way, resemble the life his parents had mapped out for him? Hindsight, she told herself, knowing as she did the suffering the little boy had endured. The tears fell then, hotly splashing on her hand and she hurriedly fished a handkerchief out of her bag.

Still the old man said nothing but continued to sit there holding the exquisite little portraits of Queen Marie Antoinette and her son in a tender clasp, but when Charlotte, much moved, tucked her hand tentatively but gently into his arm, she was aware of a slight relaxation of tension in the body held so rigidly upright.

Time was passing and Charlotte was aware that Elaine and Jackson would soon be expecting her to join them for the short ride to the railway station. If I am to say these things, she faltered, then I must say them now, or hold my peace for the rest of my life.

She released his arm and rose quietly, and stationed herself in front of him, first making sure that there were no passers-by, or guests from Waterloo House in the vicinity. There must be no prying, watching eyes for this moment. She took a deep breath and as he looked up at her with startled eyes, dragged from his reverie, she sank in a deep, reverent curtsy.

'*Monseigneur*,' was all she said.

He leaped to his feet with the speed and agility of a much younger man, the two miniatures still clutched in his left hand.

'No, my child,' he exclaimed, his voice roughened by emotion. 'No, not that, never that, I beg of you,' and he took her hand and raised her up.

Charlotte let out a long, quavering sigh. So it was true. She resumed her seat beside him, still retaining the clasp of her hand in his. Their eyes met and their cheeks were wet with tears. He tried to speak, not once but twice, but the words would not come and she reached out and took both his hands, still holding tightly to his treasure, and clasped them in her own, the tiny pictures cradled gently between them.

'You have my word,' she told him, on a half sob. 'You know that I will never, ever, tell anyone about this. Not a single soul.'

At that he abandoned the attempt to restrain his emotion and let the difficult tears of old age trickle down his cheeks. But only for a moment, and as he began to search in his pocket, Charlotte mutely held out her own handkerchief.

'So,' he said presently. 'So here we are.' He put his arm round her and for a moment she leaned her head against his shoulder. She was reluctant to break the companionable silence that lay

215

between them but there was something else she must mention so she screwed up her courage and turned to him.

'*Mon* . . . I beg your pardon, M. de Kersac,' she began, correcting herself even as he raised an elegant eyebrow at her. 'There is something I must tell you. Something of the utmost seriousness.'

She hesitated for so long that he prompted her.

'Then you had better tell me, *ma chère.*' He encouraged her with a faint smile and, as she met his eyes, she understood that he knew very well what she had discovered and what it was she had to tell him.

'Mr Jonas Tibbins,' she said haltingly. 'I don't know if he said anything to you, but I must tell you, sir, that I believe he had been commissioned to discover you. He was a detective and he told me that his quarry, as he put it, was known to be visiting Waterloo House at this time. I believe he knew who you were.'

She took his hand in hers once more and turned a face brimming with questions to him.

'You know . . . you have my word though I do not believe you ever required it . . . that I will never speak of this.' She indicated the locket, now folded into a neat velvet parcel on his knee, with a hand laid gently over it as though he could not bear to relinquish his touch. Her eyes glowed with love for him, along with a dancing mischief. 'But my dear, dear sir, you know that if you could bear to tell me about it, I should be so much interested.'

He was smiling at her too. 'What is it that the English say? There is a proverb, is there not? Something about curiosity killing the cat?' Their eyes met again and he nodded, the amusement dying away. 'Tell me, dear Charlotte, what is your own reasoning? You who have so cleverly deduced so much that was previously impenetrable? Why do you believe that Mr Tibbins was searching for a ghost? An old man who matters only to a few people in a tiny far away corner of the world?'

She looked away, towards the hills just visible between the houses opposite. 'That last morning,' she said slowly, choosing her words with care, 'at breakfast when Mr Tibbins had, if you recall, secreted one of his unsettling little notes to you and to some of the other residents at the house. I saw the word, *Monseigneur* and thought, for a while, that it meant you were a renegade cardinal. . . .'

His head jerked up sharply and he gave her an incredulous look and she shrugged. 'I know how foolish that sounds now and I soon abandoned that idea, but then I recalled that Mr Tibbins had said something about exile. I remember now. It was the night before, when Lady Buckwell was so scathing about exiled royalty and you made some remark to her about not trespassing on her goodwill.'

He nodded but waited in silence while she gathered her thoughts. 'Yes,' she said, remembering the detective's voice, half mocking, half serious. 'He said something about us all being exiles here at Waterloo House and he quoted the words of Psalm 137: '*By the rivers of Babylon . . . we wept as we remembered Zion.*' And then he looked round at us all and – I believe he said – "What is it that we think of when *we* remember Zion?" And he looked straight at you, *monsieur*.'

His continuing silence was a little unnerving, but she was too much in earnest to back away now. 'I think that Mr Tibbins's clients must be members of some secret society dedicated to the removal of any remnants of the *Ancien Régime*. Fanatical Jacobins, perhaps? Or their descendants, they would surely be too young to have been *sans-culottes* themselves but perhaps there was a family tradition?'

He interrupted her then with an abrupt shake of his head. 'No, you deserve an explanation, my dear, but it is not easy for me to explain.' He faltered a little then gathered confidence. 'You are partly correct in your assumption; there is indeed a secret society, but they are not rabid revolutionaries. Far from it, though had Mr Tibbins's employers succeeded in their ambition, the result would have resounded upon the world stage and could have precipitated yet more decades of revolution and war.'

He cleared his throat then took her hand, looking away towards the trees. 'What they desire more than anything else, is the restoration of the Bourbon monarchy. The *true* monarchy. They wish, either by peaceful methods or, if necessary, by force of arms, to remove from the throne of France its current incumbent, the Emperor Napoleon the Third and his empress, the beautiful Eugénie. And in their place it is proposed to reinstate the rightful king of France, son of King Louis and Queen Marie Antoinette, the Lost Dauphin, in fact. King Louis the Seventeenth.'

His head was bent and silence fell between them for a few moments, then he continued, 'I do not know the name of Mr Tibbins's client, but he and his fellow conspirators had learned, from what exact source I cannot even begin to guess, that the young Dauphin did not die in the Temple Prison as was reported at the time, but that his gaolers, Simon and his wife, were bribed most heavily, to smuggle out the child and to put in his place a child from the slums; a child of a similar age and appearance who was already far gone with consumption. That child was given shelter and food and rough kindness until his death, far more so than he would have received in the gutter where he was discovered.'

The sad, quiet voice tailed away and he sighed. 'At least . . . that is what I was told later, much later, when I was in a condition to ask. Was it the truth?' He shrugged and his eyes were bleak. 'Who can tell at this distance? One can only pray that it was so. As for the other child, known to his gaolers as Louis Capet, he fell into so severe a fever that his life was despaired of and he was conveyed, by a roundabout route, to a small fortified manor house in a remote corner of Finistère, far away in the west of Brittany. There he was brought up as the acknowledged child of the elderly Count de Kersac who was said to have married unsuitably, thus explaining the previous silence regarding the child's existence.'

'They wanted you to take the throne?' Charlotte whispered. 'But what did Armel think of that? Did he know?' She was aghast at the thought of Armel de Kersac, forced to leave forever the *manoir* and the farm and his beloved fairy stones. 'And Marianne too? Oh no, not the child, she would be destroyed . . .'

218

She read the answer in his eyes. 'He doesn't know, does he? Armel – you haven't told him? And Marianne? Her full name . . . it is Marie Antoinette, is it not?'

'Of course,' he spoke simply. 'She is the image of my mother as I believe you deduced when you came upon the miniature. And as, indeed, I suspect the detective recognized also. No, my dear, I have not told Armel. In fact, I never even told my wife, but I have written down my story for him to read after my death.' A wry smile twisted his mouth. 'My dear wife was always curious as to why I laughed at the suggestion that the old Breton name was a variant of Arthur, the 'once and future king'. It afforded me some satisfaction that Armel should have such a name for at that time I had no intention of ever revealing my life story to anyone.'

'Mr Tibbins spoke to you, I believe. Did he not explain how he had tracked you down?' Charlotte ventured to ask. 'He had the locket, I know, but the likeness is surely not enough.'

'He hinted merely, but there have always been rumours in monarchist circles.' He shrugged. 'Some of them were founded upon nothing but wishful thinking, but there is no such thing as a complete secret. The details were not generally known but money talks always and hints were dropped. It was necessary that not one whisper of my whereabouts should reach anyone, royalist or revolutionary alike, and to that end my prolonged illness was a blessing in disguise. A sick, possibly dying child, dressed as a girl as an added disguise, could be moved from house to house, village to village and I bore no resemblance to that little boy in this picture.' He touched the bundle with a gentle finger. 'I was gaunt, almost skeletal I believe, though I have no recollection of that time. By the time I was rational again I was Louis, the acknowledged but, probably, natural son of the Count de Kersac in a spot so remote that nobody ever raised a weapon in anger.

'It was not only the *sans-culottes* who were a threat to me, you know.' He spoke at first in a conversational tone, rising to anger. 'My foster father was informed, many months later, that there was a known plot to kill me; a plot that emanated from followers in the train of my uncle, he who was known as Philippe l'Égalité, champion of the masses, and traitor to his family, God rot his filthy soul.'

His passion startled her; he had seemed so quiet, so resigned as he told her his story. He shook his head and gave her an apologetic smile.

'Forgive me, dear Charlotte, what am I thinking of? So heated and yet so long ago.' They fell into a gentle conversation in which she told him something of her own history until a shout from across the road alerted them. 'Ah, it is time. And so we must take our leave, but first I must confess to you. I am not a violent man, I have seen too much of death, but I am wholeheartedly grateful to whoever murdered that detective. I think I might have been able to kill him myself, to save Armel and Marianne, but I shall be eternally grateful that I did not have to take that step.'

She was too startled to respond by more than an upward glance. Should she mention her suspicions as to the perpetrator of that murder? But no, she had made a vow to herself to keep silent on that subject, and she would not break her word, even to him. I could set his mind at rest a little, she thought, and related Lady Buckwell's conversation with Mr Tibbins's henchman. He nodded sagely, but said nothing, so they rose to their feet and walked slowly towards the group at the door of Waterloo House, her hand once more tucked into his arm and his own hand, the one not holding his household gods, stroking her fingers with a light caress.

'I am very sorry for Armel,' he told her again, 'but I knew all along you were not for him. But I will say this, my dearest girl, if I were forty or even thirty years younger I tell you I myself would have proposed marriage to you with all my heart.'

The mischief in his pale eyes struck an answering light in her own hazel ones. 'If that had been the case, dearest M. de Kersac,' she said lightly, 'I should most certainly have accepted.'

He was surprised into a look of pleasure and he smiled even more warmly. 'I am only seventy-three,' he informed her with a shrug and another smile at his own involuntary vanity. 'Even now I—'

'Excuse me, sir.' It was Jackson, bobbing a curtsy to the gentleman and turning to Charlotte. 'Mrs Knightley is ready in the carriage, Miss Char – Mrs Richmond I should say, and you have precious little time in hand when it comes to catching that train.'

Charlotte had reached the carriage by now and she nodded a greeting to Elaine while holding out her hand to this collection of people who, while perhaps she could not call them all friends, were certainly now more than mere acquaintances. To Mr Chettle and Dora Benson she spoke a brief farewell with a promise of a meeting in Hampshire very soon, while some commonplace politeness was all that was required for Captain Penbury and his droopy bride-to-be, who would return to Finchbourne in a day or so, along with Mr Chettle and Dora.

Lady Buckwell (*Aunt Becky indeed!*) took her hand, bestowed a kiss on Charlotte's cheek, to the manifest astonishment of the assembled company, and smiled, merely saying, 'I will write to you, my dear, and you must do the same to me. I will not lose you too.' Then the lady turned on her heel, perhaps overcome by an unaccustomed and uncharacteristic rush of sentiment, and trod briskly up the steps and into the house.

And so she came to the de Kersac family and her heart swelled with love and sorrow as she held out her arms to the small Marianne and mopped up her tears. She held out her hand to Armel de Kersac but her voice shook too much for coherent speech. Finally she was clasped in a warm embrace by the old man and for a moment they were alone, the rest of the group having moved away a little.

'My child.' His eyes were filled with compassion as he looked at her. 'There is something I need to say to you, I forgot it earlier when we were . . . otherwise occupied.' She gazed at him in surprise, her eyes wet with tears. 'I believe I know something that troubles you, even now.' He hushed her exclamation. 'No, say nothing. If I am correct I suspect that you torment yourself daily with guilt, the guilt of having survived when your loved ones have died. Is that not so?'

Her astonished gasp was answer enough. 'I thought so.

Indeed I spoke more truly than I knew at our first meeting, when I told you we were akin.' He took her hand once more. 'We live by the same rules: trust no one, watch your words, be always on your guard, but more than that, what we both crave is forgiveness, absolution perhaps, redemption if you prefer, for the unwitting sin that we committed in our youth. That of living when all that we held dear was gone before and left us with our grief and guilt. But you must let them go, my child, and live for yourself now.'

'Oh.' She could say no more and he gave her another fatherly kiss on the cheek followed by a low and courtly bow as he kissed her hand with great elegance. Then he pushed her gently towards the carriage. 'You may tell *la princesse lointaine* everything we have discussed,' he told her, surprising her greatly. 'She will never mention it and indeed, I think she will have little time to do so. But she is a great lady and you will need to talk to someone. She is the most fitting person.'

He nodded at her incredulous glance and bowed regally to Elaine who was watching them with considerable interest, but she made no remark, either in the bustle that ensued, nor once they had boarded the train. Only when they were a bare half hour from Salisbury did she allow her curiosity to overcome her tactful silence.

'You have made a most interesting friend, have you not, dearest Char? In the person of that charming elderly Breton gentleman?'

Charlotte took a sharp breath as she recalled M. de Kersac's words, spoken with gentle melancholy, about Elaine, the *princesse lointaine*, as he had christened her, who would never tell his secrets or indeed have time to do so. A shiver ran down her spine but Elaine was looking at her with lively curiosity written all over her delicately beautiful face, so Charlotte moved across to sit beside her friend. She gave a very brief, almost curt explanation of the passions and secrets stirred up by the American detective among the residents of Waterloo House and then startled Elaine even further by disclosing the sad and strange history of the Lost Dauphin of France.

'My dear Charlotte,' Elaine exclaimed when Charlotte's voice tailed away. 'If I did not know you to be an exceedingly sensible young woman, not in the least given to flights of fancy, I should think you to be planning to write a Gothick romance! But I see that you are in earnest and that all these events happened right under my nose while I sizzled gently in young Mr Radnor's electrical baths. And although you have not asked it of me, I do assure you that this will remain between us. Your kingly admirer was right to perceive no threat from me.'

She thought for a moment then raised her head at the sound of the engine's whistle. 'We are nearly there. I shall be so glad to see Kit and I hope he will be pleased with my progress in Bath.'

Charlotte was looking out of the other window now, but she withdrew her head, scrubbing smuts off her face with a grimy handkerchief, glad of an excuse to wipe away her tears for the little lost boy king who, for a brief moment, had become her friend.

'The old gentleman was not your only admirer was he, dear Char?' Elaine gave her a quizzical smile. 'You have been so exceedingly tactful but I could not mistake that crestfallen look on the younger count's face. For my part I am glad not to lose you to France, though he would have loved you well, I'm sure of that.'

Charlotte nodded. 'When I first came to England in the spring,' she said thoughtfully, measuring her words. 'I would have leapt at such a proposal. Oh, not for love, Armel knew I did not love him, but because I was so desperate for a place of my own and a family to love me. Now I have that place and that family and I know I am loved, but it wasn't just that. When he asked me I had already begun to have some inkling of the truth, outrageous as it seemed. It was the little portraits with their likenesses, so surprising and yet so convincing. How could I have saddled him, the rightful heir to the throne of France, even if he does not know it, with a bastard wife born to a convicted and transported felon, not to mention my godmother and my stepfather and their – eccentricities?' She heaved a sigh. 'I do regret the little girl Marianne,' she admitted. 'I love her with all

223

my heart and I confess that, for a moment – a very short moment – I could have been tempted at the thought of becoming her mother.'

Her serious mood fell away and she stood up to crane her head out of the window again. 'I think I can see the station in the distance,' she said, scrubbing at her face again and straightening her bonnet, then looking back over her shoulder for a final word.

'Oh well . . .' Elaine rejoiced to hear the laugh once more in Charlotte's voice. 'I may have almost witnessed a murder, had an attempt upon my own life and discovered a grandmother of my very own, but what I shall recall most vividly from this adventure of ours, Elaine, is that I might have been the rightful Queen of France!'